Shepherds of Destiny

KIEL BARNEKOV

LitPrime Solutions
21250 Hawthorne Blvd
Suite 500, Torrance, CA 90503
www.litprime.com
Phone: 1-800-981-9893

Published by LitPrime Solutions   10/13/2022

ISBN: 979-8-88703-067-8(sc)
ISBN: 979-8-88703-069-2(hc)
ISBN: 979-8-88703-068-5(e)

Library of Congress Control Number: 2022918145

Contents

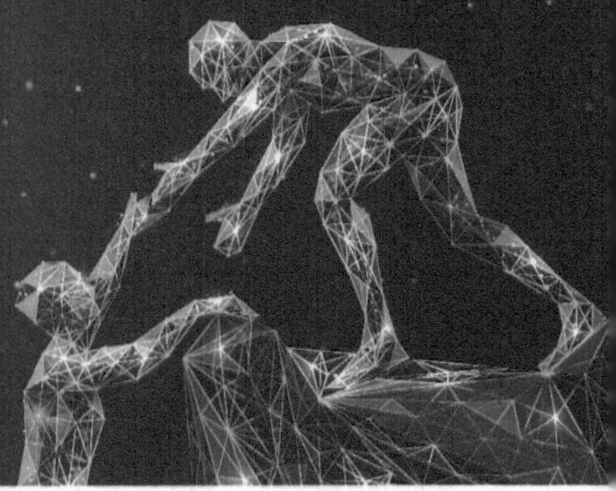

Prologue

In the late 2030s, a cyborg body had been developed by a Defense Advanced Research Projects Agency (DARPA) team led by Dr. Ansley Barnett that fully resembled the human body. To the untrained eye, the cyborg body was indistinguishable from a human body. The cyborg was controlled by a human mind, downloaded to the cyborg brain from a patient irreversibly incapacitated by a disease or an accident. The cyborg could eat and drink when desired in order to better blend with the human population. Food was 'digested' by the synthetic body by reducing anything ingested to a gas and cleansed of any odor before excretion. Its senses mirrored the senses of a human. It did not require sleep although it periodically needed to rest the human mind it was hosting and recharge its advanced battery array, which was located where the kidneys are located on a human body. It was able to enjoy having sex.

Kristian Barnett, a billionaire through inheritance of his parents' estate, and CEO and Chairman of the Board of Barnett Industries which developed, manufactured and implemented advanced transportation systems globally, fell ill at the age of thirty-three with amyotrophic lateral sclerosis (ALS), also known as Lou Gehrig's Disease.

Dr. Savannah Richards, Neurosurgeon and Research Scientist at the Stanford Neuroscience Health Center was developing a means to preserve the brain of a patient whose body had been irrecoverably destroyed but whose brain was unharmed. Concurrently, Dr. Ansley

Barnett, wife of Kristian Barnett, was leading the development of a cyborg body indistinguishable from a human body for DARPA.

Soon after Kristian's brain was removed and placed in stasis, he was approached by The Guardian. The Guardian was a spiritual being who watched for timelines that were going astray and threatening the existence of humanity. The Guardian needed Kristian's mind, untethered from his corporeal body, to control the actions of key individuals. While in his current spiritual state, Kristian was able to travel to any period in the past or the future with The Guardian in order to affect changes to a timeline gone astray.

With Kristian in tow, The Guardian traveled back in time to the U.S. Civil War where the timeline in which the Union won the war was in jeopardy. With Kristian's mind in brief control of one key individual, the catastrophe was averted, and history continued its pre-destined course. Aaron Adams, also suffering from advanced ALS, was approved as a candidate for the brain extraction procedure. But prior to the procedure his mind would be scanned and stored for download to a cyborg body. The download was a complete success and Aaron was introduced back into society under a new identity. Aaron was also approached by The Guardian as his mind was also separated from his corporeal body. His assignment from The Guardian resulted in the timeline being maintained in which the Allies won World War II and defeated the Axis Alliance of Germany, Italy and Japan.

Commander Erik Richards, captain of the Mars spaceship USS Elon Musk, was returning to Earth from Mars when the ship experienced a catastrophic hull breach that led to the deaths of four of her crew and inflicted extensive wounds on Erik. The prognosis for Erik was that he would not recover beyond his quadriplegic state. Erik was therefore, approved to receive a synthetic cyborg body.

Kristian Barnett and Aaron Adams, under the guidance of The Guardian, traveled forward to the year 2052. The CEO of Find Corporation and two multi-billion-dollar telecommunication moguls had developed a new smartphone supporting an advanced communications technology. This technology enabled the ability to control a user's thoughts and actions without the knowledge or consent of the user. The new smartphone and communications technology were promoted to the military as a means of controlling the actions of an enemy. The intent of the billionaire cabal was to use the technology to ultimately establish a dystopian world in which the billionaire elites and their ruling class government puppets would live in opulence while the masses were enslaved to serve their masters.

The demonstration of the technology to senior government officials, including the Secretary of Defense, was a failure due to the intervention of Kristian and Aaron taking brief control of the test subjects' and SecDef's minds.

Although successfully stalled, the CEO of Find vowed to correct the cause of the failure and offered to fund whatever amount was necessary. The threat of human domination by evil tyrants continues.

Chapter 1

"Tyler, Aidan, thanks for coming to the mansion on short notice this weekend. I trust you brought your families," said Kristian Barnett, standing in the great foyer of the Barnett House mansion under a huge crystal chandelier.

"Mine wouldn't miss a chance to experience the mansion's amenities," replied Tyler. Aidan nodded with a widening smile.

The Barnett House mansion boasts a hundred-thousand- square-feet of living space, including multiple outbuildings, and is located in Bel-Air, California. It has twenty bedrooms, thirty bathrooms, a four-lane bowling alley, three infinity pools, a wine room, a seventy-seat movie theatre, an indoor/outdoor nightclub, and, of course, a helicopter pad. An invitation to spend a weekend at Barnett House is something very few mortals will ever receive.

Barnett wasted no time in getting to the primary reason he'd invited his personal physicians to spend the weekend. "Doctors, I have been having, hmm, shall we say, some health-related issues of late."

Dr. Aidan Sullivan responded, "Kris, we recently completed a full physical for you. Looked at every system and organ in your body using the latest diagnostic techniques and found no issues. You're in perfect health."

"Yes," said Barnett. "However, I have been experiencing occasional weakness in my legs. Just this morning I dropped a pitcher of orange juice while pouring juice into a glass. And it didn't slip. It seemed that my grip went weak on me for no reason.

I have also experienced twitching in my arms and shoulders." "Those symptoms come with a plethora of ailments. But it sounds like it could be neurological," said Dr. Tyler Sullivan. "Has Ansley noticed your symptoms?" Ansley Barnett, Kristian's wife, has both a medical degree and a Ph.D. in bioengineering and is actively working on top secret projects for the Defense Advanced Research Projects Agency (DARPA). Ansley was a confirmed genius with an IQ north of 160. She finished her undergraduate degree at 19, completed Harvard Medical School at 23, and received her Ph.D. at 26.

"No, not really. But we're so busy we hardly have time to notice anything subtle that is happening to each other."

"Have you been experiencing any unusual stress? Are you sleeping well? Have you been able to maintain your exercise program?" questioned Tyler.

"Doctor, my stress level is always high, as you know. I generally sleep well if not enough. And I swim laps multiple times a week and bike around the hills on the weekend," replied Barnett. "When I'm not experiencing these unusual symptoms, I feel great."

"I suggest we consult first with a neurologist we know who is top in his specialty to get advice on where we should start looking. As I said, what you are describing are symptoms related to several different issues," said Tyler.

"Gentlemen, I would appreciate you looking under my hood, so to speak. While not life-threatening, these symptoms are becoming a cause for concern," replied Barnett. "Now let's go enjoy the weekend."

"Tyler, great to see you again," said Ansley as she gave him a cordial hug. "Glad you could come and spend the weekend with us."

"Thanks, Ansley," Tyler replied. "You look terrific, as usual. Have you noticed anything out of the ordinary recently with Kristian?"

"Well, now that you mention it. Yes, he seems a little moody, withdrawn lately, like something is on his mind."

"Physical problems?" asked Tyler.

"He does seem a little more off balance than usual. Dropping things and occasionally slurring his words. I haven't thought much about it though, probably because we both are so busy."

"Hey there!" Kristian said as he and Aidan walked up to Ansley, Tyler and Tyler's wife, Rachel. "Let's head up to the pool deck for cocktails. After all, it's past five on a beautiful Friday evening and we should have a pitcher of Miquel's margaritas waiting for us." The mansion's pool deck was an open-air lanai that overlooked the California hills. Facing west, sunsets viewed from this deck were amazing. Hues of gold, red, orange, and green peeking between wispy clouds made the sunset a calming and memorable experience.

On the pool deck, Miquel had prepared a large pitcher of his special margaritas, a recipe he had initially developed for Kristian's father. Miquel had been the Barnett's' facility director, head butler, and bartender for more than twenty years. His cocktail recipes were legendary among the Barnett's' friends and business associates.

"Thank you, Miquel," said Kristian. "I'll take it from here," as he reached for the large pitcher. He turned to Tyler's wife Rachel and began to pour. Just as he started to fill her glass, the pitcher crashed to the pool deck, breaking into hundreds of pieces of glass, drink splashing on his guests. Kristian just stood awestruck, realizing what had happened after a few long seconds.

"I...I don't know what happened. It's as if my hand just fell off the pitcher. I lost all feeling! Oh, I am so sorry and embarrassed. Ansley, please call Miquel and request he bring a crew up here to clean up.

Then take Rachel to our pool dressing room so she can change." Kristian then slumped down in a nearby chair, head in hands.

Tyler and Aidan walked over to Kristian. Placing his hand on Kristian's shoulder, Aidan said, "We now see firsthand some of the problems you have been experiencing. Tyler and I will get on this first thing on Monday, but you should prepare for a battery of tests. Do you know if anyone in your family has had Parkinson's Disease?"

"Not that I know of," replied Kristian. "With my father's side of the family, it had always been heart and coronary issues. Mother's family all seemed to just die of old age, most living well into their nineties. Of course, we shall never know any health issues mother and father might have experienced in old age since they both died in their late forties in the plane crash." Kristian's parents, Silicon Valley billionaires, were killed in a crash of the family Learjet when Kristian was 23 years old. The cause of the crash was believed to be a sudden cabin depressurization at high altitude, rendering the passengers and crew unconscious. The plane simply flew, unresponsive to air traffic control, until it ran out of fuel over the Pacific Ocean. Neither the plane nor the remains of the passengers and crew were ever found despite an extensive search by the U.S. Navy and Coast Guard. Weather in the area believed to be where the plane likely went down was poor, with heavy wind, rain, and twenty-foot seas. Kristian was their sole heir.

Within what seemed like just minutes, Miquel's crew had cleaned up the mess from the spilled pitcher and had returned with a new one. Ansley and Rachel returned from the dressing room with Rachel sporting a new outfit.

"Miquel, this time I will let you pour," smiled Kristian. After the second round of Miquel's margaritas, the incident was all but forgotten

Chapter 2

Monday, May 1, 2028. 11 AM.

Dr. Tyler Sullivan dialed Kristian Barnett's personal smartphone. "Hello," answered Kristian.

"Good morning, Kristian. I have some news. I have contacted Dr. James Stanley at Stanford's School of Neuroscience regarding your symptoms. He will be setting up a series of tests that he can use to arrive at a diagnosis. Stanford is one of the best neuroscience schools in the world, and Dr. Stanley is one of its top neurologists. The tests will likely span two to three days and be performed at Stanford's Neuroscience Health Center. When do you think you will be available to schedule?"

"I will clear my schedule as soon as Stanford can accommodate me, Tyler," replied Kristian. "I need to find out what this thing is, and the sooner the better."

"They can accommodate you for the recommended tests on Tuesday, May 9, at 11:30 AM. Will that work for you, Kris?" Anticipating Kristian's response, Dr. Sullivan had already requested the earliest available schedule for the tests.

"Absolutely."

"Great. I'll confirm the schedule with Stanford. I assume your staff will handle the travel arrangements."

The Barnett's personal twelve-passenger Learjet Challenger 650 landed at the Palo Alto City Airport and taxied to meet the limo that would take Kristian to the Stanford Neuroscience Health Center. As Kristian disembarked, he nearly stumbled descending the stairs from the jet to the tarmac but caught himself using the handrail before he fell.

"Damn!" he exclaimed. "I am feeling more and more like a feeble old man."

"Nonsense," replied his executive assistant and vice president, Noel. "Those steps are treacherous for anybody."

Arriving at the Stanford Neuroscience Health Center, Kristian was greeted at his limo to ensure privacy and security. Kristian, always averse to spontaneous press inquiries, did not want to arouse any speculation on the reason for his visit.

"Hello, Mr. Barnett," greeted a sharp-looking young woman dressed in a blue suit and white lab coat. "My name is Lauren Thompson and I will be your test coordinator for your visit with us this week. If you will follow me, we will enter the facility through an entrance that bypasses our public check-in office." Kristian, accompanied by Noel, followed Lauren through a side entrance and down a hallway to Lauren's office.

"You must be Noel. Nice to meet the person behind the voice. It was great working with you to get Mr. Barnett's schedule arranged," said Lauren.

Noel replied, "Yes we really appreciated your assistance, Lauren."

"Mr. Barnett, Dr. Stanley has ordered a number of tests that will lead to a diagnosis of your condition. First, we will be conducting an MRI of your head and neck this afternoon to rule out a herniated disc in your neck and a tumor on the brain. Either can cause the symptoms you are experiencing.

"Tomorrow we will conduct electrophysiological tests. Doctors use them to determine how your muscles and nerves are reacting to various stimuli. The first will be Electromyography. EMG is one of the most important tests we use for muscle irregularities. Small electric shocks are sent through your nerves. Your doctor measures how fast they conduct electricity and whether the nerves are damaged. A second part of the test also checks the electrical activity of your muscles."

"Next we will perform a nerve conduction study. The results of this test can also suggest several diagnoses."

"Finally, we have scheduled a muscle biopsy. You will be given something to numb the area before the tissue is taken. On Thursday morning you will meet with Dr. Stanley regarding the results of the tests and a possible diagnosis. Your appointment with Dr. Stanley is at 10:45."

"Lauren, aren't these tests given when the suspected cause of the problems is Lou Gehrig's disease?" questioned Noel.

"This series of tests is used to determine a diagnosis, Noel. That diagnosis could point to a number of possibilities, or none." "You mean I could have ALS?" questioned a visibly concerned Kristian.

"Let's not jump to any conclusions," said Lauren. "As I said, these tests are used for multiple suspected causes. If you have no further questions at this time, we have arranged for lunch to be brought into our private dining room. After lunch, you will be taken up to the imaging lab for your MRI. Please follow me."

After the MRI, Barnett and Noel were escorted to their limo and driven to the Four Seasons Hotel where a penthouse suite had been reserved for Mr. Barnett. Noel was accommodated in her own suite.

Kristian tipped the bellman who delivered his bags and immediately picked up his smartphone and dialed Ansley's private mobile number. Ansley answered on the second ring. "Hi, Kris, how did your tests go today? Are you in your hotel?" "I had an MRI this afternoon," replied Kristian. "I have several more tests tomorrow. Ansley, I need you to plan on being here on Thursday when I get the results of the tests." "We discussed my being there all three days, and I had multiple appointments I really couldn't miss. That's why Noel went with you," replied Ansley.

"Ansley, I'm afraid this thing may be...serious. The tests they are giving me are those used to diagnose ALS."

Silence on the other end for what seemed like minutes but was only a couple of seconds. "Oh my God!" exclaimed Ansley. "What time do I need to be there on Thursday? Or do you need me to come sooner?"

"No, they are mainly doing tests tomorrow. Thursday will be fine. My appointment with Dr. Stanley is at 10:45."

"My last meeting tomorrow is at 4 PM. I will arrive in Palo Alto tomorrow evening," replied Ansley.

Barnett rang Noel's room and asked her to bring his laptop up to the penthouse. Noel was at his door in less than five minutes.

"Kristian, here's your laptop. Do you need my assistance with anything?" she asked.

"No, no thanks, Noel. I will be dining in my room this evening. I need to catch up on a couple of … issues. Oh, and Ansley will be joining us in our meeting on Thursday with Dr. Stanley."

"I see," said Noel. "You seem stressed over the possible test results."

"Well, I guess you could say I am somewhat concerned. I mean ALS? I'm only in my thirties for heaven's sake."

"I understand," said Noel. "Try not to stress too much. You have several tests tomorrow. As Lauren said, there are several possible diagnoses that these tests may point to."

Kristian immediately began researching ALS symptoms, tests, and treatment. What he found at the National Institutes of Neurological Disorders and Stroke website was quite disturbing, given his symptoms. Several of the symptoms listed were familiar ones that he had experienced the past few months. Muscle twitches in the arm, leg, shoulder, or tongue were among the symptoms that had plagued him, particularly twitches in his arms and legs. Muscle weakness was also identified. Kristian recalled the evening with Tyler and Aidan at the mansion where he dropped the pitcher of margaritas.

The MRI he had this afternoon, as well those he was scheduled for on Wednesday, were the standard tests for ALS. He also found that an estimated 90 percent of ALS cases were "Sporadic ALS," where there was no relation to family history of the disease. He read how the disease progresses as muscle weakness and atrophy spread to other parts of the body. Individuals may develop problems with moving, swallowing (dysphagia), speaking or forming words (dysarthria), and breathing (dyspnea). Individuals with ALS will have difficulty breathing as the muscles of their respiratory system weaken. They eventually lose the ability to breathe on their own and must depend on a ventilator. Affected individuals also face an increased risk of pneumonia during the later stages of the disease. Besides muscle cramps that may cause discomfort, some individuals with ALS may develop painful neuropathy (nerve disease or damage). One somewhat encouraging note he discovered was that people with ALS usually retain their ability to perform higher mental processes such as reasoning, remembering, understanding and problem-solving. However, since they are aware of their progressive loss of function, they may become anxious and depressed.

"At least I may still have my mental health until near the end," Kristian thought. As he continued his research, he found that there is still no cure for ALS. It was one of the few remaining diseases for which a cure had not been found. Treatment consists of drug therapy to reduce damage to motor neurons by decreasing levels of glutamate, which transports messages between nerve cells and motor neurons. Physicians can also prescribe medications to help manage symptoms of ALS, including muscle cramps, stiffness, excess saliva and phlegm, and involuntary or uncontrollable episodes of crying and/or laughing, or other emotional displays. Drugs also are available to help individuals with pain, depression, sleep disturbances, and constipation. Pharmacists can give advice on the proper use of medications and monitor a person's prescriptions to avoid risks of drug interactions. Other treatments included physical and speech therapy. Some progress had been made in delaying symptoms, but still, no cure had been discovered. Kristian concluded his research for the evening around 9:30 PM. Not feeling hungry, but feeling he should eat, he ordered a bowl of The Four Seasons clam chowder, a small loaf of bread, and a bottle of wine from room service. He believed the combination of a light meal and wine would help him get some needed sleep.

After being poked and prodded for the better part of the day, Kristian was glad to return to his suite at the Four Seasons around 4:30 PM. The Center had done a good job of protecting his privacy. So far, no media hounds had bothered him.

Kristian heard the buzz of his smartphone indicating he had received a text message. "I should be at your hotel around 7 PM," stated the verbal text from Ansley. "Would you like to have dinner? I hear there is a pretty good steakhouse near the university."

Kristian typed his reply on the smartphone keypad, "Gr8, glad you are coming today. Should we go out or will we be subject to media scrutiny?"

In a few minutes, a verbal text reply from Ansley stated, "I think we'd be OK to go to a restaurant. If any media discovers us, you are at the university to discuss business with the president of the university."

"OK, let's risk it. Do you know the name of the restaurant? I will ask Noel to make arrangements for us."

"Sundance the Steakhouse," replied Ansley.

Not wanting to draw attention, Kristian and Ansley decided to catch a driverless Uber car to the restaurant rather than take a limo. However, the limo would pick them up at a discreet spot a block away from the restaurant when they were done. The reservation Noel had made for them was for 8 PM.

"May I take your drink order while you look over our menu?" said the waiter who was dressed in a white shirt, black slacks, maroon vest, and bowtie.

"I'll have the Sundance Margarita," replied Ansley. "And I'll have a Moscow Mule," said Kristian.

"Should you be drinking?" questioned a surprised Ansley. "Tests are over, Dear. No reason I can't," replied Kristian, smiling at his wife's concern while knowing he had polished off two-thirds of the bottle of wine the night before.

"I will get those drinks right out to you," said the waiter, turning and walking towards the bar.

"So, tell me all about your tests, Kris," said Ansley. "Did they give you any hint as to what the diagnosis may be?"

"Well, no, actually. When I asked any of the hospital staff if they saw anything, or knew anything, the reply was the standard, 'Dr. Stanley will review the tests with you in the morning'," replied Kristian. "However, I did some research on my own last night in the hotel and it doesn't sound promising. I seem to have several of the major symptoms associated with ALS according to what I found on the NIH website."

"What symptoms?" asked Ansley. "I've only seen you stumble a couple of times. Then there was that Margarita pitcher you dropped at the pool that evening with the Sullivans."

"Oh, my stumbling has been more frequent, particularly the past couple of months," replied Kristian. "I almost fell deplaning when we arrived at Palo Alto on Tuesday. Fortunately, Noel caught me, or I might have been visiting the hospital for other reasons. I've also experienced tingling and numbness in both legs and in my right arm more frequently lately. Unfortunately, our schedules keep us apart too often, so you wouldn't have noticed the number of.... incidents."

The waiter returned with their drinks. "Are you ready to order?"

"I guess we haven't looked past the appetizers," replied Kristian. "But we'll start with a half-dozen raw oysters and the Tempura Gulf prawns."

"Very good, sir," replied the waiter who turned and left their table.

"The only thing I've noticed is that you seem to be more distant lately," said Ansley. "I thought that maybe the pressures of running a multi-billion-dollar corporation and the estate were weighing on you, so I didn't question you. Are you saying that it was these... symptoms that have been bothering you?"

"Quite honestly, Ansley, I haven't realized that I've been 'more distant' as you describe it. But I have had a growing concern that something wasn't right with me for some time. That's why I contacted Tyler and Aidan a couple of weeks ago."

The waiter returned with the appetizers and again asked if he could take their dinner order. Having just finished perusing the menu, Ansley said, "I will have the 7-ounce filet with a baked potato."

"I will have the 12-ounce prime rib with mashed potatoes," said Kristian. "Also, we would like a bottle of Silver Oak Napa Valley 2013 to be served with our entrees." Kristian often spent more on a bottle of wine than the cost of their two meals. The Silver Oak was no exception at two-hundred-and-thirty dollars.

"Excellent choices. Any soup or salad?" questioned the waiter. "None for me," replied Ansley.

"I'd like a Caesar salad," said Kristian.

Chapter 3

Dr. Stanley, tall, thin and balding, stood up behind his oversized mahogany desk and reached out to Kristian to shake his hand. "Mr. and Dr. Barnett, good morning. I hope our staff here at the center has made your visit comfortable. Have a seat and we'll go over your test results."

"Good morning, Dr. Stanley," replied Kristian as they sat in the leather desk chairs facing Dr. Stanley. "I hope these tests will reveal the cause of the symptoms I've been experiencing."

"Well, in that regard, yes the tests are pointing to a diagnosis," replied Stanley. "I'm afraid your test results indicate that you have amyotrophic lateral sclerosis," he paused. "That's ALS." Both Kristian and Ansley were stunned. Ansley let out a slight moan.

Dr. Stanley continued, "You are in the very early stages of the disease, but it is likely your condition will worsen over time and the prognosis for ALS patients is not good."

"I did some reading on the disease while in my hotel these past couple of days and things do not sound promising for an active future, " replied Kristian. "Just how fast will I become a vegetable, doctor?"

"The speed of physical decline is unpredictable," Stanley replied. "It is different for every patient and can span from a couple of years to a decade or more. Recall that the renowned physicist, Stephen Hawking, suffered from the disease for decades and lived past 70. Although, I will say that Hawking was an exceptional case."

"What can I expect, given a typical case?" questioned Kristian.

Dr. Stanley described the disease and its toll on the body.

"Motor neurons reach from the brain to the spinal cord and from the spinal cord to the muscles throughout the body. The progressive degeneration of the motor neurons in ALS patients eventually leads to their demise. When the motor neurons die, the ability of the brain to initiate and control muscle movement is lost. With voluntary muscle action progressively affected, people may lose the ability to speak, eat, move and eventually, breathe. The motor nerves that are affected when you have ALS are the motor neurons that provide voluntary movements and muscle control. Examples of voluntary movements are making the effort to reach for a smartphone or step off a curb. These actions are controlled by the muscles in the arms and legs."

"My research indicates that there is no cure for this disease," said Kristian. "What is being done to achieve a cure or at least improve the quality of life for those who are afflicted with ALS?" Dr. Stanley replied, "Recent years have brought a wealth of new scientific understanding regarding the physiology of this disease. Studies all over the world, many funded by The ALS Association, are ongoing to develop effective treatments and cures for ALS. Although there is not yet a cure or treatment that halts or reverses ALS, scientists have made significant progress in learning more about this disease. In addition, people with ALS may experience a better quality of life in living with the disease by participating in support groups and attending an ALS Association Certified Treatment Center of Excellence or a recognized treatment center. Such centers provide a national standard of best-practice multidisciplinary care to help manage the symptoms of the disease and assist people living with ALS to maintain as much independence as possible for as long as possible. I recommend that we try to find a program for you, that considers your need for privacy and confidentiality, to prepare you for what you will ultimately experience with this disease. To that end I want you to meet someone who I believe you will find to be a great resource in the management of the disease."

Pressing a button on his desk phone, his assistant responded. "Yes, Dr. Stanley."

"Please ask Dr. Richards to join us in my office."

"Dr. Savannah Richards is one of the best research scientists on the planet dealing with neurological conditions," stated Stanley. "Her team of research scientists and physicians led the development of the cure of Alzheimer's Disease and similar dementia. They are probably the foremost group involved in finding new treatments, and, ultimately, a cure, for ALS."

"Savannah Richards?" asked Ansley. "Oh my God, she and I went through medical school together!"

Dr. Savannah Richards entered the office. "Good morning, Savannah, I want you to meet the Barnett's, Kristian and Ansley. I understand you know each other."

Savannah Richards and Ansley Barnett embraced briefly as did Kristian and Savanah. "How is Erik doing, Savannah?" said Ansley. "Is he still competing for a spot on the Mars expedition?" Erik Richards, Savannah's younger brother, is a lieutenant in the U.S. Navy and is a top F-35 pilot.

"Oh, Erik is doing fine. He is one of the finalists for one of the four pilot positions on the USS Elon Musk. He should know any day if he won the position." Then, she quickly changed the subject. "Kris, I hear you have been going through some tests. How are you feeling?"

"Well, to be honest, not too well at the moment," replied a dejected Kristian. "Dr. Stanley here tells me I have ALS. It's not easy being handed a death sentence at my age."

"I can empathize with your feelings, Kris," said Savannah. "However, we are making progress in managing the disease and may be as close as five years away from a cure. If you will allow my team to review your specific condition based on the tests, we can come up with a plan that manages the disease all through its various stages."

"Five years for a possible cure!" exclaimed Ansley, tears forming on her eyes. "My God, Kristian may not have five years."

"Given Kris's age and otherwise good physical condition, I believe five or more years is a very possible expectation," replied Savannah. "We are working with older patients who have had the disease for over a decade that still have some motor capabilities. I suggest we adopt a positive outlook going forward that will help both Kris and you."

"Ansley, please, let's not allow our emotions to overcome our desire for a good outcome," said Kristian.

"Sorry," said Ansley. "All this talk of the disease and its horrible impact on someone got hold of me, I guess. I'll try to be positive going forward. On that note, will this possible cure reverse the damage done to Kristian's body?" Ansley thought immediately of her top-secret work with the Department of Defense and DARPA, restoring damaged tissue for soldiers injured in combat.

"We are focusing on stopping the progress of the disease first," replied Savannah. "However, there is considerable ongoing research to restore neurological function following a traumatic loss."

"Savannah, you do know that money is no object in beating this thing," said Kristian. "If there is a way we can help financially, or any other way, please don't hesitate to let us know."

"Thanks, Kris," replied Dr. Richards. "We will certainly keep that in mind as we design your treatment plan."

"Also, I want to ensure that my treatment plan protects my privacy. I don't want the world to find out about my condition until it is absolutely unavoidable," said Kris. "I would like to build, or otherwise convert, part of the mansion into the most advanced treatment facility for ALS in the world. As you develop my plan, please include what will be needed to achieve this. Again, money is no object."

"Savannah, I would like you to take charge of this project and supervise both my treatment as well as the design of our new ALS facility," continued Kristian. "Any resources, both physical and human, that you require will be placed at your disposal. And whatever they are paying you here at Stanford, I will triple it."

Chapter 4

It had been three years since Kristian Barnett had been diagnosed with ALS. His condition had declined to the point where he required a cane to walk, could only walk short distances, and spent most of his time in a motorized wheelchair. He still had about sixty-percent function in his right arm, but his left was now ninety percent immobilized. He retained about eighty percent of his speech capability but was on a diet of soft foods to accommodate difficulty in swallowing.

An advanced treatment facility, incorporating all the latest technology and equipment, had been built on the Barnett mansion property. At $120 million and still climbing, the facility, built under the supervision of Dr. Savannah Richards, enabled her to move her research in dementia reversal and brain-body extraction and preservation techniques to the Barnett Center for Neurological Restoration. A healthy donation to Stanford by the Barnetts had erased any objection the university had allowing Dr. Richards to relocate.

In the meantime, Dr. Savannah Richards, Director of the Barnett Research Foundation, was concluding tests on a procedure that would remove the healthy brain of a patient suffering from a terminal disease or from a disabling accident and keep the brain alive, in biostasis, indefinitely. As one might imagine, the procedure raised serious ethical questions such as at what point in the patient's condition should the brain be removed from the body, given that it must be removed prior to death before the brain is damaged irreparably. Testing the procedure on animals had demonstrated that it was highly successful. The brains continued to live indefinitely in an induced coma. But with a human, how will the procedure affect the mind of the patient when and if the brain could be restored to a human or cyborg body? These issues were now being debated at the highest levels and it would be some time before an actual living human brain would be removed and placed in biostasis.

Dr. Savannah Richards arrived at Barnett Place, arriving in a pod that made the three-quarters of a mile trip from Barnett Center to the mansion in five seconds. The pod system developed by Barnett Industries and named "The Transporter" was essentially a vacuum tube between the facilities that worked virtually like the tube in a bank drive-in window. The pod system was being built in multiple cities in the U.S., as well as in Tokyo, Japan.

"Hello, Kristian, good to see you," said Savannah. "How are you feeling?"

"Given the circumstances, I'm feeling good," replied Kristian. "Thanks for coming up from the Center. I have a couple of things I'd like to discuss. First, tell me about this brain extraction procedure you are developing. Sounds like something out of an old Frankenstein horror movie."

Savannah replied, "It does sound bizarre, but I assure you, it is based on sound science. Essentially, the patient is placed in a coma while we transfer the brain to a biostasis cube which maintains the brain at optimum temperature and nutrient supply. The skull is removed from one side of the brain and we sever the brain from the body just below the medulla oblongata. This sounds simple, but, believe me, it is one of the most complex procedures ever developed. Just think of all of the nerves that must be accounted for."

"What happens to the brain of a patient once their brain is placed in this ... biostasis cube? Do they still have thoughts? Can they still hear or feel?"

"First, we have not performed the procedure on a human, so we don't know how the mind will react to its new surroundings.

Second, the patient is in a coma and will be until we have a vehicle to return the brain to," replied Richards.

"A...vehicle?" said Kristian, somewhat stunned at what he was hearing.

"A body," said Richards. "There are several possibilities for this. One could be a brain transplant. A body in which the brain has been destroyed by disease or accident but is otherwise healthy. Another could be immersion in a body grown from stem cells of the original body, essentially a clone. And a third procedure could involve downloading the mind to a cyborg brain."

"The problem with the human transplant," Richards continued, "is if the donor's brain is destroyed there is an extremely short window to transfer the brain from biostasis. I consider this to be the most complicated and least feasible method and the ethics involved are likely insurmountable."

"So, essentially, this is a one-way trip to...nowhere... for the patient," said Kristian. "You get put into a coma with no hope of ever waking up."

"Well, no," said Richards. "Look at it more like a journey where you don't know how long you'll be traveling. With the advancements currently achieved in cloning technology and cyber enhancements, we may not be that far out from a fully- cloned or cyborg body that could accommodate the brain in stasis or download the mind into a cyborg brain. We are now growing virtually all organs, except the brain, using stem cell technology. This has nearly eliminated the issue of organ rejection for transplants."

"Artificial limbs, that are difficult to distinguish from flesh and blood limbs, controlled directly by the brain are now commonplace," continued Richards. "And we are now able to cure paralysis caused by spinal injury, restoring the quality of life for many quadriplegics and paraplegics."

Pondering this information, Kristian responded, "Could you replace my limbs with artificial limbs so I could return to a better state of health?"

"Good thought," replied Savannah. "Problem is, with ALS, you could not control the artificial limbs any better than you can control your natural limbs. The disease affects the nerves that control your motor functions."

"Savannah, you've addressed my first question. Now for my second: could I be a candidate for your brain extraction procedure?"

"Kristian, I don't believe we are far enough along to answer that question. First, you still have much of your motor capability. You can still walk with assistance; both of your arms are still functional. You do not have difficulty breathing when you speak."

"I don't mean today, Savannah," said Kristian. "But we both know that given my rate of decline, I will be a vegetable in a just a few years. Once that likely outcome is nearly upon us, I would be willing to take the risk with the procedure. In the meantime, the advances you spoke of will be closer to reality. So, my.... journey, as you put it, may not be too long.

Chapter 5

Three years had passed since Kristian had raised the possibility of the brain extraction on himself with Savannah Richards. His condition had declined further. He could no longer walk, both legs were now paralyzed, and so he was confined to his motorized wheelchair. His left arm was fully paralyzed. His right still had about 20 percent motor function. He was virtually unable to swallow so he was being fed intravenously. He was able to speak with computer-aided assistance, where a chip had been surgically implanted on his vocal cords and wirelessly connected to a speaker. Yet he still retained full mental function and that made fighting depression his main challenge, aside from his dying body of course. In the meantime, the FDA had granted the Barnett Research Foundation limited permission to begin testing brain extraction on humans. The ethics finally came down to the conclusion that if people who were terminal could elect assisted suicide, which was now legal in forty-two states including California, they could elect the alternative of Brain Preservation, as the procedure had come to be known.

Kristian and Ansley were watching the sunset from the rooftop garden atop the mansion. "Ansley, I think the time has come to go forward with the procedure," said Kristian.

"Oh, Kristian," Ansley replied. "I am having a hard time visualizing your brain being removed from your body while you are still alive. I don't know if I can deal with that."

"Ansley, I am close to becoming a vegetable with death not far behind," said Kristian. "Noel has been running business operations for Barnett Industries and the Barnett Research Foundation for over a year now, leaving me to contemplate my demise. I would officially appoint her as CEO. You would be named executive chairman over both to await the possibility of my eventual return. I believe I am ready, but I want your blessing to proceed."

Ansley contemplated Kristian's request, knowing that her work with DARPA was going to result in a cyborg capable of downloading the human mind into its electronic brain in less than a decade. The cyborg body, which was virtually indistinguishable from a human, had nearly been completed. The technology to download the human mind was the next hurdle but was progressing well.

"Kristian, if this is really what you want to do, standing in your way would be selfish of me," said Ansley.

"Ansley, there is an … issue I think we should discuss and get cleared up before we go much further," said Kristian. "It may be several years, if ever, until I can return to being a … fulfilling husband. I don't expect you to be," he paused before slowly continuing …"I don't expect you to remain faithful to me."

"Kristian, you've been … incapacitated for over three years and counting. I have accepted the situation and am willing to endure it as long as necessary," replied Ansley.

"But we are looking at … ten years or longer before my brain is restored into some sort of body. And we have no idea whether that body will have any sexual ability. What I'm saying is I'm willing to set you free if you want. You could remain married to me if you wish, and otherwise have all the benefits of marriage. But I think it would be selfish of me to demand your celibacy. It would be like medieval knights going to the crusades and locking their women in chastity belts."

"So, you think I should have male … concubines?" Ansley replied somewhat smartly.

"Well, that image is not one I envisioned, but if you had the … opportunity … to have some enjoyment in your life while I was a brain in a bottle, I wouldn't hold it against you," said Kristian.

"As long as I'm in that bottle, what you do in that regard is of little consequence to me."

"What I want, Kristian, is to be artificially inseminated with the sperm we took from you when you were still viable," said Ansley. "I know you said you don't want to take a chance at passing your disease onto your offspring, but you also said that there is less than a 10 percent chance of that happening. I want to have our baby before you go into the brain bottle. I want you to see your child before you go away on your 'journey.'

"I see," said Kristian. "If that is what you want, it is what I want too."

Approximately ten months later Ansley gave birth to a healthy, beautiful baby girl. Kristian and Ansley named their daughter Kristen Elaine, after Kristian and Ansley's grandmother.

Chapter 6

Dr. Savannah Richards arrived at the mansion in the transporter and was met by Kristian and Ansley at the docking port. "Savannah, thanks for joining us," Kristian said through his electronic voice. "We would like to review the possibility of my undergoing the Brain Restoration Procedure. Ansley and I have discussed it at length and we both agree that now is probably the optimum time for the procedure."

"I understand," replied Dr. Richards. "I suggest we meet at the Center and allow me to walk you, step-by-step, through the procedure. This would include viewing animated films of exactly what will be happening to you before, during, and following the procedure. " As she spoke, she could see that Ansley was visibly upset, near tears.

"Ansley, is there anything you need to help you get through the procedure? I can see that you are still anxious when we discuss it." Ansley replied tearfully, "I am just having some difficulty comprehending what is going to happen to my husband, the love of my life. I mean, removing his brain and placing him in an indefinite coma. Will I ever see him again?"

"At this point, Ansley, that is our hope and prayer," replied Richards. "But you must go into this procedure knowing there are no guarantees. I suggest we walk through the procedure at the Center before we make any final decisions."

"OK," said Kristian. "When could we do the walk-thru?"

"I will work with Noel to get it scheduled, Kristian, if that's alright with you."

The year is 2037, nine years after Kristian Barnett was diagnosed with ALS. Kristian has given his full consent to the Brain Restoration Procedure developed by Dr. Savannah Richards. Savannah Richard's prediction of a cure for ALS has not panned out and is still likely several years in the future. Kristian awaits Dr. Richard's final consultation prior to the procedure in a suite in the Barnett Center. Kristian is now completely paralyzed and requires the use of a respirator to breathe. He is fed intravenously. He retains his mental faculties and communicates with the aid of a computer.

"Kristian, we are ready to proceed," said Dr. Richards. "Are you prepared based on what you have been shown regarding the procedure?"

Kristian indicates that he is prepared.

"Ansley, are you prepared for Kristian to undergo the procedure?" Savannah asks.

"Yes."

Twelve hours later, Dr. Richards, still in blood-stained scrubs, approached Ansley Barnett. "Ansley, the operation has been completed. Kristian's brain is healthy and in biostasis. All our monitors indicate everything is working fine – as planned. He, of course, will be unconscious indefinitely, in an induced coma."

"I understand. And thank you, Savannah. We can only hope and pray that somehow he will be returned to a physical body soon," said Ansley, tears streaming down her cheeks. She turned her head as she thought about the progress her team was making with the DARPA effort to create an artificial human body. The body was essentially complete and undergoing testing, but the challenge of scanning and downloading a human mind into its electronic brain was still a major challenge.

Chapter 7

"Kristian…Kristian…Kristian," Kristian heard as he seemed to awaken, at first in a dense fog that began to slowly give way to a bright light. Then, within the light, he could see a glowing figure that seemed to slowly move closer. Still unaware of his surroundings Kristian thought that something had gone wrong with the Brain Restoration Procedure, and he was coming out of anesthesia. He said, "Where am I? What's happened with the procedure?"

Then, the glowing figure showed itself to be a tall figure with a fair complexion, thick, blue eyes and wavy shoulder-length blond hair. He was dressed in an open leather trench coat that reached below his knees and under the trench coat, Kristian could see a T-shirt, jeans, and boots. The figure raised its arm and pointed. Following the figure's arm, Kristian saw the biostasis cube, and within it saw what looked like a human brain. "That is what remains of your corporeal body. Your brain, your spirit is alive, but your body is not. You are the first human to be trapped between the physical and spiritual worlds. This means your spirit can pass between the two worlds."

Kristian tried to contemplate what he was hearing from the being in front of him. "I thought I was to remain in a coma until they figured out how to restore me to a functioning body. How is it that my brain is in a bottle, but I am here talking to a stranger?" "In your current form you are what humans call a spirit.

However, your spirit is restricted from fully entering the next level because your mind is technically still tied to the corporeal level," replied the being.

"So, now what am I supposed to do?" replied Kristian. "Am I to remain in limbo until somebody figures out how to bring me back? Am I supposed to be a ghost haunting those who are trying to help me?"

"You are not a ghost, as you call it," said the being. "Some spirits remain earthbound for a period after they pass. But they have fully passed and have stranded themselves by choice in their earthly surroundings. Eventually, most ascend to the next level." "The reason I am with you is that you have work to do while you are in this state. The best description of what I am, in your vernacular, is a guardian. My siblings and I exist to see that the timeline remains aligned with the predestined outcome that the Creator has envisioned. As your species has speculated, there are no coincidences. Everything happens for a reason."

Still quite confused at what he was hearing, Kristian said, "tell me more. What am I expected to do? Are you an angel? What do I call you? You look like a character in a motorcycle gang."

The being responded, "You may call me Guardian. I have been called many things throughout the centuries. Angel is one of those references. My appearance to you is intended to put you at ease. My true appearance would damage and may destroy your brain in biostasis. Again, what we do is to watch over the timelines and induce corrections when they go off course. You see, there are many like you who are between worlds and therefore can assist us in correcting errant timelines."

"Wait, you said I was the first human to be in this…state… as you call it," said Kristian.

"You are, but there is something you should know about the next level. There is no time there as you know it. All at this level can exist at any point in Earth's timeline, past, present, and future. In the future, there are many more like you who are assisting with timeline guardianship."

"So, how can the timeline, or timelines you refer to, go off course if the Creator has established them?" questioned Kristian. "Simple. Man was endowed by the Creator with free will," replied the Guardian. "Human actions can and will alter a timeline. Most of the time these alterations are of little or no consequence. But sometimes they can be catastrophic. It is these situations we focus on."

"In this form am I able to communicate with those still alive, like my wife?"

"No, in fact in your current state, you can only interact with me and others like you. I will guide you to that which you should see to further your education as it pertains to your assignments. You cannot communicate with anyone else on either side of the veil without my explicit involvement and assistance. Now I will begin to show you what you will need to know.

Chapter 8

The Guardian began by saying, "I will begin by showing you the ramifications of the timeline uncorrected. You need to understand this fully as it will give you strong motivation to complete your mission." Then, in his mind, Kristian saw an altered flag of the United States of America flying above the U.S. Capitol. The red and white bars on the flag appeared to be the same but the white stars on the blue background were replaced with the image of the Stars and Bars of the Confederacy. Images of statues honoring Robert E. Lee, Jefferson Davis, J.E.B Stuart, Stonewall Jackson, and other prominent Confederate generals passed through Kristian's mind. Images of black men and women laboring in the fields and serving elites in their plantation mansions followed next. An image of Ulysses S. Grant surrendering his sword to Robert E. Lee flashed quickly, along with Abraham Lincoln surrendering the White House to Jefferson Davis. The images all portrayed the fall of the Union because of the Confederate victory in the Civil War. But these images were only the beginning of what Kristian was to see.

With the Confederate victory and southern congressional representatives returning to Washington, state's rights became the battle cry in Congress. Laws were passed limiting the federal government's domination over state legislatures. Many issues, but especially slavery, were left up to the states to determine. Of course, all the southern states quickly established slavery as an acceptable practice based on economic needs.

As time went by, agendas and programs that were to be promoted by more liberal factions never occurred. Women did not gain the right to vote in federal elections, although this was finally achieved during the Calvin Coolidge administration in the 1920s. The 14th Amendment to the Constitution was never enacted, therefore Blacks who were freed never achieved the full rights of citizenship, including the right to vote. A black person who attempted to escape from a slave state to a free state faced serious consequences including extended time in prison. Prohibition never happened and social programs including Social Security never passed. The 17th Amendment failed to pass Congress, leaving senators to be appointed by state legislatures. Again, the policies enacted for some fifty years after the war supported state's rights and the block in Congress defending severely limited government remained too strong to allow consideration of federally-run programs.

During the Gilded Age, from 1870 to 1900 there wasn't much change from the known timeline aside that most of the presidents who served were former Confederate officers. Jefferson Davis served until 1876. In fact, until the presidency of Woodrow Wilson, none of the presidents were the same as in the Union victory timeline. During this period little serious legislation was passed. Between 1875 and 1896 only five major bills made it through Congress to the President's desk. Even discussion of the graduated income tax, by any definition a revolutionary measure, failed to arouse much interest or public debate. All the same, there was wide voter participation and interest in the political process and most elections saw about an eighty- percent turnout.

Yet the unprecedented dilemmas created by industrialization, urbanization, and the huge influx of immigrants were met with passivity and confusion. Congress was known for being rowdy and inefficient. It was not unusual to find that a quorum could not be achieved because too many members were drunk or otherwise preoccupied with extra-governmental affairs. The Senate, whose seats were often auctioned off to the highest bidder, was known as a 'rich man's club,' where political favors were traded like horses, and the needs of the people in the working classes lay beyond the vision of the exalted legislators. The Senate dominated the federal government during the Gilded Age, often calling the tune to which presidents were required to dance.

Woodrow Wilson was president in the altered timeline and kept the United States out of World War I until 1917 when German aggression on the high seas forced his hand to petition Congress for a declaration of war. Wilson was also a known racist and segregationist, something that sat well with the Democratic Party leadership. However, Wilson and the Democrats continued to alienate many Americans outside the South.

By 1919 the Democratic Party was in disarray. The southern Democrats, unlike their colleagues in the north, were adamantly against most of the progressive policies passed in the timeline where the North won the Civil War. The election of 1920 saw the first Republican president since Abraham Lincoln take office in 1861, as voters reacted to Wilson's failure to keep the U.S. out of World War I and his desire to outlaw slavery. Defeating Democrat James Cox in a landslide, Warren G. Harding was elected along with Calvin Coolidge, Harding's vice president.

The timelines in the 1920s generally paralleled each other. Harding was elected and then died suddenly in 1923. Harding's brief administration was plagued with scandals in both timelines. Coolidge assumed office and was re-elected in 1924. Coolidge essentially cleared up the corruption in the federal government including the Tea Pot Dome scandal. Coolidge declined to run for re-election in 1928, stating that ten years in office is too long for anyone. The two biggest accomplishments under the Republican administrations in the 1920s were the passage of the 19th Amendment giving women the right to vote and the ratification of the 13th Amendment which abolished slavery. The 13th Amendment was passed by Congress in January 1865, but ratification was blocked by the Southern states after the Union fell to the Confederacy in April 1865.

Herbert Hoover was elected in 1928 in both timelines and was blamed for the Great Depression, mainly by Democrats in both timelines. Hoover resisted intervention in the failing economy by the federal government which became his undoing as President. Hoover was defeated in a landslide by Franklin Delano Roosevelt in 1932.

Now the timelines began to diverge. In the Confederate victory timeline, Roosevelt was heavily influenced by the southern Democrat block in Congress. Many of the progressive programs created in the Union victory timeline were either not, or only partially implemented. Nevertheless, Roosevelt did attempt to provide relief to the millions of unemployed and farmers during the era. Programs and legislation implemented in the Union victory timeline under Roosevelt, including the Securities and Exchange Commission, the National Labor Relations Act, the Federal Deposit Insurance Corporation, and Social Security were never enacted.

Where the timelines grew further apart involved the U.S. and World War II. In the Confederate victory timeline, Roosevelt succumbed to severe pressure from both Republicans and many Democrats to avoid entry into the war. Aware of this resistance, the Japanese not only decimated the U.S. Pacific Fleet at Pearl Harbor but continued the invasion onto the U.S. West Coast. The coastal states of California, Oregon, and Washington fell to the Japanese. Because of poor funding of the U.S. military during the Roosevelt years, the U.S. response to this invasion was weak and ineffective.

Roosevelt, in both timelines, was an admirer of Mussolini and the way he essentially took control of Italy. The mutual admiration between Roosevelt and Mussolini led Roosevelt to lean against entering the war against Germany as Mussolini was allied with Adolph Hitler and Germany. Little did the naïve Roosevelt know that Hitler and Mussolini had been conspiring against the United States. As the Japanese attacked the U.S. West Coast, Hitler and Mussolini, allied with Japan, attacked the U.S. East Coast and overcame New York City, Boston, and Philadelphia, as well as Norfolk and Charleston in the South. The U.S. had been attacked on both coasts. Defending its own shores, the U.S. never joined the allied forces in Europe, which allowed Hitler to conquer Britain and develop a four-engine jet- powered bomber with which to attack the United States.

Fighting continued until the German-Italian invasion captured all major U.S. cities east of the Mississippi River. And in the West, the Japanese controlled everything west of the Rocky Mountains. What remained of the U.S. was essentially a no-man's land between the Mississippi River and the Rocky Mountains.

Chapter 9

Kristian awoke from the dream state imposed by The Guardian in horror. "What could possibly cause this alternate timeline to manifest?"

"You saw that the Confederacy won the Civil War," replied The Guardian. "The Confederacy was winning the war until Stonewall Jackson was killed by his own men in a horrific mistake. The combined genius of Jackson and Robert E. Lee proved too much for the weak leadership of the Union forces. In the altered timeline, Jackson endured only a minor wound and returned to Lee's side in only a couple of days. Lee and Jackson were subsequently victorious at Gettysburg and later captured Washington D.C. You just saw the remainder of the history in the dream I sent to you."

In the Union victory timeline, Major General Richard Ewell was promoted to lieutenant general and assumed command of the Army of Northern Virginia's Second Corps at the death of Stonewall Jackson. Ewell initially performed well. On July 1, 1863, Ewell's corps approached Gettysburg from the north and smashed the Union XI Corps and part of the I Corps, driving them back through the town and forcing them to take up defensive positions on Cemetery Hill south of town. When General Lee arrived on the field, he saw the importance of this position. He sent discretionary orders to Ewell that Cemetery Hill be taken 'if practicable.' Historian James M. McPherson wrote, "Had Jackson still lived, he undoubtedly would have found it practicable. But Ewell was not Jackson." Ewell chose not to attempt the assault.

In the Confederate victory timeline, Jackson did indeed survive his wounds and led the victorious assault on Cemetery Hill. From there, Lee and Jackson, along with Generals Longstreet and Hill were victorious at Gettysburg, dealing a deathblow to the Union Army. From Gettysburg, the Confederates marched on Washington and the result was as I previously described."

"What about the Union forces in the South?" questioned Kristian. "Sherman swept through the South like a demon and razed Atlanta."

"Sherman and his army were recalled to Washington after the defeat at Gettysburg. Sherman never made it to Atlanta."

"So how does the timeline get put back on track?" asked Kristian.

"That will be mainly up to you, Kristian," replied The Guardian. "You must assume the identity of the Confederate officer who issued the command for his troops to fire on Stonewall Jackson. The man hesitated to give the command to fire which resulted in only one shot grazing Jackson's arm. You need to eliminate that hesitation in giving the command to fire." "How do I assume this man's identity in a manner that gives me control of his thoughts and actions?" questioned Kristian. "Are you just going to drop my spirit into his body like Whoopie Goldberg in the movie Ghost? If you do that, how will I know where I am and what I'm supposed to do?"

"You will shadow Confederate Major John Decatur Barry prior to the shooting of General Jackson. You will be with him from the beginning of his military career in July 1861 through the incident at Chancellorsville on May 2, 1863.

"Shortly before the incident at Chancellorsville, where Jackson was shot, you will take possession of Barry's mind and be in control of his actions. You will issue the order without hesitation to fire on what you believe are Union cavalry. Once the shooting is complete you will return Barry's mind to his control. Barry may experience some side effects of the transition as he will die in 1867, still absorbed and depressed over his actions at Chancellorsville. He will never resolve, in his mind, how he could have given the command to fire. And he will correctly believe that his actions ultimately contributed to the loss of the war by the Confederacy."

Chapter 10

The intercom buzzed on Ansley's desk. "Dr. Barnett, Dr. Stephens wants to see you in her office at 3 P.M.," said Rachel, Dr. Stephens' secretary.

"Hi Rachel, no problem. I will be there. Thanks," replied Ansley, wondering what the director wanted. She hoped it wouldn't be another discussion on funding for her project developing the transition of a human mind into a cyber body. The project had fallen behind schedule due to the complexities associated with electronically digitizing the seemingly infinite thought processes of the human mind.

Several attempts had been made at downloading the mind of a chimpanzee to a cyber body designed to emulate that of a living chimp. Each attempt initially appeared to be successful. But after a few days, the cyber-chimp would begin to display erratic behavior. Ultimately the electronic brain had to be purged of the downloaded chimp's mind or it would destroy its cyber body. There appeared to be no damage or side effects to the living chimpanzee whose mind was being scanned and downloaded. It, of course, had no memory of waking up in a cyber body.

"Hello, Ansley, come in and have a seat," Dr. Brenda Stephens said. "Can I offer you anything, coffee, water?"

Ansley entered the large office of the Director of DARPA and took a seat in the leather side chair in front of the director's desk. "Hi Brenda, no thanks. I had a late lunch," replied Ansley. "What can I do for you?"

"Well, Ansley, you know we have fallen behind on the cyber-mind-download project. We are getting pressure from above to essentially show progress, with threats to our funding."

"Brenda, I know I don't have to remind you that this is probably the most complex project ever undertaken by DARPA, or anyone else for that matter. Do they realize that a successful download of a human mind into a cyber body could eliminate death as we know it? Throwing it all away now would be … an egregious waste of medical and scientific advances."

"Ansley, they have heard all about the wonderous potential associated with this project for years. It appears they've grown numb to these arguments and are looking for something, anything, to give them reasonable justification to present to the military and Congress. I'm not sure how we can fend off the growing threat of politics associated with this project."

Both Ansley and Brenda sat silently for a few moments when Brenda questioned Ansley. "Is it possible that you are too emotionally involved, given the situation with your husband? It certainly would be understandable if you were."

"Of course, I have a personal stake in the success of this project. I think about it every day. But I believe it provides me even greater motivation to succeed," said Ansley.

"Regarding the recent tests with the chimpanzee brain, is it possible the chimp lacks the mental capacity to understand what is happening to it as it attempts to learn how to manage its cyber body? I believe your current tests essentially 'light up' the cyber body with the chimp's mind all at once. Is that true?"

"Essentially, yes. Are you suggesting that we limit activation of the cyber body to one major system at a time – sight, hearing, feeling, motion? Wouldn't the chimp's mind believe its body was somehow damaged if, after the download, its bodily functions were limited? Our procedures allow for a slow awakening of the cyber chimp, strictly controlling the pace at which full consciousness is restored."

"I see," replied Brenda. "Did the problem with the chimp's mind adapting to the cyber body manifest at all during the simulations? We should have seen these reactions before we attempted the download into an actual cyber body."

"No," replied Ansley. "Maybe we should look at the simulations and determine how well they portray the experience. We probably focused more on what the experience would be from a human perspective without factoring in that we were dealing with a much more ... primitive mind than that of a human. But that will take more time and funding..."

"Well, here's the real reason I asked you up here today. Should we just abandon the tests with the chimpanzee and go straight to a human test? We know that if we experience any problems, we can just erase the cyborg's electronic brain without affecting the patient in any way. Perhaps a human mind would be able to cope with existence in a cyber body as it would be aware of what was happening."

"Whoa!" exclaimed Ansley. "Even if what you suggest is the next logical step in the project, the ethics would be formidable. What if the download is successful and the donor mind accepts its cyber body? How do we terminate the human living donor? Ethically, I don't believe we could allow both the donor and the cyborg to exist indefinitely having the same mind."

"What if we select a donor whose body is ...dying? They would have to agree that if the download is deemed a success that their human body would be euthanized. Perhaps we could solicit the participation of someone who has requested to be euthanized. Someone in a physical state like your husband prior to his Brain Restoration Procedure with a fully functional brain but a body that is essentially dead."

"Are you thinking that Kristian would be a candidate for the download?" questioned Ansley.

"Not for the first download," replied Brenda. "At the risk of sounding cruel, in Kristian's current state, unable to communicate, we don't know the state of his mind should it be brought back to consciousness. We don't know if maintaining his brain in biostasis, outside of his body, will result in ... unexpected consequences.

I recommend we seek a subject who is fully conscious and can communicate. An extensive interview process should be conducted to determine if the subject would want to live if he or she could survive his or her physical affliction."

Chapter 11

Ansley waited at the mansion Transporter port for Savannah to arrive, which happened in just a few seconds. "Hello, Savannah, great to see you, how are you doing?"

"I'm doing fine," replied Savannah. "What can I do for you, Ansley?"

"Let's go up to my office. I have some news I need to share, and I need your help going forward."

Ansley's office in the mansion was decorated in a modern motif of glass and aluminum. Her desk was mostly glass on a polished aluminum frame. The desk chair was a teal leather high back. The two side chairs were also teal leather and aluminum. "As I said, Savannah, I have some important news to share. But before I can share it, I need you to sign these non-disclosure agreements that bind you from sharing what I am about to tell you."

"Sounds very … cryptic," replied Savannah. "Let me have a look at what I am signing." Savannah read the document and saw no objections, particularly since she held much of what had been done with Kristian in total confidence. "OK, I don't see where this will hurt me by signing," she said as she reached for a pen.

"Savannah, you know I have been working with DARPA for a number of years developing cyber limbs for use by wounded soldiers. What you don't know is that research has led to the development of a fully functional cyborg body. If you saw one you probably wouldn't immediately identify it as an artificial human body. Now for the interesting part of the project. We are working to download a human mind to the cyber body." Ansley stopped momentarily to allow Savannah time to absorb what she was saying.

"So … a person's mind can be implanted in an electronic brain?" said Savannah.

"Yes, but we need to move into testing the procedure with a human subject. Our thinking is to offer the opportunity to someone whose body is irreparably failing, giving them the opportunity to return to a relatively normal life."

"Wow, this could eliminate the need for the Brain Restoration Procedure. The individual's mind could be downloaded directly from the living brain."

"Yes, but not in all cases. Emergency situations, such as those experienced in an accident that has resulted in imminent death of the body, there wouldn't be time to scan the brain and capture all the thoughts and memories for download. In those cases, removing the brain and placing it in biostasis would allow time for the scans to be completed," said Ansley.

"I see. Tell me about this cyber body you've created. You said it was virtually indistinguishable from a human body. "

"Yes, it is fully functional, including an ability to have sex," smiled Ansley, as she thought of the possibility that Kristian could fully return.

"So, hypothetically, if a mind can be downloaded to a cyber body it could vastly extend one's lifespan. I guess, in theory, if the mind was backed up in a secure database, death itself would need to be redefined. Even if the cyber body was destroyed the mind could be restored in a new body."

"Exactly," replied Ansley.

"So, what is my involvement here?"

"We need a test subject. Someone who is terminal, near death and has requested the Brain Restoration Procedure. Someone like Kristian."

"I see," repeated Savannah. "I have both a man and a woman that we are discussing the procedure with. Neither has committed, but I believe they are close to moving forward."

"The cyber body is only available in male form at this time as most combat soldiers are male, but we will be creating a female version soon. Do you think it would be possible to discuss this alternative with your male patient?"

"Yes, I am confident that he will appreciate being offered an option to having his brain put into a bottle. But what happens should the download fail or the cyborg is destroyed days or even weeks later?" said Savannah.

"That is why, for our test, we recommend that you perform the Brain Restoration Procedure after the download. Then, if the cyborg fails at any point, the patient would have another chance at a future download. In addition, the download process includes the creation of a backup of the patient's mind that is stored in a secure data center."

Ansley and Savannah met in Savannah's office at the Center. After the customary greetings, Savannah pressed the screen on her workstation and asked her assistant to bring in Aaron Adams. "Hello, Mr. Adams," said Savannah, as he was wheeled into Savannah's office. "I'd like you to meet an associate of mine – Dr. Ansley Barnett."

"Hello, Doctor," Adams replied using his computer- aided voice. "Pleasure to meet you. Wait, aren't you Kristian Barnett's wife? Wow! You've made this amazing center possible. Outstanding!"

"Hello, Mr. Adams, yes my husband's estate funded this entire center."

"Mr. Adams, we have an exciting proposition for you that could completely change your life. We want to tell you about it, but first, we will need you to sign a non-disclosure agreement. What we are hoping to share with you is a top-secret project sponsored mainly by the U.S. Military." Ansley placed a plain, sealed manila envelope on the desk in front of Adams. "When do you think you could give us your answer?"

"Please, call me Aaron. If you can give me thirty minutes to review these documents, I'll give you my answer today. But I will need someone to turn the pages for me." Savannah buzzed her assistant to come in and turn the pages for Adams as he read the document.

"Of course. Ansley, let's go for a cup of coffee while Mr. … while Aaron reviews the documents. Aaron, you are welcome to use my office."

Ansley and Savannah returned to Savannah's office. "Aaron, have you had enough time to review the NDA?" said Savannah.

"Yes, and I am willing to sign. I had a top-secret clearance when I was in the military, so I am familiar with this type of NDA. I will need a pen and I will need to hold it in my mouth. I can no longer use my hand as it is nearly 100-percent paralyzed." Savannah put a pen in Adams' mouth and he was able to move his head enough to make a barely-legible mark on the signature line.

"Good," said Savannah. "Ansley, please describe your project and what it could mean for Aaron."

"Aaron, as you gleaned from the NDA, this project is under the direction of DARPA. It is a top-secret project that is targeted with restoring seriously wounded soldiers to full and complete health. But its applications offer tremendous possibilities for anyone who is suffering from disease, like you, or for those infirmed by a serious accident. You see, we have developed a cyborg body that resembles the human body so closely the untrained eye is unlikely to detect that it is an artificial body. This cyborg body, which is only available as a male, has been my primary project for the past twelve years. What we need to do now is to provide it with a human mind."

"So … let me get this straight. You have developed a cyborg body that looks human. And rather than provide it with an electronic brain, you can … download the mind of a human being to it?" asked Aaron.

"Actually, the cyborg has an electronic brain, but the brain will assume the mind of a human. Remember, we developed the cyborg as a replacement for a severely injured human body. While a fully electronic brain is feasible, it would in the end, be essentially a robot. This project is not about creating a "Mr. Data," the emotionless cyborg from Star Trek. While a robot could do many, many things including fight battles for the military, it offers nothing for the minds of trained soldiers who have been injured in combat."

Ansley continued, "We have reached the point where we would like to attempt a download with a human patient. The cyborg would resemble your healthy human body to the greatest extent possible. We would conduct a scanning process on your brain that would capture every thought you have ever had. All your memories, both good and bad, would be captured by the scan and stored in a secure data center. We would also give you a battery of tests that would be repeated when the download was complete to ensure that we have captured the essence of your mind. The process would be completely painless."

"Well, given my current condition, end-stage ALS, what do I have to lose?" said Aaron. "But what happens if the download fails or, six months or a year later, the cyborg body fails, or my mind goes off the rails?"

"I'm glad you asked that question, Aaron," replied Savannah. "First, the mind at the point of the download is stored and periodically backed up from the cyborg's brain in a secure data center, so it could be restored to this or another cyborg body. Second, we recommend that you proceed with the Brain Restoration Procedure where your physical brain is removed from your body and stored in biostasis where it will be protected from any further decline in your physical body due to ALS. That will give us the ability to rescan and download if needed."

"How will I control the cyborg body... like its sight, speech or movement?

Ansley replied, "Your mind will issue the necessary instructions for the electronic brain in the cyborg body to respond as you intend. Essentially, in the same way, you were able to control your human body before you became ill."

"How do you know this? Has this been thoroughly tested?" questioned Aaron.

"Yes, we have been testing the scanning and download processes, most recently using chimpanzees. The chimps have received the download well but, in full disclosure, began to reject the cyborg chimp body in a few days. We do not understand why that is happening but theorize that the chimp mind cannot adapt to its cyborg body. We believe that a human mind could overcome any … issues related to adaptation of the cyborg body. Also, when we erase the downloaded mind from the chimp cyborg body the actual chimp has no memory of what has occurred. So, the chimp isn't harmed in any way."

Aaron continued to explore the proposition before him. "My mind will be scanned and stored in a secure data center. The scan will then be downloaded to a cyber body where it will control the electronic brain. How long will I exist in the cyborg body?"

"The cyborg does not age, Aaron. And the human mind does not age. So, the honest answer is we don't know how long you'll live. It could be years, decades, or longer," replied Ansley.

"Well, seeing as my alternative is essentially a miserable death, I am willing, in fact, I am excited, to proceed. When can we do this?"

Chapter 12

Dr. Ansley Barnett entered Aaron Adams' suite at the Barnett Center for Neurological Restoration. "Hello, Aaron. We have good news. Your brain scans have been completed and successfully stored in our data center. We are ready to download to the cyborg body. But you will need to complete the Brain Restoration Procedure with Dr. Richards before we perform the download. I've spoken with Dr. Richards and she is ready to schedule the procedure. Are you ready to proceed?"

Adams, who is by now declining at an increasingly rapid rate, replies through his communicator, "Yes. I am ready to get the hell out of this failing body. The process is the only reason for me to stay positive given my condition. Without it, I would be looking at euthanasia."

"Very well, I will notify Dr. Richards. Her staff will be getting with you today to review the procedure and arrange the schedule."

Ansley was sitting at her desk eating a salad when the phone rang. "Hello, this is Dr. Barnett," she said without looking at the video screen on her office phone.

"Ansley, Savannah. The procedure for Aaron has been completed. His brain is in the biostasis cube and all indications are positive. You can proceed with the download at your discretion. We'll update you should any anomalies surface in Adam's brain, but we do not anticipate any at this point."

The DARPA facility housing the cyborg lab, as well as Ansley's team, looks like the operating room in a *Star Trek* movie. High-definition screens hang in an oval around a stainless-steel operating table. The screens reflect the status of the cyborg body lying on its back on the table. All bodily functions are normal. An array of instruments is suspended above the table for use in performing surgical procedures on the cyborg. Doctors and technicians have no need for surgical caps, gowns, and masks as the cyborg is invulnerable to bacterial and viral infections. A thick cable runs from the floor below the table, through the table, and is connected to the back of the cyborg's neck. The port is normally hidden seamlessly by the cyborg's synthetic skin when not needed for downloads, charging, or backups.

Dr. Ansley Barnett and four technicians, who have replaced nurses in this cyborg operating room, entered the OR. "Ladies and gentlemen," began Ansley, "let's review the checklist one more time before we initiate the download. Janice, please begin reading the checklist."

"Yes, doctor," replied technician Janice. As Janice reads the checklist the technician responsible for each item on the list responds.

"Data network." "Online and stable. Download speed at 78 Tbps," (terabits/per second.) At this speed more than a thousand high definition movies could be downloaded in one second. Anything under 50 Tbps is considered unacceptable for the download. At this speed, approximately 90 seconds will be needed to complete the download.

"Data distribution processing," someone said.

"Ready," said another. This process will seed the downloaded data into the proper areas of the cyborg's brain and will take approximately thirty minutes.

"Systems status monitors."

"Ready and functioning. All cyborg systems active."

"OR systems and redundancy."

"Running at optimum." The systems supporting the OR have backups that, in the event of a system fault, can take over processing instantaneously.

"Checklist complete, Doctor."

"Prepare for download," commanded Ansley. "Download test file."

"Test file downloaded successfully," a technician replied in no more than two seconds.

"Initiate download," said Ansley.

"Download processing," said the technician at the console monitoring the download.

The technician counted out the download time, "Thirty seconds, 1 minute, 90 seconds. Download complete, time 97 seconds. Download verification beginning now." 90 seconds later – "Verification complete. Initiating data distribution."

Thirty-three minutes later, "Data distribution complete." "OK, now we get to see if all of this really works. Let's activate the cyborg," said Ansley. Ansley then gave the activate command followed by a key phrase that verifies the command is authentic. The cyborg's eyes opened, its fingers twitched as it looked around the room and then at the faces, all wide-eyed, looking down at it. Ansley, standing over its head, says "Aaron?" Aaron replies, "Yes."

Chapter 13

Kristian was in awe at the combination of horror and beauty that surrounded him now. It was a beautiful spring day in North Carolina, a light breeze fluttered through the blooming dogwood trees and the great oaks cast their shade over the 18th North Carolina regiment as the soldiers came to attention. The 18th was under the command of Brig. Gen. Lawrence O'Bryan Branch and was one of six brigades in Maj. Gen. A.P. Hill's Light Division.

General Branch waved his hand and his aide stepped forward and said, "Private John Decatur Barry, please come forward." Barry stepped out of line and walked smartly to stand at attention in front of General Branch.

"Private Barry, in recognition of your fine duty to the Confederacy you are being promoted to the rank of Captain. Congratulations," General Branch said and extended his hand. Barry smiled and shook the General's hand. While it was uncommon for a private to be promoted to captain, in the period it was not unheard of. Also, the 18th North Carolina had just been reorganized by Branch's superior, Major General A.P. Hill, commander of the Light Division. Branch's brigade was one of six under General Hill's command.

The 18th North Carolina marched to Virginia where in June 1862 General Robert E. Lee's Army of Northern Virginia prepared to repulse Maj. Gen. George B. McClellan's Army of the Potomac's threat against Richmond. Kristian was in awe of the conditions of the period where troops marched great distances, depended on local farms for food and some supplies, and slept on the ground, sometimes with no protection from the elements. Officers often were provided horses or brought horses of their own and Captain Barry was no exception.

The 18th saw action throughout the Seven Days' Battles, suffering two-hundred-and-twenty-four casualties of the four- hundred men engaged. Kristian observed Barry's courage and coolness in battle even after he was grazed by a musket ball on his left leg just below the knee. But the fierceness of the battles was very difficult for Kristian to witness. Men, wounded by cannon, musket, and bayonet lay writhing in the dirt, blood often pouring from their wounds, severed arms and legs lying feet and yards away from the bodies strewn about. "How can men do this to each other?" Kristian wondered.

At the conclusion of the day's battle, Colonel Robert H. Cowan congratulated Barry for his courage on the battlefield. "Captain Barry, that was fine work you did today. It is apparent that you've commanded the respect of your men. I will be including a statement recognizing your performance in my report to General Branch."

"Thank you, Sir. I am blessed to have very fine men under my command," said Barry.

When McClellan's Peninsula Campaign faltered, Branch's brigade moved north with Stonewall Jackson's Second Corps and fought at Cedar Mountain and Second Manassas with light casualties. The brigade participated in the siege and capture of Harpers Ferry during the Maryland Campaign and was charged with patrolling the Federal garrison. The 18th was held in reserve during the Battle of Antietam while the remainder of the brigade withstood Maj. Gen. Ambrose Burnside's late afternoon attack, when Branch was killed. Colonel James H. Lane assumed command and was later promoted to brigadier general.

In the warm summer evening, Colonel Lane mustered the troops for an important announcement. "Gentlemen, it is with my sincere regret that I must inform you that General Branch gave up his life for his country during today's battle. As some of you know, Branch arrived on the battlefield in time to help stop the Union advance, thus saving General Robert E. Lee's right flank from a crushing defeat. Soon after this victory, Branch stood talking with fellow brigadier generals Maxcy Gregg, Dorsey, Pender, James J. Archer, along with Hill and General Lee when a federal sharpshooter, seeing the group, fired a shot that hit him in the right cheek and exited behind his left ear, killing him instantly. General Branch was a fine officer and a great leader whom we will surely miss. For now, I will assume command of the 18th. That is all. Captain Barry, dismiss the troops."

"Captain Barry," said a young soldier who looked about fourteen years of age. "General Lane wants you to meet at his tent at 5:00 PM."

"Did the General say what this meeting was to be about?" replied Barry.

"No, sir."

"Captain Barry, please come in," said the General. "I continue to hear good things regarding your command and your personal performance on the battlefield. Your men have a lot of respect and admiration for you. I have a note here from Lt. Colonel Purdie. Purdie desires that special mention should be made of Captain John D. Barry of Company 1 for his coolness, gallantry, and devotion to duty. I will include said recommendation in my report to General Hill. Also, I am a strong supporter of good, talented officers so I am promoting you to major." Lane then reached for a bottle of Jack Daniels and two glasses. Pouring about two-fingers into each, Lane smiled and said, handing Barry a glass, "Congratulations, Major."

Barry was promoted to major after the Maryland Campaign. "Lieutenant-Colonel Purdie, who bravely commanded the 18th in most of these engagements, desires that special mention should be made of Capt. John D. Barry, of Company I for his coolness and gallantry and devotion to duty," Lane noted in his report to General Hill on the campaign.

Chapter 14

It had been six months since Aaron's mind was downloaded to the cyborg. The time had been filled with exhaustive physical testing as well as mind-numbing mental evaluations and tests. Physical tests had measured things like strength, endurance and speed. This cyborg body was tuned to blend in with the human population so, although likely capable in many respects, it won't perform super-human feats like the Six Million Dollar Man. Future cyborgs that host the minds of soldiers may see their physical capabilities enhanced beyond human performance limits.

At the quarter-mile track at the DARPA test facility where Aaron had just completed a mile run, Ansley said, "4.77 minutes, not bad."

Aaron, not at all winded after the run, said, "I feel that I could run much faster, Dr. Barnett. I feel like I have a governor on my legs that won't allow me to go any faster."

"You do have a governor of sorts, Aaron. Remember, you will be released into the general population soon. Our desire is that you blend well with people your age and not be a super athlete, which would subject you to press scrutiny and a strong desire to evaluate you medically."

"So, this body can perform at a higher level," said Aaron.

"We feel that your strength and speed have been tuned to the proper level for a healthy male of your age and physique. Given where you came from, isn't that enough?"

"I guess we'll see," said Aaron. "Don't get me wrong. I'm eternally grateful for this second chance at a normal life. Now speaking of a 'normal' life,' there is yet one test that we have not performed."

"I … I'm not sure what test you are referring to, Aaron. We've been testing every aspect, every detail of both your body and your mind now being hosted by this body."

"No," said Aaron. "There is still one test that involves both physical and mental capabilities that we haven't performed. I haven't had sex with a completely human female. How will I know if … it will work in a humanly natural way?" Aaron has had feelings for Ansley since the first time they met in Savannah's office when he was all but paralyzed by ALS.

"So, what are you suggesting, Aaron? Should we send you to Las Vegas and get you a prostitute to prove your manhood?"

"No, you've been with me throughout all of my tests for the past six months. I … I would like it to be you who performs this final test with me, Ansley."

Ansley, taken aback and speechless for what seemed like minutes but was only seconds replies, "Aaron, that is simply not possible. First, I am a married woman, and I am saving myself for Kristian's return. Second, I don't believe we, or at least I, are emotionally attached in a way that could result in having sex. Our relationship is purely professional. Haven't the simulations demonstrated that you are functional?" Simulations had mainly involved sessions that, when you came right down to it, were simply masturbation.

"I can understand, Ansley, that you may not have feelings or desires to be with me in that way. But I have been harboring feelings for you ever since we met in Dr. Richards' office. That is the real reason I want to perform this test with you and not some prostitute."

Ansley began to blush at the words she was hearing from Aaron. "Aaron, I'm flattered that you find me attractive but that doesn't compensate for the fact that I remain a faithful married woman. As you know, with ALS Kristian suffered from ED for most of the nine years he suffered from the disease. Throughout that time, I remained loyal … and celibate. Now, that he may be close to returning in a cyborg body like yours, why would I not wait a short time longer?"

"Just because my human-cyborg body may perform well doesn't mean Kristian's will. I never existed as a brain in a bottle. My brain was simply a backup vessel in case something went awry with the download. Kristian's brain, his mind, has been in that bottle for what, three years? And you know the act of sex is a concentrated effort involving both the mind and the physical body. Plus, don't you want to know what to expect should Kristian return fully functional?"

"I ... I need some time to think this through," replied Ansley. "How about we sit down with dinner and a bottle of wine?" While the cyborg body didn't require food or drink and got its energy from an advanced set of batteries, it could ingest both food and drink. Alcohol had no effect. This was mainly to facilitate social interaction in situations that involved food or drink and to allow the human mind to experience the pleasures of eating and drinking. Any food that was consumed was "digested" and expelled when convenient.

"As I said, Aaron, I need some time to think."

A few days had passed since Aaron attempted to seduce Ansley Barnett when Aaron picked up his smartphone and dialed Ansley. After three rings Ansley picked up. "Hello, Ansley, have you given any thought to my ... idea regarding the final test of my new body? The dinner invitation is still open if you want to discuss it."

Ansley waited a few seconds to respond and then, "Yes, Aaron. I have given it some thought. I am still strongly against your idea, but I am willing to discuss it face-to-face with you." "Great! I'll pick you up at seven."

"Wait, how will you pick me up? You have no car and no driver's license."

"Uber, my dear, Uber."

Ansley spent the afternoon trying to justify meeting with Aaron. Three times she picked up her smartphone to call and cancel, and three times she put it back down. After all, Aaron had some valid points. What will it be like making love ... no, having sex, with a cyborg? Should she prepare for Kristian's return by knowing what to expect? Could an experience with Aaron allow her to coach Kristian in adapting to his cyborg body? As the afternoon wore on, she seemed to be warming to the idea of a one-time fling, the first between a human and a cyborg. After all, Kristian had given his blessing should she desire to venture outside of their marital bed.

As Aaron and Ansley stepped into the self-driving Uber car, Aaron said, "Bel-Air Restaurant. Turning to Ansley, "I hope you like this restaurant. I haven't eaten there before but it has great ratings."

"I've eaten there a few times and found it quite good," said Ansley.

They were seated right after entering the restaurant and the waitress asked if she could take their drink orders. "Water for me, with lime," said Aaron.

"Could I see your wine list?" asked Ansley.

"Of course," said the waitress as she handed the wine list to Ansley. "I'll come back in a few minutes to get your wine order."

The tension between Aaron and Ansley was intense. Neither of them spoke for what seemed like minutes. Finally, Aaron broke the ice. "It has been years since I've been in a restaurant. I'm still in awe over the fact that I have been resurrected from the nearly dead and now exist in a near-perfect, possibly immortal body. That I won't face the decline that comes with age." Ansley looked up from the wine list and her eyes caught Aaron's blue eyes. "Yes, that is quite astounding when you think about it. The implications for science and space exploration are amazing. One of the possibilities we envisioned were cyborg- astronauts traveling to the stars at near-light speeds, taking centuries to reach planets that offered the possibility of life. Of course, the true unknown is not the cyborg body but the human mind it is hosting."

The waitress returned to take the wine order. "I'll have the Burgess Chardonnay 1980," said Ansley. "Aaron, does that wine meet with your expectations?"

"Yes, sounds good."

The conversation was still awkward as Aaron asked, "How is your little girl doing?"

"She's doing fine, thanks. She's growing up so fast. I hope Kristian returns while she is still a little girl so he can see her grow up."

The waitress returned with the wine, poured a bit for Ansley to taste. Then poured a glass for Ansley and Aaron. Ansley took a rather large gulp right away to soothe her emotional thirst and calm her nerves.

"Can I take your dinner orders?" the waitress asked.

"I'll have the Stone Fruit and Pecan Salad, and the Ahi Tuna for the main course," said Ansley.

"Any appetizers or sides, miss?" said the waitress. "No. No thanks," said Ansley.

"Sir?"

"I'll have the grilled lamb chops," said Aaron. "Appetizer or salad?"

"Let's go with the fig and goat cheese salad."

"That's quite a meal you ordered considering you don't need food," smiled Ansley.

Aaron replied, "Hey, I've got to fully test out this body, right? I'm supposed to be able to eat like a human. I experience taste like a human and never have to worry about indigestion." This opened the door to the discussion that they had been avoiding since Aaron had picked up Ansley.

"Speaking of fully testing this body, any more thoughts on my proposal?" asked Aaron.

"Well, yes, I've been debating with myself for three days. You make some valid points, but I keep going back to the fact that I am a loyal married woman, married to a man who, through no fault of his own, is clinging to life with his brain in a bottle. The scientist in me can almost justify what you are proposing, but the wife and woman in me abhors the thought of betraying my husband."

"Ansley, no one is or will accuse you of betraying Kristian. I don't expect you to become emotionally attached to me, although I have feelings for you. If you can justify the experience from a scientific basis, set your emotional reservations aside for this one-time meeting."

As they progressed through dinner, Ansley consumed more of the wine and consequently began to relax a little more than she had intended. In fact, Aaron nursed his glass of wine through the meal, so Ansley downed three glasses to finish the bottle.

"How about we go to your place ... for a nightcap?" said Aaron, as they finished their meal.

"I would rather get a hotel room," replied Ansley. "I really wouldn't feel right taking you to the mansion under these circumstances."

A rather surprised Aaron immediately grabbed his smartphone to book a reservation in a nearby hotel.

Having checked into their room, Aaron asked, "Would you like me to order anything from room service? A bottle of wine, perhaps?"

"No, I've probably had too much wine already. Any more and I would just fall asleep. We'd better get right to it before I change my mind and call Uber to take me home."

"OK, Let me step into the bathroom while you ... prepare yourself and get in bed."

Aaron waited a few minutes, then tapped on the door. "You still here, Ansley?" he said, half joking. Ansley replied with a tepid yes, turning out the lights.

Aaron had stripped to his boxers in the bathroom and walked over to the bed and hesitated. "You OK?"

Ansley hesitated, then replied, "Yes," as Aaron climbed into the bed.

Both lay on their backs facing the ceiling. "I feel like a teenager having sex for the first time," said Ansley.

"I know what you mean. I haven't felt this nervous since my mind was downloaded to this body," said Aaron. "How about we just ... hold each other to try and set the mood?"

Ansley and Aaron slowly turned to face each other. It was awkward at first but as skin began to touch skin, both felt their bodies begin to relax. Aaron began to have sensations of an erection as he could feel her breasts on his chest. Ansley began to have sensations she had not experienced in years. The physical sensations continued to grow and nearly consume them as Aaron made intense love to Ansley. And surprisingly, Ansley responded just as intensely.

By the time they were through, Ansley was exhausted and fell asleep in Aaron's arms. Aaron, however, was not the least bit tired, and as time passed, his desire for Ansley grew. After a couple of hours, Aaron began to lightly caress Ansley's shoulder, hoping to awaken her. At first, Ansley just moaned but still appeared to be sleeping deeply. Then, slowly, she grabbed Aaron's hand and put it on her breast. That was enough to cause Aaron to get another erection. The second session was nearly as amazing for both as the first. In the end, Ansley again fell into a deep sleep.

As dawn began to break and first light enter their room through the window, Aaron was successful in raising Ansley from her slumber for a third session. Again, Ansley was quite willing and blissfully enjoyed the event for the third time.

After they were through lovemaking, the sun had risen, and the bright light shown along the edges of their room-darkening curtains. Aaron said, "That was quite a night. I hope I passed this final test."

Ansley replied, "Yes, if there was a grade higher than A+, I would give it to you."

"Would you be willing to repeat the test … for purely scientific reasons, of course?" said Aaron through the big grin on his face. "My body is screaming 'yes' but I really can't, Aaron. I could almost justify the one-time carnal test on scientific grounds. But given the outcome, I no longer have that option. So, this is our one-and-done. Please don't raise this question again."

As Ansley dressed in the bathroom, Aaron summoned two Uber cars to take them both separately, her to the mansion and him to the test center. She was adamant that no one discover their last night's rendezvous.

Chapter 15

Aaron is seated in Ansley Barnett's office at the Barnett Center where a gentleman he has not met sits on his right in the side chair by the desk. Ansley is seated at the desk. "Good morning, Aaron," said Ansley. "I'd like you to meet Brad Williams. Brad is head of DARPA's security group." Brad appears to be in his late thirties or early forties. He's a little more than six-feet tall, with brown hair, brown eyes, and is dressed in a grey suit, white shirt, and red tie. Aaron silently wonders if Brad's dress is a government uniform.

"Good morning," said Aaron, as he extended his hand to shake Brad's.

"Aaron, as you know, we have been planning for your release into the general population. Brad is here to explain that process to you and to answer any questions you may have," said Ansley.

"Hello, Aaron," Brad said. "The process by which you will re-enter the general population has been carefully developed to ensure both your privacy and safety, as well as to protect DARPA's highly-classified cyborg program. I'm sure you've heard of the federal witness protection program where informants involved in major crime activity are placed in a manner to ensure their safety. Your re-entry will be managed in much the same way. You will receive a new, fully documented identity including a Social Security Number and Passport. You will receive a driver's license for the state in which you will be placed. You will also be provided a position in a software engineering firm that does business with the federal government. You will receive a salary and benefits commensurate with your experience and the cost of living in the location where you will settle. You will be provided a residence, apartment or house depending on where you choose to locate that will have all necessary secured Internet connectivity needed to support your cyber body. Any financial accounts you currently have will be closed and the funds transferred to similar accounts in your new name.

Death certificates will be created for Aaron Adams and distributed where necessary. Since you have no heirs, this will be fairly straightforward. Finally, you will be provided an online bank account in the amount of $100,000, as well as an American Express credit card account to fund your transition to your new location. Do you have any questions?"

"Wow! That is a lot to take in," said Aaron. "Being released to the 'general population' sounds like I'm going to prison, Brad. Let's not repeat that phrase again. Essentially it sounds like you're killing Aaron who has been reborn as ... I didn't catch the name." "Your new name is Phillip Geoffrey Preston. I suggest you start saying that over and over to yourself, so you become comfortable with it. When people speak your name, you need to react as if you have always been ... Phillip Preston. From feedback received from people in witness protection, one of the toughest things to get used to is people calling you by your new name."

"So, where are you relocating me?" said Aaron. Do I get any say in the matter?"

"Yes, we are prepared to offer you three choices for relocation. The first is Austin, Texas. The second is Portland, Oregon. The third opportunity is in Silicon Valley. All three opportunities are with startup companies deemed as visionary by DARPA and that have DARPA contracts. Job stability will be about as good as it gets in your field of expertise. If you like, I can provide you with materials on each of the companies as well as general information regarding their DARPA projects to aid you in your decision. All three companies have reviewed your resume under the name Phillip Preston, and they are all excited about the possibility of you joining them. We will arrange interviews for you at each of the companies. The purpose of the interviews is to give you an opportunity to evaluate the company and those who run it, more so than for the company to evaluate you. Acceptance of you by the company you choose has already been … arranged."

"Yes, that would be great, Brad. Can you also provide information on my options for housing and neighborhood demographics in each of the three locations?

"Yes, of course. Aaron, we will need your decision soon after your interviews, so we can finalize living arrangements, both temporary and permanent."

"I think I can give you an answer a couple of days after the interviews and I receive the material we agreed on," said Aaron.

"You will have all the information we discussed today, including information for the three companies," replied Brad. "My assistant, Jennifer, will be making the arrangements for your interviews and will be back to you today or tomorrow with your itinerary."

"Ansley, Brad, thank you," said Aaron. "Please know that I am still in awe over the prospect that I will be living a near-normal life again, at least in the near term. I am eternally grateful."

Aaron completed interviews with all three companies over the course of a week and was able to explore the communities he was considering. All three companies were pretty much as Brad Williams described. Aaron's software engineering background would allow him to fit in well at any of the three. Politically, all three companies were located in areas of heavy liberal demographics. However, Aaron had never been much of a political animal. Housing in the two West Coast communities would be apartment living. Housing in Austin would allow him to rent a condo or single-family home.

Sitting in Ansley Barnett's office across from Ansley, Aaron described his trips to the three companies, the interviews, and exploration of the communities he visited. "After reviewing the three opportunities, Ansley, I feel that I am best suited to accept the offer for Silicon Valley. After all, I am a Californian, born and raised, lived here all my life. Portland is too cold and wet, Texas too hot and dry. And I seemed to gel with the folks at the company better. Heck, maybe we do have a culture unique to California," he mused. What was left unspoken was he would be in relatively close proximity to Ansley should the situation with Kristian not pan out. He still harbored strong feelings for Ansley. "Shall we go out for a small celebration of my re-entering the 'general population'?"

"No, Aaron, we have had enough celebrating," replied Ansley as she tried to hide a small smile by looking down at a file folder on her desk. "Besides, we are working on the plan to download Kristian to his cyborg body. I expect that could happen as soon as a few months. I will notify Brad of your decision. Expect a call from his office in a day or two with instructions for your move."

Aaron was sitting on the sofa in his suite at the Barnett Center when his smartphone buzzed. "Hello, Mr. Preston. This is Jennifer from Brad William's office. Would this be a good time to go over the instructions for your upcoming move?"

"Hi Jennifer," Aaron replied, hesitating a moment at being addressed as Mr. Preston. "Yes, that would be great. Let me grab a pen and some paper."

"We have placed a deposit in your name at the Avalon Silicon Valley apartments for a two-bedroom luxury apartment. I know you were considering Mountain View but the rentals there simply weren't up to what we believe you would enjoy. The apartment has 1163 square feet and rents for $6,525.00 per month. We will furnish the apartment. I will send you some catalogs to use in selecting your furniture. I can send you all the details and floor plan to your email."

"Your commute to the office will be about thirty minutes depending on traffic conditions, but I understand you will be working from home at least some of the time. Grocery shopping is about two blocks from your apartment. The grocery there will deliver your orders so no need to go to the store. We have subscribed to an Uber driverless car service to take you to and from work. You can manage that subscription and setup your travel at the website I will send you. Please let me know if this will be satisfactory so I can complete the arrangements for your move. We are planning for your move to be October 1st. That only gives us a couple of weeks to get everything arranged, including the modifications needed to accommodate the equipment necessary to support your special technical requirements."

"Jennifer, thank you. Everything sounds good. I will review the information you send as soon as I receive it and expect to get back to you in a day or two. I will check out the apartment first, so any modifications required can be completed by move in."

Chapter 16

"Wow, this apartment rocks," thought Aaron as he crossed the threshold for the first time on Saturday, October 1st, 2039. "Very spacious, and the furniture I picked out fits well." Aaron spent the weekend unpacking items he'd delivered to the apartment. He had previously given his digital assistant a list of dishes he liked for which he ordered groceries and had them delivered. While he didn't need to eat, he enjoyed eating. For dinner Saturday night he ordered take-out from a Thai restaurant he found online. To end the evening, he dialed up a movie on Prime. Finally, he lay down in the master bedroom to recharge and let the backup process.

Aaron had never remembered having a dream while in a semi-conscious state during recharging. So, when, in his mind, he saw the figure of a man approaching him he tried to come fully awake. Unable to do so, and seemingly in a state of complete paralysis, the figure spoke to him. "Aaron, do not be alarmed. Yes, you are seeing me with your mind's eye as if in a dream. I am a Guardian and I am here to give you information that you will need to perform the tasks which you will be assigned."

Speaking with his mind Aaron replied, "What … who are you? Guardian of what? What tasks?"

"Your mind has separated from your corporeal body. Normally when this occurs your mind transitions to the next level of existence. You exist as an immortal being. In your case, your mind remains bound to the earthly realm by your cyborg brain and you are unable to transition to the next level. But, with my assistance, your mind can transition between the earthly realm and the next level. This provides you the ability to exist in spirit form at any point in time and space."

"Guardian, why do I need to exist at any point in time and space? This must be a bad dream. I wonder if something has gone wrong with my cyber brain."

"There is nothing wrong with your cyber body or brain. You see, timelines are very fragile, constantly changing. Something done, or not done, in the past can affect the present and the future, sometimes profoundly. We Guardians of time must oversee the timelines and attempt to correct those gone awry. In essence, we are shepherds of human destiny."

Chapter 17

Kristian noted that dusk on May 2, 1863, had ended the highly successful assault for the day by General Jackson's Second Brigade on the Union army at Chancellorsville. The evening was clear and pleasant with a light breeze out of the west rustling the leaves on the trees. As Jackson and his staff were returning to camp, they were mistaken for a Union cavalry force by the 18th North Carolina Infantry regiment. "Halt, who goes there?" was heard from the regiment.

The Guardian then told Kristian it was time for him to act, to possess Barry's mind. Barry went completely blank for a second. When his eyes opened, Kristian was in control.

The regiment fired as frantic shouts by Jackson's staff identifying the party were replied to by Major John D. Barry with the retort, "It's a damned Yankee trick! Fire!" A second volley was fired in response. Jackson was hit by three bullets, two in the left arm and one in the right hand. Several other men on his staff were killed, in addition to many horses. Darkness and confusion prevented Jackson from getting immediate care. He was dropped from his stretcher while being evacuated because of incoming artillery rounds. Because of his injuries, Jackson's left arm had to be amputated. Jackson was moved to Thomas C. Chandler's plantation named Fairfield. He was thought to be out of harm's way; but unknown to the doctors, he already had classic symptoms of pneumonia, complaining of a sore chest. This soreness was mistakenly thought to be the result of his rough handling in the battlefield evacuation, and he died on May 9.

Immediately following Barry's command to fire, Kristian left Barry. Again, Barry went blank and nearly fell. But he recovered quickly and continued to hear pleas from Jackson's staff. Barry, pausing a few seconds because of the supernatural intervention by Kristian, then issued the command to cease fire. Barry suffered from severe headaches for the next several days. News that his regiment had killed perhaps the greatest of the Civil War Confederate generals resulted in notable depression. However, Barry did recover and continued to fight at Gettysburg. He returned home after the war and died two years later. Those who knew him claim he died of a broken heart caused by depression from his role in the death of Stonewall Jackson and the fall of the Confederacy.

"You did well. You have accomplished your first task successfully, Kristian," said the Guardian. "The timeline has been restored."

"First task?" questioned Kristian. "You mean there will be more?"

"Yes," replied The Guardian. "Many more."

Chapter 18

The year is 2040 and it is the month of August. Kristian's brain has been in stasis for four years. Ansley Barnett calls Savannah Richards who answers immediately.

"Savannah, Ansley. Kristian's cyborg body has completed testing and is ready for the mind transfer. We can schedule it as soon as tomorrow morning. Will you be able to fit that into your schedule?"

"Ansley, of course. What time will you start the process?" "We will begin the final verification for network connectivity and system availability at 8 AM. The download initiation sequence is at 9 AM."

"I will be there at 8 AM."

The advanced cyborg lab is like a scene out of a science fiction movie. Ten large, maximum definition screens surround an operating table where a cyborg body lays motionless. Highly trained technicians are assigned to observe specific monitors and report on progress and any anomalies that arise. Wireless sensors are placed at strategic locations on the body to effect monitoring of body functions and responses that will be reflected on the hi-def screens. Designed by Dr. Barnett, the cyborg bears a full resemblance to Kristian at the age of thirty-three. Even a small scar on its knee is present from a skiing accident Kristian experienced at twenty-one.

Dr. Ansley Barnett and four technicians, who have replaced nurses in this cyborg operating room, enter the OR. "Ladies and gentlemen," begins Ansley, "let's review the checklist before we initiate the download. Janice, please begin reading the checklist."

"Yes, doctor," replies technician Janice. As Janice reads the checklist the technician responsible for each item on the list responds.

"Data network." "Online and stable. Download speed at 78 Tbps," (terabits/second.) At this speed over 1,000 high-definition movies could be downloaded in one second. At this speed, approximately ninety seconds will be needed to complete the download.

"Data distribution processing." "Ready." This process will seed the downloaded data in the proper areas of the cyborg's brain. This process will require approximately thirty-three minutes.

"Systems status monitors."

"Ready and functioning. All cyborg systems active."

"OR systems and redundancy."

"Running at optimum." The systems supporting the OR have backups that, in the event of a system fault, can take over processing instantaneously.

"Checklist complete, Doctor."

"Prepare for download," commanded Ansley. "Download test file."

"Test file downloaded successfully," a technician replied in no more than two seconds.

"Initiate download," said Ansley.

Approximately ninety seconds pass when "Download complete" is stated by the observing technician. The time required for data distribution of Kristian's mind in the cyborg brain seems to take longer than the estimated thirty-three minutes, but it is completed soon after.

"Data distribution complete. All systems are in the green, functioning normally," stated technician Janice.

Ansley approached the head of the operating table, leaned over and said "Kristian, can you hear me? Kristian?" At first, there was no response, no indication of awareness. Then, in a response programmed into the cyborg when it detects sound, the eyes opened. Ansley emitted a slight gasp. "Kristian, it's me, Ansley. Can you hear me?" No response, no movement.

Although Kristian's eyes are open there is no movement of the eyes. Kristian appears to be staring straight up at the ceiling with no awareness of his surroundings. Ansley continues attempting to arouse awareness but to no avail. "Systems check!" she yells at the technicians. One-by-one the technicians indicate all systems are in the green including the cyborg's brain. Ansley shines a small flashlight on Kristian's pupils and they respond normally.

In the meantime, Kristian's mind is attempting to adjust to its cyborg brain, but he is fully aware that something just happened. When the cyborg's eyes open, he can see the ceiling of the operating room and motion on the periphery of his range of vision. He can hear Ansley as well as the technicians responding to systems status. He remains unable to move or blink his eyes.

"Let's give him some time to adjust to his new environment," said Savannah Richards. "After all, he's been in an induced coma for four years and may need some time to respond."

"I seem to have regained consciousness," thinks Kristian. "I am able to see and hear so I must be in a functioning body. But I am unable to move. I can't even move my eyes."

Ansley comes into Kristian's view. "Kristian, I don't know if you can see or hear me. Your mind has been transferred to a cyborg body. The body is a perfect replica of your corporeal body at the age of thirty-three, before you became ill. The year is 2040. You have been in a coma for four years. If you can hear me, please try to give me a sign. You will need to concentrate on controlling your cyborg body. Your mind has been disconnected from a physical body for some time and it may require time to adapt to the cyborg. Please don't be frightened. You can do this. Concentrate on moving one thing at a time. Blink your eyes or wiggle your finger," she said as she fought back her emotions and tears.

Several hours pass with no visible response from Kristian. Technician Janice enters the operating room to check on the systems monitoring Kristian and to check on Ansley. All systems remain in the green. "Dr. Barnett, can I get you anything? Is there anything else I can do to help? Can I get you something to eat?

"I'm not hungry, but I could use some hot tea," replies Ansley.

"No problem. I'll run over to the dining room and be back in a few minutes," replied Janice.

Ansley begins to lose control of her emotions and starts sobbing. "Kristian, what have we done to you?" she says aloud.

Kristian hears Ansley sobbing and speaking. He continues to concentrate on moving his eyes and eyelids but to no avail. Emotionally he is becoming more concerned that he may be trapped in a body he cannot control. What will they do with him if he is unable to revive this cyborg body? Will they just turn it off and let his mind die? Do they have a backup of his mind that they can retain until these problems are resolved?

Janice returns with a cup of hot tea and some pastries and cheese on a plate. "Dr. Barnett, I know you don't feel like it, but you should eat. You will need to maintain your strength through this."

"Thank you, Janice," replies Ansley as she sips the tea and picks up a pastry.

Just as she bites into the pastry, something seems to happen with Kristian. Ansley drops the pastry and comes into Kristian's view. "Kristian, Kristian, are you there? Can you hear me?"

At first, no response. But then Kristian's eyes blink together. "Kristian, please blink once if you can hear me!" shouts Ansley, loud enough to startle Janice.

A few seconds pass when Kristian blinks once. "Oh my God!" screams Ansley. "He is … in there! He's alive!" "Kristian, can you see me?" Kristian moves his eyes, so he is directly looking at Ansley. His eyes blink once.

Ansley takes his hand. "Kristian, can you feel my hand in yours?" Kristian's eyes blink once. "I think he's coming around!" said Ansley. "Janice, please call Dr. Richards and see if she can join me."

"Kristian, this is Savannah Richards. Do you recognize me?" Kristian's eyes blink once, and his lips seem to quiver. "Kristian, I want you to concentrate on your ability to speak. The cyborg has been developed to mimic your voice as it was before you became ill. I know this may take a lot of effort, but if you can speak, we can better assist you in gaining control over the cyborg body."

Several minutes go by and then Kristian's lips part slightly and a groan is heard coming from the cyborg's throat. "Good," said Savannah. "Try again." Several more minutes transpire, and Kristian says "Ansley", slowly, in a very low whisper.

"I'm here," said Ansley. "Keep focusing on trying to talk to us." Kristian then utters the word 'alive,' perhaps trying to give confirmation that he is recovering. "Yes," said Ansley. "You are alive. You are like a newborn that must learn how to control its body. But you are alive."

Kristian then says 'daughter.' "Kristen Elaine," said Ansley. "She is a beautiful young lady who resembles her daddy. She will be in kindergarten starting next month and is very smart." The beginnings of a smile form on Kristian's lips, as tears well up in Ansley's eyes.

Although Kristian's development of his control of the cyborg body accelerates slowly over the days that follow, it will take weeks, perhaps months, before he gains full control.

Chapter 19

Aaron, a.k.a. Phillip Geoffrey Preston, finished watching the latest Star Trek film starring Chris Pine as Captain Kirk on his 120-inch 3-D wall projection video screen, thinking that Pine is getting a little long in the tooth to be galivanting about the galaxy. Aaron goes to his bedroom and lies down on the recharging bed that will charge the batteries that enable operation of the cyborg body. His mind will also be backed up in order to preserve it against any anomalies that could negatively impact the cyborg including accident, power surge or any other emergency.

Aaron connects the cable from the processor to the port just under the skin on the back of his neck and lies down, shutting his eyes. While he doesn't sleep like a human body, he does allow his mind to assume a restful, dreamlike state. He often experiences dreams, as if his mind is cleansing itself. After an unknown period, he begins dreaming. But this dream is unlike his usual dreams, in that it is so vividly real. In his dream, he sees the being he saw several months ago, the being that called himself 'The Guardian.' Dressed in blue jeans and white T-shirt, wearing a long leather coat, black motorcycle boots with his wavy, golden shoulder-length locks descending from a leather Stetson, the figure addressed Aaron. "Hello, Aaron. Do you remember me?" "Yes," replied Aaron, hesitantly. "You are the Guardian. Why are you here? What do you want with me?"

"I have come to engage you in your first assignment. A timeline that, if not corrected, will result in the destruction of everything you know, and possibly even yourself. The timeline altered by Kristian presented a very similar threat. Now you have been chosen to address this dilemma."

"I will show you the result should the altered timeline remain dominant over the timeline you know." Images of battles appearing to be of World War II flashed across Aaron's mind. A map appeared depicting the Nazi advance through Western Europe. The Swastika is seen growing brighter while the Norwegian, Belgium, and French flags burned. British troops amassed at Dunkirk are seen trying to flee the brutal Nazi war machine to no avail. Nazi aircraft and artillery devastate Dunkirk where British casualties are shown in the hundreds of thousands. The British army is effectively destroyed at Dunkirk.

Next, visions of British leaders appear, including Churchill, Neville Chamberlain, Lord Viscount Halifax, and King GeorgeVI. A vision of Parliament appeared where a vote to accept a peace settlement with Hitler, negotiated by Mussolini, is approved. Next, the Nazi Swastika is seen flying over Buckingham Palace and Parliament. Number 10 Downing Street has a large Swastika banner hanging above the door. The governments of Scotland and Ireland also submit to the peace agreement in order to avoid attack by the Nazis.

The surrender of Great Britain to Hitler affected the outcome of World War II. The United States never allies with Great Britain to fight the Nazis in Europe. Instead, Hitler sets his sights on the United States. He knows if he can take the USA, he will have the resources needed to conquer Russia and drive out Stalin. German U-Boats patrol the Atlantic, sinking several U.S. warships and cargo ships. Hitler's new four-engine long-distance jet bomber inflicts horrendous suffering on America's East Coast. Hitler is also rumored to be developing an atomic bomb to place atop his secret V-3 rocket which is purported to be capable of flying across the Atlantic from Ireland to targets in North America.

On December 7, 1941, the Japanese attacked Pearl Harbor. Visions of Japanese planes bombing the fleet passed by Aaron's vision. Hitler, emboldened by the Japanese attack, orders his navy to sail for the U.S. East Coast where they will prepare to support an invasion. Following the success of the attack on Pearl Harbor, the Japanese fleet steams to the US West Coast. The Japanese Flag and the Nazi Swastika are growing brighter as seen by Aaron in his vision while the United States flag is fading.

Seen next in Aaron's vision is the US Capitol being enveloped by a mushroom cloud. The White House, the Capitol, and virtually all government administration buildings including the Pentagon under construction are effectively destroyed. However, most congressional representatives are not in Washington, they're at home for the holidays. President Roosevelt is in Warm Springs, Georgia, for the holidays and Vice President Truman is at his home in Ohio.

Next Aaron sees the Nazi invasion force landing at strategic points on the US East Coast. Japanese battleships and destroyers are bombarding the ports of Los Angeles and San Francisco. Fighting continues for several years when President Harry Truman accepts the terms of surrender from Germany and Japan. The US is no longer a country. A band of resistance fighters continues to plague mainly German forces from their positions between the Rocky Mountains and the Great Plains.

Mesmerized by the visions sent to him by the Guardian, Aaron is terrified. "Guardian, what can I possibly do to prevent this disaster? How can we change the past?"

"Aaron, as I said before, since you are a disembodied mind, you can travel to any time, past, present, and even the future. With my guidance, you will enter the next level of existence to move about the space-time continuum. As for your assignment, King George VI is wary of Winston Churchill, fueled by Viscount Halifax's dislike of the Prime Minister. However, His Majesty appoints Churchill to the position in spite of Halifax's objections."

"Halifax and former Prime Minister Neville Chamberlain are pressuring Churchill to engage the aid of Mussolini in negotiating a peace settlement with Hitler. Churchill does not believe Hitler will abide by the terms and remains resistant to any peace agreement. In the meantime, the Nazis have taken Norway and Belgium, and are poised to take France. Three hundred thousand British forces are trapped at Dunkirk with no apparent escape path back to England. The British High Command is painting a dire picture for Churchill's War Cabinet should the British not attempt a negotiated peace settlement. The British Army is facing total annihilation at the hands of Hitler's war machine."

"Churchill, however, cannot be persuaded to capitulate. He orders the High Command to issue a notice requesting owners of boats thirty feet in length and longer to cross the English Channel to Dunkirk to rescue the stranded British soldiers."

"Halifax and Chamberlain threaten Churchill with their resignations from the War Cabinet. This would set the stage for a vote of no confidence in the House of Commons and end Churchill's term as Prime Minister. Finally, against everything he felt, Churchill agrees to open discussions with Mussolini regarding the terms of a peace agreement."

"Halifax and Chamberlain brief King George on Churchill's acquiescence. Because of his friendship with Halifax, the King accepts the news and offers to help in any way that he can. But after Halifax and Churchill depart Buckingham Palace, the King decides that he should speak with Churchill personally. Although late in the evening, the King has his coachman take him, without fanfare, to Number 10 Downing Street.

"Winston, Dear, you have a visitor," says Winston's wife, Clementine. Winston is sitting on the duvet in his study pondering his speech scheduled for the next day to Parliament. In that speech, he plans to announce that he will be pursuing peace negotiations with Hitler using Mussolini as an intermediary.

"Who is it, dear?" asks Churchill.

"The King," replies Clementine, just as King George appears in the doorway.

Chapter 20

"Good morning, Kristian. How are you feeling today?" said Ansley, as she entered Kristian's suite at the Barnett Center. Months have passed since Kristian's mind was downloaded to his cyborg body. Progress in gaining control of his new body was slow in the beginning. Regaining speech and mobility were the greatest initial challenges. But as those abilities were mastered, progress came more easily and rapidly. Kristian was now able to perform basic functions such as walking, dressing, feeding himself on occasion when he desired food and was improving his ability to use his laptop, both vocally and by using the keyboard. "I'm well," said Kristian. "Ready for another day of therapy and tests. I also feel I am ready to move back into the mansion."

This was the first time Kristian had expressed the thought of returning to the Barnett mansion.

"Kristian, are you uncomfortable staying in the Center?" asked Ansley. "We still have numerous tests and therapies to perform. In the Center, we also have all the equipment needed to preserve your mind in the event of an emergency and perform repairs on the cyborg if needed."

"Ansley, at the mansion I am a brief Transporter ride back to the Center should something happen. Charging and backup facilities can be installed at the mansion. I can come to the Center as often as needed for tests and therapies. I would be like … an outpatient."

"I'd like to discuss it with Savannah," replied Ansley.

"Why?" replied Kristian irritably. "What does Savannah have to do with this? She was the biological support for this project. That phase of the project is complete."

"Savannah runs the Center, Kristian. Out of respect, at least, she should be consulted."

"OK, I see your point. Please set up some time for the three of us to discuss this. I believe returning to a more normal environment would hasten my recovery."

"I'll see if she's available today," replied Ansley. "Now for today's schedule. We will be measuring your strength and ability to run. The cyborg body is capable of extra-human physical performance and may need to be calibrated to closely align with the strength and performance of a healthy thirty-three-year-old human male."

"I still don't see why I need a 'governor' for this body. How can I be the *Six Million Dollar Man* if you restrict my abilities?" said Kristian, smiling the whole time he referred to the 1970s television series of that name.

"Exactly," replied Ansley. "I don't want a superhero, just a healthy husband."

Chapter 21

The Guardian begins to explain to Aaron exactly how he will use King George to correct the errant timeline and its impact on the world post-1941. "At the moment the King speaks the words "… I've come to discuss the possible peace settlement…" you will assume control of the King's mind. This may briefly affect the King physically, but the effect will abate without notice of Churchill. While in command of the King's faculties you will use the King to ask Churchill for his true opinion regarding the peace settlement. In the end, you must state your support for Churchill refusing the negotiation in his speech to Parliament the next day. You should also tell Churchill to consult with the people before his speech. Then conclude the discussion and, as you are leaving the room, return control to King George by exiting his mind. This, again, may cause a brief physical response but it will pass immediately. Are you clear on your mission, Aaron?"

"Damn, that is some mission! Are you telling me the fate of the world as we know it is at stake? Will the King even remember what he has said to Churchill?"

"Essentially, what you say is true," replied The Guardian. "The King has already begun to resent the thought of capitulating to Hitler. You will essentially be solidifying his opinion by giving his support to Churchill. The King may have surprised himself a bit, but he will not reverse his decision."

"In order for you to effectively take control of the King's mind, you will shadow the King for several days prior to the necessary event. Grab my arm."

In the blink of an eye, Aaron finds himself in a large office which appears to be part of a large estate or castle. "Buckingham Palace, May 1940," says The Guardian. "Neville Chamberlain and King George VI." Chamberlain and King George, dressed in a high-ranking British naval uniform, are discussing the pending appointment of Churchill as Prime Minister.

"Neville, I remain highly concerned with Churchill," said King George. "His record indicates he is of poor judgment. The fiasco in Norway that led to some eighteen-hundred deaths is at the top of my list. Why in blazes am I being forced to choose Churchill over Halifax?"

"Halifax has refused to consider himself, at least formally," replied Chamberlain.

After a brief pause, the two men rise. The King extends his hand to Chamberlain and says, "I accept your resignation as Prime Minister." Chamberlain then departs the office of the King.

Remaining in the room are two gentlemen. One appears to be a butler; the other is King George VI.

"Show Mr. Churchill in please," says the King.

Winston Churchill appears at the door and bows to the King. "Come in, Winston." Churchill walks to and faces the King directly. "Winston, I would like to invite you to take up the position as our next Prime Minister. Will you form a government?"

"I will," replies Churchill. "I believe we are to meet regularly, your majesty."

"Might I suggest Mondays at 4 PM?" says the King.

"4 PM. I nap at 4 PM."

"Is that permissible?" asks the King.

"No, but it is necessary," says Churchill. "I work late hours."

"Then how about lunch?"

"Lunch on Mondays. Yes, lunch would be good," replies Churchill, knowing that he will receive an excellent lunch at the palace. Churchill then departs, backing up still facing the King (as demanded by etiquette) until he reaches the door.

Aaron turns to the Guardian and says "Wow! Churchill does speak his mind freely, doesn't he?"

"Yes, and typically, it doesn't matter to whom he is speaking." In his first weekly luncheon with Churchill, the King doesn't appear to be eating much while Churchill is enjoying the meal and the accompanying champagne. "How do you tolerate drinking so early in the day? No wonder you need to nap at four o'clock," asked the King, smoking a cigarette. "Takes practice," replies Churchill, as the King's butler refills his champagne glass.

"Should I consider evacuating my family to Canada?" said the King. The possibility of a German invasion and its possible impact on Great Britain is weighing heavily on King George.

Churchill responds while handing table scraps to a dog underneath the table, "Keeping the Royal Family safe is paramount. You must do as you see fit in that regard. As for your Prime Minister, prime ministers come and go quite often around here so I plan on staying."

Aaron and the Guardian continue to shadow King George, but also shadow Churchill as he deals with his War Cabinet, particularly Viscount Halifax. They watch and listen to Halifax, with Chamberlain in tow, as he attempts to force peace negotiations on Churchill. Finally, after several heated discussions, Churchill acquiesces, stating that he will approve approaching Mussolini to obtain Hitler's terms for a peace settlement. Churchill states that consideration could be given provided Britain's independence is assured.

Aaron next finds himself standing in a room where Churchill is seated on a duvet. The room appears to Aaron to be an attic, of sorts. Sparsely furnished with a desk, a chair and a few boxes scattered about, Aaron believes this may be a room where Churchill comes to ponder his circumstances. Just then Churchill's wife, Clementine, enters the room.

"Winston, dear, you have a visitor," says Clementine. Then seeing the look of utter despair on her husband's face, she says

"Winston, you look as if you have the weight of the entire world on your shoulders. You must remember that everything that you have done, right or wrong, up until now has prepared you to bear the responsibility before you." Pausing for a moment she then says, "Shall I show him in?"

"Show who in?" questions Churchill. "The King."

"Which King?" says Churchill absently. Then, "Oh, our King, yes by all means."

King George enters the room and closes the door. Churchill rises, still in his stocking feet. "Your majesty."

"Winston, please excuse this late-night visit. I have something on my mind we should discuss." Just then the King hesitates and blinks as Aaron takes control of his mind. "Lord Halifax has just informed me of your decision to pursue terms of a peace settlement with Hitler."

Aaron allows the King to continue the conversation with Churchill. "I will go to Parliament in the morning to inform of our intentions to begin to initiate peace talks with Herr Hitler," said Churchill. "I should like to know Your Majesty's thoughts regarding the matter."

"I should like to know your mind first," says King George.

Churchill looks away from the King and says quietly, "I should like to know it myself. History has shown us that nations that go down fighting rise again. Countries that surrender do not."

"Are you afraid, Winston?"

"I am most certainly terrified," replies Churchill. "Support within the War Cabinet for resistance has collapsed."

The King then rises from his chair and sits beside Churchill on the duvet. With Aaron in control of the King's mind the King whispers, "You have my support."

Churchill looks at the King, surprised. "Your Majesty?"

"You have my support," the King repeats, louder. "I cannot bear the image of a Nazi Swastika flying above Buckingham Palace, above Parliament. At first, I admit that I had doubts about you in the role of Prime Minister. But I've come to realize that you are exactly what we need. Why? Because Hitler fears you more than any other European leader. Anyone who can put fear into the heart of that brutal man is who I want to lead us at this crucial time."

"There is not much support for resistance in Parliament, Your Majesty."

"Let me give you a bit of advice. Go to the people. Do not spare them any of the reality of what we face both by surrendering and by resisting. Let them empower your spirit to do what is best for them and for Britain."

"But I have few with whom I can speak who are not biased with their own perception of what is good for themselves."

"Well, we now have each other with whom we can speak candidly," says the King, rising to leave.

As the King heads for the door he hesitates, looks straight ahead with a blank stare not visible to Churchill, and then continues his exit. Aaron has departed the King's mind.

Aaron turns to the Guardian. "Well, did I just save the world?"

The Guardian replies, "We're here aren't we?"

The next thing Aaron realizes is he has just awakened from the strangest dream he ever had.

Chapter 22

"KB, what is my schedule today"? asked Kristian, standing on the balcony of his suite at the mansion enjoying the morning sunlight and cool air through the millions of sensors embedded in the artificial skin of the cyborg. KB is the personal assistant built into the house and available through an interface between his cyborg body and his mind when away from the mansion.

"You have a psych evaluation at 10 A.M. at Barnett Center. Lunch with Ansley at 12:30 P.M. followed by tests of your athletic abilities beginning at 2 P.M.," replied KB. Recall that eating is optional but still pleasurable for Kristian. Any food consumed will be processed by his cyborg body and waste eliminated through the air. Kristian occasionally tells Ansley that he needs to go fart after a meal, referring to the way the cyborg eliminates waste.

"Please start the cleaning machine," said Kristian. Cleaning the cyborg body involves standing in an enclosed shower stall while a chemical mist that cleans the cyborg's skin is sprayed from multiple outlets. No water, soap, shampoo or otherwise conventional washing products are used. After the chemical mist spray, compressed air is blown to dry off the cyborg body. The whole process takes about ninety seconds. Afterward, Kristian dresses and heads for the hyperloop to Barnett Center.

Kristian arrives at the office of Dr. Samuel McKensey, who is the psychiatrist evaluating him as he continues to adapt to his cyborg body. Dr. McKensey is the same psychiatrist that evaluated Aaron Adams and approved his return to the general population. Thus far,

Dr. McKensey approved Kristian's move back to the mansion but wanted to conduct more tests on Kristian before he can be allowed to integrate freely with the public.

"Good morning, Kristian," said Dr. McKensey. "Feeling well today?"

"Couldn't be better," replied Kristian.

"I want to review the results of the tests we performed last week. Everything looked great with one exception. The results indicated you experienced a very stressful situation while your brain was in stasis. Do you recall anything between the time your brain was put in stasis and you awoke in your cyborg body?"

"I don't recall much of anything after I went under anesthesia to have my brain removed," said Kristian, breaking eye contact with McKensey and deliberately avoiding any discussion of his mission with The Guardian.

"Perhaps the trauma we are seeing was associated with having your brain removed," said McKensey. "Are you sure you don't recall anything that may have frightened you, stressed you, irritated you, or angered you? The scans indicate that the event was quite real and stressful."

"Well, I do recall having some strange dreams," said Kristian, again attempting to defuse McKensey's questioning.

"Dreams about what, Kristian?" asked McKensey.

"I seem to recall having been a soldier in what appeared to the U.S Civil War," replied Kristian. "I think I was on the Confederate side, maybe an officer. We were in the midst of a battle at dusk and I was giving the order to fire on the enemy. Gunfire was everywhere and cannon firing could be heard in the distance. Some of my men were falling, dead and wounded. Then the dream suddenly ended. I still have no idea why I had the dream. It is the only one I remember."

"Well, we still don't know much about dreams and what causes them. But that your dream was foreign to any life experience you've had raises my curiosity. Did you ever study the Civil War in detail, read about the life of any particular soldier or soldiers?

"Nothing more than what we were taught in high school," replied Kristian.

"Have you had any similar dreams since the one you recall?" asked McKensey.

"While in my charging/resting state I recall having dreams, but none like that one. It was so vivid, so real. I believe that the dreams I have now are associated with my mind resting and rejuvenating."

"Yes, very possible, even likely," replied McKensey. "I think that will be all for now. Your progress thus far has been very good. I believe we have concluded the psychiatric portion of your tests. If I have any additional questions, I'll give you a call."

"Sounds good to me, Doc," replied Kristian as he rose to leave and shook the doctor's hand.

"So how did your session with Dr. McKensey go?" asked Ansley as they sat down in the Center dining room to eat lunch. Ansley had a chef salad and Kristian had a hamburger and fries, washed down with a chocolate shake. Kristian enjoyed eating any kind of junk food knowing he wouldn't gain weight or harm his body. "It's not fair that I have to eat like a rabbit while you chow down on all that fat, carbs, and calories," she said.

"Well," replied Kristian. "He said my psych eval is complete." "Is that all he said?" questioned Ansley, suspiciously.

"We had a discussion about dreams," said Kristian, munching down on his burger.

"What dreams? You haven't mentioned dreams to me. You have dreams?"

"When I'm in my charging/resting state, I let my mind go where it wants. Whether it is just my imagination running loose or I am really dreaming, I have no idea. I told McKensey that I believe my mind is just purging itself of old thoughts that are no longer needed."

"And what thoughts would those be?" questioned Ansley, continuing to press the point.

"I dunno. Do you have dreams that you think have any real meaning?"

"Of course, I have dreams. I had lots of dreams that I hoped had meaning when you were … under," said Ansley. "Some were good, even great. But some were horrifying nightmares."

"So, when are we going to be able to relive some of your 'good' dreams, Ansley? I need to see if this body will react to my mind in all situations, including making love."

"I was wondering when you would get around to asking that question," said Ansley. "I was beginning to think you had lost interest. Your cyber body is designed for rigorous sex. It should be quite pleasurable for you. But I didn't want to put any pressure on you for sex that you may not be psychologically ready for."

"Sounds like you planned for a 'reunion' for us in the design of the cyborg body," Kristian joked. Let's plan a second honeymoon at a five-star resort in the South Pacific."

"That will be fine once you're cleared for interfacing with the public. But in the meantime, a dinner and rendezvous at the Mansion would be intriguing."

Reacting to Ansley's suggestion, Kristian immediately began preparations for an extravagant dinner at the mansion. He called the mansion chef and issued orders for a dinner for two to be served at sunset on the mansion's highest balcony overlooking the Bel-Air hills. A waiter, dressed formally, would serve and oversee the event. Fine wines from the mansion's wine cellar would be served to compliment the appetizer, main course, and dessert portions of the meal. And, of course, none of this was to be shared with Ansley.

Chapter 23

Kristian, Ansley, and Savannah met for lunch two days later. "Ansley, do you have possible candidates for the Brain Restoration Procedure and cyborg activation?" asked Savannah. "Not as of yet," replied Ansley. "Apparently our current state of peace throughout the world has limited the number of military candidates. Do you have any patients that would meet the criteria for the procedure?"

"No, not at the moment. There are a couple of patients whose ALS has not advanced to the point to justify the procedure. As we get closer to a cure for ALS, I don't want to jump the gun on what could be a possible recovery from the disease."

Listening intently to the conversation, Kristian asked, "Was I the first to undergo the transformation to a cyborg body?"

Ansley and Savannah both looked surprised and stared at each other for a long second. Then Ansley answered, "no," still staring at Savannah.

Savannah said, "yes."

"Well, that is interesting," Kristian said, the sarcasm in his voice quite evident. "So which version of the story am I to believe?"

Savannah responded first, stammering a bit, "You were the first to have your brain removed from your diseased body and put in stasis."

"But you are not the first successful download of a human mind to a cyborg body," said Ansley. "There is one other who was created months before we downloaded your mind to your new body."

"So, you made me wait months longer than was necessary to resurrect my consciousness?" replied Kristian, his tone reflecting anger and confusion. "Why?"

"Kristian, downloading a human mind to a cyborg body was a ground-breaking feat, something that had never been attempted. I did not want to place all the risks on my husband. I had to be sure, confident, that the procedure would work before I attempted it on you."

"Who was the first to receive his cyborg body? What were his, and I am assuming it was a male, problems that justified the risk of being the first?" said Kristian.

"I cannot divulge his identity, Kristian. He has been released back into the general public with a new identity, under a witness protection program. He has a career and is now healthy. He suffered from the same disease as you," replied Ansley, solemnly.

"Neither of you, or for that matter anyone else, has experienced what the first cyborg and I have gone through!' exclaimed Kristian. "I demand to be allowed to communicate with this other cyborg! You can keep his identity from me but there should be no harm in he and I discussing our experiences."

Ansley and Savannah looked at each other for several moments, after which Ansley said, "We will look into establishing a communication session for you, but I will need to run it up the chain with DARPA. I suspect the answer will be 'no' since there is a risk that the other cyborg will reveal his true identity during the session."

As the afternoon and evening wore on for Kristian, the idea that another cyborg existed continued to occupy his thoughts. He really wanted to know if the other cyborg had encountered The Guardian. He recalled that The Guardian had told him there were others, with other missions associated with maintaining timelines. He wondered if he could summon The Guardian during his rest/recharge session and decided he would attempt to make contact.

Chapter 24

Kristian was swimming laps in the Mansion infinity pool, with a beautiful sunset in progress, when Ansley appeared on the deck still wearing her lab coat. "Kristian, I have been summoned to DARPA HQ in Washington, D.C. to brief the brass on the status of our program. I must leave in the morning and will be gone for two or three days, minimum. Will you be OK while I'm away?

"Certainly, I'm not a child, you know," replied Kristian, wiping the water dripping down his face.

"Of course, I know," replied Ansley. "I just want to make sure you have everything you need."

"Sorry, I understand. Any chance you could take me along? A real live cyborg would sure beat any 3D video-slide presentation you've whipped up."

"I wish, but I'm told this meeting was requested by the Secretary of Defense, with a specific set of attendees. Probably not a good idea to rock the boat with an uninvited guest, even a real live cyborg. Each attendee at these meetings must be vetted with an FBI background check in advance."

Kristian thought perhaps while she's away, I can do a little research into the identity of the first cyborg.

Indian Summer had descended on Washington D.C. the last week of September and the weather conditions were warm and humid. Humidity is not something Ansley was used to, and as she exited the black, unmarked government SUV and ascended the steps to the entrance to DARPA, she could feel herself breaking a sweat.

The security checkpoint at the entrance to the facility was not busy at 10 A.M. so the security screening was quick and uneventful. On the other side of the checkpoint, a tall, muscular man in a dark suit with an earpiece planted in one ear immediately recognized and approached her.

"Dr. Barnett, please affix this visitor's badge to your clothing above your waist and follow me," said the Secret Service agent. "Of course," replied Ansley.

Ansley was led to a bank of elevators. The Secret Service agent pressed the UP button. The door opened and they both stepped inside. Another woman attempted to enter the elevator, but she was blocked by the agent. "Sorry, ma'am, only approved personnel on this elevator," the agent said curtly. The agent pushed a button that said '5-RESTRICTED' and faced a small camera lens that verified his identity. The elevator rose quickly and stopped on the fifth floor. Ansley and the agent exited to the right and approached a glass door with an access-control device on the adjacent wall. The agent faced the device while it captured a scan of his face. Ansley heard the door click. The agent opened the door and passed through while Ansley followed. The agent then stopped and told Ansley to hold her security pass up to the camera on the wall. "You may proceed" was heard from a bodiless voice.

Ansley and the agent then walked down the long hallway to a set of double doors. The agent opened both doors, stepped inside the large conference room, and said, "Dr. Ansley Barnett." The Director of DARPA, Jim Hanson, greeted Ansley.

Hanson was wearing a dark blue suit, white shirt, and red tie, the uniform of many high-level government executives. The blue suit complemented his blue eyes and salt-and-pepper hair. "Dr. Barnett, thank you for coming all this way on short notice. I trust your flight and accommodations were satisfactory."

"Good morning, Director," said Ansley. "Yes, the trip was quite comfortable. I hope this meeting will be positive, but I have the sense I will feel some turbulence based on the list of attendees."

"Well, hopefully, we can keep the turbulence to a minimum and have a positive outcome."

The Secretary of Defense (SecDef), William Bonner, was the last to arrive at the meeting. He entered the room briskly, stopped just inside the door and scanned the room. He too was dressed in the blue suit uniform and his dark eyes, amplified by his shaved head, were penetrating as they fell on several attendees including Ansley. Already seated at the oblong conference table were The Chairman of the Joint Chiefs of Staff, Director of DARPA, Deputy Director of Medical Research for DARPA, and the Secretary of the Treasury. Several assistants were also seated in chairs against the walls bordering the conference table. SecDef took his seat at the head of the table opposite the Director of DARPA. Ansley was strategically seated in the middle of the table, which was the best position for the brass in the room to levy verbal attacks.

"Good morning, all," started SecDef, curtly. "Dr. Barnett, can you enlighten us as to the status of your cyborg project? Do we have any military personnel injured in battle that has undergone the ... procedure?"

"Yes, sir," replied Ansley. "We have successfully completed the transformation to a cyborg body on two patients, both of which are controlled by a human mind. These patients were in the advanced stages of ALS, close to complete paralysis and nearing death but as cyborgs they are now in excellent health. One has been released to return to the public under a new identity. The other is in final testing and anticipating certification to return to the public."

"But, neither of these two ... patients were military personnel, much less few military personnel injured in combat. Correct?"

"That is correct."

"Why have we not attempted the procedure on a military candidate, Dr. Barnett?" said SecDef, sternly.

"Mr. Secretary, we have not been given any military personnel to evaluate for the procedure," replied Ansley.

SecDef's gaze immediately shifted to the Chairman of the Joint

Chiefs. "Admiral Tucker, why haven't any candidates been provided for the procedure?"

Admiral Tucker, surprised at the quick question from SecDef, hesitated, then cleared his throat, "Quite frankly, sir, we have not had any serious injuries these past several months that would warrant the procedure. The current state of peace we are enjoying globally has not produced any candidates."

SecDef's face began to redden. "You mean to tell me we have had NO serious injuries to military personnel in the past year that would qualify for this procedure?" he said with his voice rising through the sentence.

"Not injuries resulting from combat, Mr. Secretary."

"What about non-combat injuries, Admiral? Surely, in the combined forces of the United States, there have been serious injuries resulting from combat training. What about flight training? We just had an F-35 overshoot a landing on the USS Donald Trump where the pilot was seriously injured! Where is that pilot?

"Dead, sir," stammered the admiral. "He died from his injuries forty-eight hours after the crash."

"Could this procedure have been used to save this man, Admiral?"

"Dr. Barnett, can you address the Secretary's question?" deferred Admiral Tucker.

Ansley took a breath and said, "I can't answer that without knowing the facts surrounding the pilot's injuries."

"Damn it, people!" exclaimed SecDef. "Greg, how much have we spent on this program to date? It has to be in the billions." "Thirteen-point-six billion to date, over ten years," replied the Secretary of the Treasury, Gregory Pate.

"Thirteen-point-six billion dollars," mused SecDef. "And we have yet to show any benefit to the U.S. military. Damn it, people, how do you expect me to explain this to the President? I am very tempted to recommend that the program be canceled!"

"Sir," said the Director of DARPA, "to cancel the program now when we have demonstrated proof that the procedure works and can be performed on a military candidate would be a tremendous waste of the resources invested."

"I tend to agree and will recommend the program continue with the caveat that a successful procedure is performed on a military candidate in time for a presentation of the candidate to this body no more than one year from today. Do you accept the challenge, Director?" said SecDef.

"Ansley, can you meet the challenge?" questioned the Director.

"If I have a candidate meeting our criteria within the next three months."

"This meeting is adjourned," said the Secretary of Defense. "Director Hanson, I want a personal briefing from you regarding this project monthly, beginning a month from today. Is that clear?"

"Yes, sir."

Chapter 25

Ansley arrived at the mansion mid-afternoon from Washington, D.C. "Hi Kristian, I'm home," she announced as she walked through the massive double doors from the portico. Receiving no response, she dropped her bags just inside the door and went up the curved staircase to the second level to Kristian's office. "Kristian?" she said as she entered Kristian's office, but Kristian was not there. Ansley then said, "KB, where is Kristian?"

"Kristian is at The Barnett Center meeting with Dr. Savannah Richards," replied the digital assistant.

"Please dial Dr. Richard's office," said Ansley.

"Dr. Richard's office, may I help you?" answered Dr. Richard's digital assistant.

"Yes, this is Dr. Ansley Barnett. I need to speak to Dr. Richards."

"I'll connect you," replied the digitized voice.

"Hello, Ansley," Savannah said. "How are you? How was your trip?"

"We need to discuss the meeting, Savannah. I'm beat from the trip. Can you do lunch tomorrow?"

"Let me just check my calendar …. Yes, I can do lunch. Where do you want to meet?"

"Let's meet at the mansion. Lunch on the pool deck. Kristian, are you free to join us?"

"Thought you'd never ask," replied Kristian. "Yes, of course."

"When are you coming back up to the mansion, Kristian?" said Ansley.

"I'll be there in a few minutes."

Back at the mansion, Kristian greeted Ansley with a big hug and long kiss. "I missed you terribly," he said. "Ever since my … absence I hate being apart from you for more than a few hours." "I missed you as well. The meeting was tough. SecDef was on a tear over the lack of a military cyborg to date. He gave us one year to produce one or he will recommend to the President that the program be canceled."

"I do want to hear more about your meeting. But, how about some good news first? I've arranged for us to have a special dinner on the upper balcony the day after tomorrow. This will be a dressy affair so pick something formal, and sexy."

"On the upper balcony?" replied Ansley. "Who is coming to this event?"

"Two very important people. You and me."

The next day, Ansley, Kristian, and Savannah met on the mansion's pool deck for lunch. Ansley and Savannah both had a shrimp salad with a slice of sourdough bread and organic butter and a glass of unsweetened iced tea. Kristian had a Philly cheese steak and fries, with a chocolate milkshake.

"Very nice, Kristian. You can down all the high calorie, high fat food you want while we must suffer over salads and veggies and suffer guilt over a slice of bread and butter," said Ansley.

"And I thank you for giving me a body that can eat whatever it wants with no harm," replied Kristian.

"Ansley, how was your meeting with the D.C. brass?" asked Savannah.

"Tense. The Secretary of Defense was looking for a fully functional cyber-soldier to appear or a scalp to present to the President. Fortunately, not all of his wrath was directed at me. He shared his frustration and anger with several in the room. He ripped into the Chairman of the Joint Chiefs, CJCS, Admiral Tucker, pretty hard. He wanted to know why the military has been unable to provide a suitable candidate for the procedure. He then ordered the military to expand its search for a candidate outside of combat casualties. Finally, he gave us one year to produce a fully-functional military candidate or he would recommend cancelation of the program."

"Canceling the program seems extreme considering the amount of money already invested," said Kristian. It has to be north of five billion.

"Thirteen-point-six billion," said Ansley. "This figure is courtesy of the Secretary of the Treasury. This, of course, just served to further infuriate SecDef."

"How are we going to find a candidate who meets the government's requirements?" asked Savannah."

"We aren't," said Ansley. "It is up to the military to provide a candidate. Fortunately, for us, SecDef ordered the CJCS to expand its search for potential candidates to training accidents, aircraft or land vehicle crashes, and other accidents."

"If we are to produce a fully functional cyborg in a year, we will need to begin the process in a couple of months," stated Savannah. "We need approximately nine months, with no hitches, to produce a thinking, feeling, functioning cyborg."

"Funny how that works," said Kristian. "Nine months. About the same as a baby."

"Yes, I made our time requirements quite clear to the attendees before the meeting was adjourned," said Ansley. "So, we wait for the military to produce a candidate."

Chapter 26

The view of the sun setting over the mansion's highest balcony was spectacular. The wispy clouds reflected a collage of orange, red, blue, and green on a pallet of blue sky, reflecting the sun's fading brilliance as it set over the horizon. The air temperature was a perfect seventy-four degrees, humidity at thirty percent, with a light breeze out of the southwest. Kristian, dressed in a black tuxedo with a red bow tie and red cummerbund, stepped out on the balcony to find the setting just as he had ordered. A round, glass table was placed in the center of the balcony with two chairs. The table was set with fine china, pure silver cutlery, and Waterford crystal water, champagne, and wine glasses. White wine chilled in a sterling silver ice bucket resting in a stand next to the table. Standing beside the table was Miquel, the Barnett's long-time head butler and bartender, also dressed formally in a black tuxedo.

"Good evening, Mr. Barnett," said Miquel. "Will Mrs. Barnett be joining you soon?"

"I hope so, Miquel. Everything looks perfect, just as I envisioned it."

"May I get you a cocktail while we await Mrs. Barnett's arrival?" said Miquel.

"No, I will wait for Mrs. Barnett," replied Kristian as he turned to walk slowly around the edge of the balcony which was bordered in ornate rod iron.

Just then, Ansley appeared in the double-glass doors leading to the balcony. Kristian turned and smiled at the image she presented.

To him, she looked like a goddess dressed in a flowing, full length pale blue gown. She wore her dark blonde hair up off her shoulders as she had done years before for their wedding.

"Good evening," said Kristian, as he could sense his cyber body ever so slightly begin to respond to the beautiful woman who was his wife. "Please, join me in paradise this evening," he said as he stepped to where she was standing. "You are every bit as beautiful as you were on our wedding day. Perhaps even more so."

"And you, sir, are just as handsome as you were on our wedding day," said Ansley.

Kristian turned to Miquel and asked that he bring them cocktails. Already knowing Ansley's favorite, Kristian had arranged the order with Miquel earlier. Miquel nodded and stepped away to fulfill the request.

"Come, look at this special sunset I ordered just for this occasion," said Kristian.

"Well, I see your modesty hasn't changed since our wedding," said Ansley, smiling.

They enjoyed their cocktails standing at the edge of the balcony admiring the sunset. "I cannot adequately express my gratitude at being able to stand here with you," said Kristian. "Without you and Savannah's genius, I wouldn't be here at all. Now I have an unlimited lease on life."

"I still have one concern, Kristian," she replied. "Your cyber-body does not age. In theory, you could look the same one hundred years from now. As I age, the person you see standing with you this evening will become old, haggard looking. Will you still love me then as you do today?"

"I am going to think positively, Ansley," said Kristian. "I believe aging is just another disease whose symptoms destroy the body in a manner not dissimilar to ALS. So why wouldn't it be possible for you to obtain a cyber-body at the appropriate time?" "That's a nice thought, Kristian, but aging is not yet accepted as a disease. It is still seen as a natural progression of human life in most circles. Ethically, I don't know how widespread adoption of cyber technology as a cure for aging will be accepted. How would candidates be selected for the procedure? How would the procedure be paid for?"

"Let's just leave this discussion as there may be a way to avoid your concerns for you and me relative to your aging. Stay positive and see what comes. After all, you are years away from showing noticeable signs of aging."

The dinner prepared by the mansion chef was magnificent, a work of art more than just a meal. Caviar was served with a rare Chardonnay from the mansion's cellar. Appetizers included baked French bread rounds topped with mashed avocado with salt, lime juice, and grilled shrimp. The main course consisted of Kobe beef filets flown chilled, but not frozen, from Japan on the Barnett jet. Done to medium for Ansley, and medium rare for Kristian, the eight-ounce filets, prepared with a touch of garlic butter and herbs, literally melted in their mouths. The main course was served with a bottle of Araujo Cabernet 2010, Eisele, Napa which goes for more than a thousand dollars a bottle in fine restaurants. Dessert consisted of pastry made from a raspberry biscuit, glaze, and mousse, with crème Brulee filling, served with a small glass of sweet dessert white wine.

Dinner concluded, Kristian said, "should we retire to our bedroom suite or have champagne here on the balcony?"

"I am feeling a little chilled out here. Plus, I am feeling a little … flushed from the wine. Let's go downstairs to our suite. Thank you for arranging this incredible dinner. It is possibly the best I've ever enjoyed."

Kristian addressed KB, the digital assistant, "KB, please light the fireplace in our bedroom suite and close the sheer draperies. We'll be there in a few minutes."

Kristian and Ansley changed into more comfortable attire. Kristian donned a full-length, black silk robe patterned in oriental embroidery. Ansley dressed in a full-length, high-waisted negligée with a matching flowing robe. Kristian opened the champagne and poured a glass for each of them.

"To our continued love of one another, may it last into eternity," toasted Kristian, smiling, as their champagne flutes clanked together.

They then sat on the Elizabethan love seat in front of the massive stone fireplace.

"We really should take that month-long journey to the South Pacific," said Kristian. "I dream of being on a secluded island where we can shut out the rest of the world for a few days. Sailing the crystal blue waters under a strong tropical sun. Beautiful sunsets that set the tone for wonderful evenings of food, wine, and you."

"Sounds delightful, Kristian, but you know I can't drop off the planet for a month right now. If the military produces a candidate for the procedure, I will be working overtime to meet the government's deadline."

"Yes, I know, but someday, we will make time for a wonderful second honeymoon."

With that, he took Ansley in his arms while they kissed. After several minutes locked in an embrace, they arose and walked slowly over to the over-sized king bed.

"KB, please close the main draperies," said Kristian. "Reduce the intensity of the fire to a minimum." The heavy draperies closed over the suite's floor-to-ceiling glass wall and the fire was reduced to glowing embers.

They embraced each other gently at first, but shortly their embrace became more feverous. Kristian removed Ansley's robe revealing a sheer negligee underneath. Ansley untied Kristian's robe at the waist and pushed it back over his shoulders until it dropped to the floor, leaving Kristian in the silk boxers that were a matched set to the robe. Kristian could feel his cyber- body responding to the sexual encounter without a noticeable difference in the way his corporeal body had responded before he fell ill. They continued to embrace as Kristian slipped the string straps of the negligee off Ansley's shoulders, kissing her neck and shoulders, then descending to her naked breasts. Kristian then stood and walked Ansley to the edge of the bed and laid her down. He then removed his boxers and slid in next to her.

They made love, slowly at first, enjoying the touch of each other's bodies, sampling their favorite sensory spots that they had discovered so many years before. They then began to move more fiercely when Ansley mounted Kristian. After an unknown amount of time, they both seemed to climax simultaneously. Ansley moaned and Kristian uttered what some would consider a guttural growl. In the end, Ansley collapsed, first down on Kristian's chest, then rolling off to his side. Kristian held her as she drifted off into a deep sleep.

Kristian, not requiring sleep, lay awake listening to Ansley's breathing while thoughts of The Guardian entered his mind. The Guardian had said he would be back with more assignments. What assignments could be in store for him? And what about the first cyborg that had been created? Had The Guardian drafted his services? Kristian then relaxed his mind, as he had learned to do, and allow it to wander aimlessly. This was the closest Kristian experienced to sleep but found his mind clearer and sharper after completing a session of rest.

After an unknown time in his mind's restful state, Kristian felt Ansley roll towards him, placing her hand on his chest. Although she still seemed to be asleep, Kristian rolled towards her, placing his hand on her hip and gently pulling her closer to him. Kristian felt his body responding, stirring to her touch. He awakened her with a gentle kiss to which she smiled, opened her eyes, and kissed him back. From there the two engaged in another love-making session. This time, he eventually moved on top of her, partially supporting himself with his arms. They caressed each other as they made love and finally climaxed together, moaning with pleasure. Ansley then fell back into a deep sleep, leaving Kristian to again return to his wandering mind.

Pre-dawn light began to appear at the seams of the draperies covering the wall of glass. Kristian leaned over to Ansley and began to kiss her, first on her cheeks, then on her lips. Eventually, he moved his head beneath the sheets, kissing her body in strategic points known to excite her. She then grabbed his head, pulling him face-to-face and kissing him on the lips. The two then continued with their third round of lovemaking, both blissfully unaware of the supernatural being, whom Kristian referred to as The Guardian, patiently watching them.

Sometime later, the two arose. Outside, the sun was already high in the sky indicating that it was late morning.

"Oh my," said Ansley. "I am late for work! But what a magical evening! I need to shower and get dressed and get down to the Center."

"Let's shower together," said Kristian.

The suite's shower, redesigned by Kristian after his parents had passed away, mimicked a grotto made of stone with multiple shower heads that provided several different water flows including a rain shower, a deep shower massage with multiple heads providing high-intensity sprays at multiple points, and a full- body rinse. On the stone wall aside each showerhead were crystal dispensers for shampoo, cream rinse, and liquid soap. Another head was set up to enable men to shave with the desired shaving device, shaving creams, etc. A fourth, water dispensing from a flexible head extending from the side of a seat, was for women to shave their legs. A wide selection of music was piped in and a couple of LED screens could be descended from the ceiling for viewing news and sports broadcasts. A shower in the mansion's suite was quite an experience.

The suite's shower, a separate facility redesigned by Kristian and separate from his cyborg cleaning station, allowed Ansley to enjoy the rain shower while Kristian received a deep massage. Ansley preferred music while Kristian nearly always activated the LED screens for news and sports. Despite their differences, the warm steam and hot water stimulated both sexually and they made love yet a fourth time. At the climax of their lovemaking, Kristian had to carry Ansley to the shower seat and let her sit down to recover. After a few minutes, Ansley looked up at Kristian through the shower steam and smiled.

"Well it seems you've passed your final test with a grade of A-plus-plus," she joked. "We will need to plan your transition back to public life. Up until now, you've been a top secret. The public believes you died years ago and now, you're back, healthy and in top shape. The demand for how this could happen will be extreme. We, together with Savannah, will have to craft a believable scenario."

"And you have been the most amazing test subject I've ever had," said Kristian, smiling. "Better yet, there does not seem to be any limit on how much or often I can make love!"

Chapter 27

"Barnett Center, how may I route your call?" said the Center's digital assistant.

"I need to schedule my annual examination," said Aaron Adams. "One moment while I connect you with a secure line," said the assistant, recognizing Aaron as one on a list of top-secret contacts.

After a click indicating the secure connection was established, the assistant said, "when would you like to report for your examination schedule, Mr. Adams?"

"I've arranged to be away from work the week after next. If they could be scheduled for that week, I would appreciate it."

"OK, I will work up a schedule for the examinations targeting the week of March 4, 2041.

"Thank you. Can you now connect me to Dr. Ansley Barnett?"

"Yes. But I see Dr. Barnett's line is busy. Shall I connect you to her voicemail?"

"Yes, please."

After the voicemail greeting provided by the digital assistant for Ansley, Aaron began his message. "Hello, Dr. Barnett, this is Aaron. I am coming to the Center the week of March 4th for my annual and expect to see you then. But please give me a call. I have a couple of questions that I'd like to discuss before I get there. Thanks."

Aaron received a return call from Ansley later that afternoon. "Hello, Dr. Barnett, thanks for returning my call. I just wanted to touch base with you on a couple of personal issues before I arrive for my annual. First, I assume that Kristian has been revived in his cyborg body. How is he doing?"

"Kristian has been successfully restored in his cyborg body. He is now fully functional and ready to announce his return to the general population. His restoration took longer than it did with you because he had been in an induced coma for so long. But he's fine now."

"Great. Do you think it would be possible for me to meet him? I'd like to share my experiences with him and learn from his."

Silence on Ansley's end for a few long moments was followed by, "No, Aaron, I do not feel that would be good," as she thought about their one-time sexual encounter. Even though Kristian once said he would not hold a sexual relationship against her, she felt it could damage her relationship with him.

"Why not, Ansley? It would seem to be an excellent learning opportunity for both Kristian and me. Are you afraid that I will let it slip that we had sex? Because I would never do that."

"I just don't believe it would be a good idea at this time," replied Ansley.

"So, at some point would you support Kristian and I meeting?"
"To be honest, I don't believe I would ever feel comfortable with that," said Ansley.

"When you say that Kristian is fully functional, do you really mean completely functional? Are you and Kristian intimate?"

"Yes, I look forward to seeing you in a couple of weeks, Aaron."
"Me too."

The thought of contacting Kristian lingered in Aaron's mind after the call with Ansley ended. He especially needed to know if Kristian had had contact with The Guardian, and whether Kristian had been given any assignments. He decided that he must find a way to get around Ansley to reach Kristian.

Chapter 28

Aaron arrived at Barnett Center late in the day on Sunday, March 3rd and reported for his first examination promptly at 8 A.M. on Monday. The staff at the Center still addressed him as Mr. Adams since that is how they knew him during his previous stay. However, they had all been required to sign non-disclosure agreements preventing them from divulging any information about him to any outside persons.

"Good morning, Mr. Adams. How are you this morning?" greeted Janice, Dr. Barnett's chief cyborg technician. Janice Goodman was also a physician and had a Ph.D. in neuro-cyber connectivity.

"Hi, Janice. Great to see you. I'm doing fine, thanks," replied Aaron.

"Let's go into my office to review your schedule for the next few days," said Janice. They walked to the elevator and rode to the second floor, then down a hallway to Janice's office. "Have a seat, Mr. Adams," said Janice.

"Please call me Aaron," said Aaron. "It's nice to hear my real name spoken for a change."

"As you wish, Mr... Aaron. Today we will be running tests on your circuitry. Testing every connection in your body to ensure everything is functioning properly. This will take most of the day, as you can imagine, given the number of connections in your body. Your part in these tests will be to provide input on what you're feeling, or not feeling. On Tuesday you will be given a battery of tests to evaluate your cognitive function. These are the same tests you took after your procedure so they will be familiar to you. We want to see if there are any changes since last year. On Wednesday, get your gym clothes on because we will be testing your physical abilities. Tests will include sprinting, distance running, swimming, rock-wall climbing, and variations of weightlifting. Treadmill tests will be used where appropriate. These tests also are those you've experienced previously. On Thursday you will meet with Dr. Barnett to get your results. Do you have any questions?"

"Not at this time, Janice," said Aaron.

"Good, then let's go upstairs where you'll begin your tests."

As they walked up to the third floor Aaron asked, "Janice, how is Savannah Richards? I haven't seen or spoken with her since I left the Center last year."

"Dr. Richards is well," said Janice. "I have heard she may be close to providing another cyborg candidate soon."

"Where is her office?" asked Aaron, thinking he may be able to use Savannah to contact Kristian.

"She's on the fourth floor, executive level of The Center. Would you like me to see if I can arrange some time for you to meet with her?"

"Oh, no, no," replied Aaron. "If I have some time between tests or at the end of the day, I'll try to reach her in her office."

Aaron's appointment with Ansley was set for 11 AM on Thursday. Ansley's office was also on the fourth Floor of The Center, at the opposite end from Savannah's. Aaron entered the reception area for Ansley's office, walked over to the unmanned desk and placed his palm on the identification reader. The reader seemed to speak to him and said, "Mr. Adams, please have a seat. Dr. Barnett will be with you shortly."

A few minutes later, Ansley greeted Aaron smiling, extending her hand to shake his. "How are you, Aaron? You're looking well."

"Hello, Dr. Barnett, I'm feeling terrific. This cyborg thing seems to agree with me," Aaron said, also smiling at the sight of Ansley, for whom he still had an attraction.

"Come in and have a seat by my desk," said Ansley. "I have your test results and they are impressive. It seems that the cyber 'thing' does agree with you."

Ansley went over Aaron's test results, all of which fell in the normal, expected ranges.

"Do you have any concerns, Aaron?"

"I know you don't like to discuss my meeting Kristian, but I really believe it would be an amazing opportunity for him and me to share our experiences. Anything I can do to convince you to bless a meeting?"

Ansley hesitated and then answered, "I really can't condone a meeting at this time, Aaron. And, no, it is not because of our one-time tryst. The cyborg program is under intense scrutiny by the feds and I can't do anything that could possibly result in increased scrutiny by them."

"I see," said Aaron, deliberately projecting sadness and disappointment.

"Well, if there are no other questions…Hey, I am meeting Savannah for lunch at the mansion. Do you have any questions for her?"

"Uh, no," said Aaron. "But thanks."

After leaving Ansley's office, Aaron waited at the indented doorway to the stairs until Ansley came out of her office to meet Savannah. He watched her walk down the hallway to Savannah's office and enter. Then he continued watching as the two of them exited Savannah's office and began walking to the elevator lobby.

"Oh, I just remembered, I need to make a quick phone call," said Savannah. "Go ahead and I'll meet you at the mansion in a few minutes." She turned to return to her office while Ansley proceeded to the elevators.

After about five minutes, Savannah exited her office and headed for the elevator. Aaron took his cue and proceeded quickly down the stairs to the first level where he exited the stairwell right after Savannah stepped off the elevator and headed for the transportation pods. Aaron followed her staying several yards behind her hoping she wouldn't see him. Savannah called a pod and stepped in. As soon as it departed, Aaron called a pod and jumped in.

At the pod terminal in the mansion, Savannah stepped out of her pod after just a few seconds that were required to arrive from The Center and rode the escalator up one floor to the mansion's foyer. Aaron saw Savannah going up the elevator and followed her at a distance. When he arrived at the top, he saw Savannah being greeted by Ansley and Kristian.

"Hello," said Aaron. "I am Aaron Adams, Dr. Barnett's first successful cyborg. I understand you are Kristian Barnett. We have much to discuss."

Ansley's face quickly reddened as her anger grew. "Aaron, I told you that this was not a good idea. What are you doing here?" she demanded.

"What is the meaning of this, Mr. Adams?" demanded Kristian. "You are an intruder in our home. KB, call security to the foyer."

"Right away, Mr. Barnett," said the digital assistant.

Holding his hands up to express his surrender Aaron said, "wait, wait. No harm intended. I am unarmed and am not a threat to anyone. I think it is a matter of utmost necessity that you and I talk."

Mansion security entered through the front door. "Mr. Barnett, how should we proceed with this intruder? Would you like him arrested or escorted off the property?"

"Ok, let's all calm down for a moment. Mr. Adams, do you realize how much you startled us with your dramatic entrance?"

"Kristian, Mr. Barnett, yes, and I offer my sincere apology. But I knew of no other way to reach you. We really need to talk."

"KB, what is my schedule for tomorrow? Am I free for lunch?" said Kristian.

"You have meetings in the morning but are free from lunch through the afternoon. Would you like to hear the details of your meetings, Mr. Barnett?"

"No, KB. Mr. Adams, are you free tomorrow afternoon for lunch?"

"To meet with you I will adjust whatever may be on my calendar," said Aaron.

"KB, please book a lunch meeting with Mr. Adams and block my calendar for the afternoon."

"Yes, sir," replied the digital assistant.

"Kristian, this is a bad idea," pleaded Ansley. "At least let me participate in any discussion between you two," she said, looking back and forth at Kristian and Aaron.

"No, Ansley. I want to speak with Mr. Adams alone. Now, Mr. Adams, if you'll excuse us, Ansley, Savannah and I have a previous engagement. If the weather is nice tomorrow, we'll meet on the pool deck at noon." He turned and began walking toward the mansion's dining room.

As Ansley and Savannah turned to follow Kristian, Aaron overheard Ansley telling Kristian that this was a very bad idea, to which Kristian said, "Ansley, that man and I are the only two people who have successfully been transformed into cyber-beings. I want to hear his story, unfiltered, from him."

Chapter 29

Aaron stepped into the pod to the mansion at 11:50 AM, both excited and nervous regarding his meeting with Kristian. As he stepped off the pod in the mansion pod lobby five seconds later, Miquel greeted him. "Mr. Adams, good morning, I am Miquel, the Barnett Mansion facility director. Please follow me."

Aaron followed Miquel to the elevator lobby where they boarded the elevator to the pool deck. Exiting the elevator, Aaron was quite stunned at the view from the pool deck overlooking the hills to the west. "This is incredible, Miquel," said Aaron.

"Mr. Barnett will meet you here in a few minutes. Is there anything I can get for you while you're waiting?" said Miquel.

"No thank you," said Aaron. "I will just take in the view for a few moments."

Kristian entered the pool deck. The two men approached each other, smiled and shook hands. They then walked to the table and sat. "I understand you were here for your first annual examination as a cyborg," said Kristian. "How did that come out?"

"Everything is fine, within expected normal limits," replied Aaron. "How long have you been a cyborg?"

"Just over a year now," replied Kristian. "It is incredible that before my brain was removed, I was literally a vegetable, physically dead. I will admit that I had serious doubts after my mind was downloaded to this body. I could not move a thing. Not even my eyelids for several days. I believe Ansley was on the verge of calling the download a failure and trying again with a new body when I was finally able to blink and answer yes and no questions. Ansley and Savannah believe my long recovery time in the cyborg body was due to being in an induced coma for years prior to the download."

"Wow, sounds like you had a rough time for a while," said Aaron. "I was able to control the body at an elementary level immediately after the download and I was essentially fully functional within a few weeks."

Kristian and Aaron shared their experiences through their testing phases, discussing progress and setbacks. Kristian was curious regarding Aaron's release to the public."

"How long was it until you were released back into the general public, Aaron?"

"It was about at the one-year point," said Aaron. "As you probably know, Aaron Adams died from ALS and "Phillip Geoffrey Preston" was born. They took care of all my affairs, transferred my accounts into my new name, issued a California driver's license and US passport in my new name. Essentially, they gave me a completely new identity. They set me up in a great job and a luxury apartment. It was the perfect witness protection process."

Kristian and Aaron continued their discussion over cheeseburgers, French fries, onion rings, and chocolate milkshakes that Kristian had ordered for the luncheon. They joked about the fact that they could now enjoy any food guiltlessly while Ansley and Savannah groused about eating 'rabbit' food. They discussed sports, discovering that they both followed professional football. Kristian was a fan of the LA Rams while Aaron supported the rival LA Chargers. Both men enjoyed tennis and swimming, deciding they should meet in the future for a tennis match. And both men loved golf, again agreeing that they should meet for a round. The cordiality between the men ignored the logistics of them meeting in a semi-public venue and the ensuing scrutiny from the media regarding Kristian's involvement with an unknown person.

"Kristian, have you experienced any unusual ... dreams since you underwent the procedure?" asked Aaron.

"Well, honestly, yes I have. But I experienced them before my download, while my brain was in stasis. Have you?"

"Yes," said Aaron. "And mine occurred after my download, while in a resting state during my nightly battery charge. I wasn't sleeping in the human sense but resting in a trance-like state. I was approached by a … being, a spirit. Some would call him an angel. He called himself The Guardian. He explained that he was a spirit that guarded the timeline and kept it on track. He then showed me that the timeline we are on now went awry in 1940 and that I needed to get it back on track. He showed me the devastating effects if the timeline was not corrected. Hitler and the Nazis invaded and conquered Great Britain. The United States was prevented from entering the war, and ultimately surrendered to Hitler." Aaron continued describing his experience to Kristian in detail. When he concluded he was visibly emotionally upset.

Kristian was silent throughout Aaron's description and silent for a few moments after he concluded. "Do you believe your … encounter with The Guardian was real or just a very vivid dream?"

"It sure seemed real to me. I mean I was actually controlling the mind of the King of England for a brief time. And I was literally sitting right next to Winston Churchill telling him I, as King, would support him in refusing to negotiate a peace settlement with Hitler. According to The Guardian, I changed the course of world history. It was very real."

"Well, I had a similar experience," said Kristian. The being calling himself The Guardian came to me while I was in a coma. He took me back to the Civil War to correct a timeline where Stonewall Jackson was wounded but was not killed. Because Jackson, perhaps the greatest general of the war, survived his wound and returned to duty, the Confederate Army defeated the Union Army at Gettysburg. They then turned towards Washington, D.C. and ultimately won the war. The effects of that victory were widespread and lingered until World War II.

The U.S. did not enter the war in Europe and the Nazis attacked and conquered the US from the Atlantic Coast to the Midwest.

Following Pearl Harbor, the Japanese fleet steamed to the US West Coast. Ultimately, the US as we know it was destroyed. My role was to enter the mind of the Confederate officer who ordered that Jackson's party be fired upon, thinking they were a Union patrol. In the errant timeline, that officer hesitated to give the order and Jackson survived his wound. My job was to take control of his mind and make him give the order without hesitation. I still harbor feelings that my actions led to the downfall of that man as he felt he was wholly responsible for the Union victory at Gettysburg and ultimately the war." "Wow, that is quite an experience," said Aaron. "Do you believe your encounter with The Guardian was real?"

"Oh, yes, definitely!" said Kristian. "To prepare for the role The Guardian had me shadow Major Barry, the officer whom I took under my control, for about three years. It was quite an education to live, so to speak, during that period. I do not believe it could have only been a dream. It was way too real for me."

"Did The Guardian tell you to be prepared for additional … assignments?" asked Aaron. "He told me there would be more assignments."

"Yes, he did. But I haven't heard from him since the first assignment concluded."

"It is quite interesting that both assignments dealt ultimately with saving the United States from conquest by the Nazis and Japanese," said Aaron. "It would seem that something … evil was trying to destroy the U.S."

"And, perhaps, The Guardian's role was on the side of good?" said Kristian. "The classic battle between good and evil?"

"If that is true, then there will definitely be more assignments as evil continues to attack good throughout time," said Aaron. "It seems as though there is more to The Guardian than correcting timelines. We may be caught up as soldiers in the unending war against evil."

"I believe that if one of us is contacted by The Guardian we should ask him to get the other one involved in a discussion regarding what our true purpose is," said Kristian.

"Agreed," said Aaron.

Chapter 30

"ISS Control, USS Elon Musk entering Earth's orbit, requesting vector and clearance for approach to Space Dock," said Commander Erik Richards, captain of the vessel returning from its third journey to Mars. Commander Richards was one of four pilots assigned to the Musk on its original Mars flight. Subsequently, Richards participated in establishing the International Mars Colony which had grown to over three-hundred personnel.

"Elon Musk, you are cleared for approach to Space Dock," said a voice from ISS Control. "We are vectoring you around space debris reported by a shuttle a few hours ago. Transmitting your flight path now. Please be alert and report anything unusual."

"Copy that, Control. Will do," said Commander Richards. "Jim, take us in," Richards told his First Officer. Lt. Commander Jim Spaulding was also one of the four original pilots on the Musk and long-time friend of Richards. Jim was a class behind Erik at the Naval Academy. Together, both men attended the US Navy's Fighter Weapons School at Naval Air Station Miramar in San Diego, California, a.k.a. Top Gun. Both men were among the best fighter pilots in the world.

A few moments passed when a loud boom shaking the entire ship was heard coming from the passenger compartment aboard the Musk. Alarms on the Flight Deck lit up and sounded immediately. "What the hell was that?" exclaimed Captain Richards. "Alarms are indicating a hull breach in the passenger section!" exclaimed First

Officer Spaulding. They are indicating depressurization and rapid drop in temperature!"

"Jim, you have the con. I'm going below to check this out!"

Among the passengers were three technical specialists and the ship's physician. One of the specialists was Arya Anderson of Sweden, the current love interest of Commander Richards. The depressurization would result in death for the four passengers if they could not be rescued in just a few minutes. The Musk responded as programmed to the emergency by sealing the hatch to the damaged compartment. Captain Richards reached the hatch and attempted to open it. He broke the protective glass covering the manual override switch on the wall next to the hatch and entered his captain's code to override the lock.

The hatch's lock released, and Erik was able to pull it open. Just as he began to move inside the passenger compartment, a large piece of the hull broke away. Erik was half-way inside the hatch when the suddenly increased depressurization slammed the hatch down on Erik, severely damaging his back and internal organs, and rendering him immediately unconscious.

Jim Spaulding was monitoring the cameras watching Erik unlock the passenger compartment hatch when he witnessed the hatch slamming down on Erik. Having called the third pilot to the flight deck when Erik went below, he turned over the Con to that pilot and dived, weightless, down the ladder to the passenger deck. Just as he reached Erik, now trapped by the hatch, he tried to pry Erik from the grip of the hatch. At first, Spaulding couldn't move the hatch due to the effect of the sudden depressurization caused by the second break in the ship's hull. However, as the atmosphere ran out of the compartment, the hatch grew lighter, and Spaulding was able to free Erik. Unfortunately, the fact that Spaulding was able to free Erik meant that the four passengers were likely dead. In fact, one passenger who had not been strapped in before the collision was sucked out of the ship into cold space when the hull breach expanded. That passenger, Arya Anderson, who had just returned to her seat from the head, was unable to keep herself from being pulled out of the ship.

Spaulding dragged Erik's lifeless body up the ladder rather effortlessly due to zero gravity. He took Erik to the ship's sick bay and strapped him down on a table. Using the handheld body scanner, he saw that Erik's breathing was shallow, his heart rate low, and his blood pressure was falling.

Spaulding spoke through the ship's AI to ISS Control, "ISS Control, Lt. Commander Jim Spaulding, now in command of the USS Elon Musk, declaring a medical emergency and requesting immediate vector and approach to Space Dock. Commander Richards has been seriously injured. We may have additional casualties."

"Roger that, Captain. Transmitting direct vector to Space Dock. You are cleared for approach," said the space traffic controller.

When the Musk docked, emergency crews removed Erik from the ship's sick bay and transported him to the ISS hospital. The remaining crew members trapped in the passenger compartment were dead.

Savannah Richards and her parents along with Ansley Barnett were in Savannah's office at Barnett Center when the video screen went live. All were devastated at the news of Erik's accident aboard the Elon Musk and were nervously awaiting word on his condition. On the other end was the chief medical officer aboard the International Space Station.

"Good afternoon, Mr. and Mrs. Richards, Dr. Richards, Dr. Barnett," said the doctor from the space station. He wasted no time describing Erik's condition. "Commander Richards, Erik, has suffered nearly catastrophic injuries to his spine and internal organs. The injuries were a result of his efforts to rescue the passengers trapped in the compartment of the Elon Musk when a hull breach occurred. We have surgically repaired much of the damage but there will be long-lasting effects resulting from his injuries. He will remain in an induced coma to allow time for his body to begin healing to the extent that it can. He will likely require special care for the remainder of his life."

"Doctor, was there any damage to his brain?" questioned Ansley, thinking immediately that there may be a way to restore Erik completely.

"Not that we have seen. There were no injuries above his shoulders," replied the Doctor. "But we won't know for sure until we are able to bring him out of the induced coma, which may be several weeks."

"When will Erik be returned to Earth?" asked his mother.

"Is there a … better hospital here on Earth?" asked Erik's father.

"We don't recommend moving Erik until he can be awakened from the coma," said the doctor. "Our hospital here on ISS has all the best equipment to deal with his injuries."

Chapter 31

After his meeting with Kristian, Aaron returned to Silicon Valley. The visit with Kristian had been a very successful risk in his opinion and he believed Kristian felt the same way. A few days later, as Aaron had drifted into his resting state during his nightly recharge, he received a visit from The Guardian.

"Hello, Aaron," said The Guardian. "We have a new assignment that will keep the current timeline on course. There is a threat, currently in the final stages of development, that presents the opportunity for severe impact to the human race."

"Guardian, you may know that I met with Kristian Barnett. He shared his experience with you, and I shared mine with him. We have questions," said Aaron.

"Aaron, this assignment will require both you and Kristian working together to defeat the threat." Just then, Kristian appeared next to The Guardian.

"How did you do ... that?" said Aaron, pointing at Kristian. "Recall that in your current state you are outside the bounds of corporeal time and space. What are your questions?" said The Guardian.

"Kristian and I discussed our assignments with each other in detail. In both cases, the United States was threatened with destruction. It seems to us that there is an evil presence threatening the US. Is that true, and if it is, how do we attack the source of this evil rather than chasing its effects?"

"Your understanding of the reality of the universe is primitive," began The Guardian. "Yes, there is what you call evil in that there is a force that is attempting to subjugate most of the human race to slavery and poverty. This force has existed since the beginning of time, just like the force for what you perceive as good has existed since the beginning. From the beginnings of humanity, the evil force has been attempting to undermine the force for good. One can see the presence of evil in the mythological tale of Adam and Eve, which forever changed the human race from one of compliant, peaceful beings to an intelligent, aware, and independent, but violent race forever exhibiting greed and envy. Evil, as we will call it, has been very successful in perpetuating the worst qualities of humans. Good, on the other hand, has been successful in battling and containing evil."

"So, what is the connection between this ageless war between good and evil and the United States?" said Kristian.

"The United States was created with strong guidance from Good. It was created to give humans the opportunity to succeed without the negative influence of monarchs, dictators, and tyrants. It was the first opportunity to give humans the ability to truly govern themselves. Consequently, Evil sees the U.S. as a major threat against its effort to destroy the human race and continually launches threats that could destroy her. The alliance of Germany and Japan in World War II was Evil's strongest threat, with the US Civil War of the 19th Century a major element contributing to that threat. With each of your recent assignments, we have derailed the greatest threats to the existence of the United States from the 20th Century. I showed you both the outcome should one or both of you had failed in your assignment."

"Are we then soldiers in the war against Evil?" asked Aaron. "Again, in your terms, you are recent additions to those like me who will continue to fight to keep the timelines on their intended courses."

"But the threats to the existence of the US as we know it continue. Post-World War II we had the threat of Communism. The Soviet Union, Red China, and a slew of despots posing threats including nuclear annihilation. What of those threats and how were they derailed? Do our continuing assignments deal with those threats?"

"Not all threats require our intervention. The threat of Communism in the 20th Century was addressed using conventional means. The Soviet Union collapsed, and China, seeing that outcome, transitioned into a world economic power. China is still a threat today but more in the economic arena. China is still very harsh with regards to human rights, but even that attitude has relaxed as global awareness of the evil of pure Communism has grown among the Chinese people."

"So, the evil of Communism has been eradicated?" said Aaron.

"Evil will continue to try to enslave the human race using those desiring to control a totalitarian state," said The Guardian. "Evil continues to develop means to achieve its goals. You will see this in your next assignment."

"What is our next assignment?" asked Kristian.

"Your next assignments deal with an ability, developed mainly under the sponsorship and direction of two major technology companies and the US Government, to exert influence and control over a human's beliefs. That you are here with me today illustrates the advances in the knowledge of how the human mind works. This development takes that knowledge several steps forward in that it enables a degree of control of the human mind using electronic signaling of messages to the brain. These messages have the ability to change a person's opinion on any issue through subliminal suggestion."

"I can see that such a technology could be a major threat. One could control one's enemies through thought manipulation. But isn't that what we are doing, albeit supernaturally?" said Kristian.

"It is likely Evil's answer to what we do," said The Guardian. "But we do not intentionally and permanently change one's thoughts and opinions."

"But we can affect a person's thoughts so that their lives are permanently changed. Look at Major Barry, for example. He forever blamed himself for the outcome of the Civil War and likely died an early death because of it," said Kristian.

"Consider that Major Barry was a soldier in the war against evil. In war, there are sacrifices. We impacted the life of one man to save the existence of millions. What Evil is close to being able to do is control the opinions of masses of people, forever changing their lives and taking away their free will."

Chapter 32

After several weeks in the hospital aboard the ISS, Commander Erik Richards, who was awakened from an induced coma, was moved via space ambulance to Bethesda Naval Hospital near Washington, D.C. to continue his long-term recovery from the accident on the USS Elon Musk. Erik's parents, sister Savannah and Dr. Ansley Barnett awaited Erik's arrival. Savannah and Ansley participated with several specialists in evaluating Erik's condition and prognosis for recovery. After approximately three days the results of this evaluation were produced.

"Good morning, Mr. and Mrs. Richards, Dr. Richards and Dr. Barnett. I am Dr. Earnest James, Chief Medical Officer here at Bethesda. Please take a seat." James opened the folder on the table in front of him. Putting on a pair of reading glasses, Dr. James read the report describing Erik Richard's injuries, surgeries, planned additional surgeries, and prognosis. "Commander Richards sustained severe, life-threatening injuries in his accident on the USS Elon Musk. His spine was broken in three separate locations and the vertebrae crushed from the thoracic disc T3 to L3 in the lumbar region. His spinal cord was severed in multiple locations resulting in total paralysis. His pelvis was crushed on the left side. Several internal organs were severely damaged. We removed his spleen, left lung and left kidney. His prognosis for recovery from paralysis is negative, meaning he will likely remain a quadriplegic for the remainder of his life. He is currently on a respirator as he is unable to breathe on his own and we don't know if he will ever be able to breathe on his own. He will remain on dialysis for two to three months while his right kidney heals from injury. Commander Richards will likely require several surgeries mainly targeted at attempting to restore some functionality including the ability to breathe on his own and restoring some mobility to his upper extremities."

The Richards party was mostly silent except for Erik's mother who sobbed all during Dr. James' report. Savannah Richards also was visibly disturbed, tears running down her cheeks. Although Savannah had participated, along with Ansley, in Erik's evaluation, hearing Dr. James describe the extent of his injuries and seeing the reaction of her parents was heartbreaking. Erik, their only son, was, along with Savannah, their pride and joy. They had two beautiful children who excelled in nearly everything they tried, who were top students, and had rewarding careers. Now, their world was crashing down on them.

Later that afternoon, Savannah and Ansley met with Director Hanson of DARPA. "Dr. Richards, given Commander Richard's condition and prognosis for recovery, do you feel that your procedures for his physical restoration can be successful?"

"Erik's injuries are extensive and permanent. His spinal injuries are so severe that our restoration procedures likely could not restore much, if any, mobility. I do not recommend that Erik undergo years-long attempts at restoration with the goal being near-full restoration."

"Dr. Barnett, have you been able to evaluate Commander Richard's mental state. Was he damaged mentality or psychologically in the accident?"

"Dr. Richards and I both conducted extensive cognitive tests on Erik together with the Chief of Psychiatry at Bethesda. We could not detect any degradation of his mental abilities. He is alert and very interested in achieving recovery. He stated his dream was to return to space," said Ansley.

"Well, Ansley, while this accident was tragic, it may have provided a means to keep the cyborg program alive. If we can convince the Chief of Space Command, CJCS and SecDef that this is a viable way to go, we may have a way for Erik to realize his dream." Hanson addressed his digital assistant, "DD, please set up a meeting with the Chief of Space Command, Admiral Tucker, and Secretary of Defense William Bonner. From our side, it will be Drs. Richards and Barnett, and me. Agenda for the meeting will be a proposed military candidate for the cyborg project. Ansley, you should be prepared to present a brief summary of the current status of the project and the condition of your two patients. This will be the Space Command's first exposure to the project."

"Understood, Director Hanson. We will be prepared," replied Ansley.

The meeting with the SecDef and the senior military staff was held at the Pentagon. Director Hanson, Ansley, and Savannah exited the black government SUV and climbed the steps to the entrance closest to the office of the Secretary of Defense. After clearing the security checkpoint, a tall gentleman in a blue Naval uniform, displaying the rank of Captain and the insignia of the Space Command, a division of the US Navy, greeted them. "Good morning. I am Captain Jeff Barnes, Naval Space Command. Please follow me."

Captain Barnes led the group to a bank of elevators, where after entering, the Captain said, "third floor – SecDef." Exiting the elevator, the group entered a conference room and were seated. Momentarily, William Bonner, Secretary of Defense, Admiral Tucker, Chairman of the Joint Chiefs of Staff, and Rear Admiral Richard Hampton, commander of the Navy's Space Command, entered the conference room. The DARPA party stood as the military brass entered the room. SecDef assumed the seat at the head of the table and said, "Please be seated." Again, William Bonner presented an imposing presence using his six-foot-four- inch height, shaved head, and athletic build to supplement his stern, deep voice. Admiral Tucker appeared stiff to Ansley as he had in their previous meeting. Admiral Hampton smiled and said, "Good morning," as he sat down across from Ansley.

"Director Hanson, I understand that you will be recommending a military candidate for the cyborg program, correct?" began SecDef.

"Yes, sir, Mr. Secretary. As you are aware, Commander Erik Richards, captain of the USS Elon Musk, was seriously injured while attempting to rescue victims of a hull breach aboard the Musk while entering Earth's orbit. Doctors, including the Chief Medical Officer at Bethesda, believe that Commander Richards prognosis is one of permanent paralysis. Dr. Savannah Richards has evaluated Commander Richards for possible entrance to the paralysis protocol at the Barnett Institute and found that he would not benefit from that protocol due to the extent of his injuries. Drs. Richards and Barnett have evaluated Commander Richard's cognitive functions extensively and have found no impairment of his mental abilities as a result of the accident. Drs. Richards and Barnett believe Commander Richards would make an excellent military candidate for the Cyborg Transformation Program."

"Dr. Richards, Commander Richards is your brother, correct?" said SecDef.

"Yes, sir," said Savannah.

"Do you feel there is a possibility that your relationship with your brother impacted your evaluation?"

"Yes, sir, my relationship and love for my brother was a consideration. Our spinal restoration procedures are the most advanced in the world. But in order for them to be effective, we need a spine to work with. Erik's spine was destroyed beyond any hope of repair in the accident. If there was any possibility that we could restore him to near-full functionality I wouldn't be sitting here today. I have worked extensively with Dr. Barnett on the cyborg program and believe that presents the best chance for Erik's full recovery. My emotional relationship with my brother will only serve to bolster my intensity to see him fully recover."

"Dr. Barnett, most of this is new to Admiral Hampton. Can you provide a brief history of the program, the current state of the program including the health of the two patients who have undergone the cyborg transformation?"

"Of course," said Ansley. Ansley proceeded with a fifteen-minute slide show including videos of the two cyborgs, Aaron Adams and Kristian Barnett, performing physical exhibitions of their abilities. Ansley emphasized, with photographs of both patients prior to the program, that both men were completely disabled by ALS. When Ansley completed her presentation, silence gripped the room for what seemed like several minutes.

"Thank, you, Dr. Barnett," said Admiral Hampton. Turning his gaze on Director Hanson, "Director, to confirm, you are recommending that Commander Richards enter the Cyborg Transformation Program at Barnett Center. How long does this procedure take?"

"The protocol for both patients to date took approximately nine months. One of the patients has been released back into the general population under a new identity. With Kristian Barnett's celebrity, we are still working on a way to announce his return to health."

"So, how will you deal with Commander Richard's return to Space Command? Knowledge of his demise was widespread," said Admiral Hampton.

"I don't necessarily see that as a major problem, Admiral. A story can be produced that illustrates his year-long recovery," said Director Hanson. "Recovery from injury is much easier to explain than recovery from an irrecoverable disease like ALS."

"Hanson, you have hinted previously at the cyborg being capable of superhuman physical abilities. Can you provide any detail regarding that possibility?" said SecDef.

"Yes, sir. The cyborg bodies to date have been limited to the physical abilities of a relatively fit male at their respective ages. But the cyborg is capable of enhanced abilities dealing mainly with strength and speed. Computer models indicate, for example, that the cyborg body is capable of running a mile in under sixty seconds and of dead-lifting over one-thousand pounds."

"Could Commander Richards' cyborg body be enabled with these enhanced performance abilities?"

"Yes, sir. We will work directly with the military regarding the specifications for Commander Richard's cyborg body."

"Mr. Secretary, Admiral Tucker, Commander Richards is an exemplary officer, a highly valued member of Space Command. If Drs. Barnett and Richards, along with Director Hanson, are confident that the transformation to a cyborg body will restore the Commander to active duty, I support it. I do have one condition. I would like to assign Captain Barnes to observe the transformation process from beginning to end. Captain Barnes will be the liaison officer between Barnett Center and Space Command. All decisions regarding Commander Richards transformation will include Captain Barnes. The captain will contact my office directly with any communication regarding decisions," said Admiral Hampton.

"Admiral Tucker, Director, Doctors, are you comfortable with Admiral Hampton's requirements?" said SecDef.

Director Hanson looked at Savannah and Ansley who both nodded positively. "Yes, sir."

"I support Admiral Hampton's recommendations," said Admiral Tucker.

"Captain Barnes, are you ready to take on this assignment?"

"Yes, sir, I'm most definitely looking forward to it, sir."

"Very well, then. Director Hanson, you have our orders. Please proceed immediately. I expect to see a fully-restored Commander Erik Richards, ready to return to active duty, no later than nine months from today," said SecDef

Chapter 33

It is February 2052, approximately nine months before the next Presidential election. Early election polls are favoring the Conservative Party including the incumbent President and both Houses of Congress. With little hope of achieving victory in the 2052 election, Members of the Liberal Party, including their billionaire supporters have realized they will need new strategies to overcome the Conservatives. Liberal corporations, led by Find Corporation, established after the breakup of Google and Alphabet, have developed a technology that may put them in power indefinitely in four years, after the 2056 Presidential election.

"Subliminal suggestion has been explored for years. The most common form demonstrated that videos that included clips that were shown too quickly for the mind to consciously see did result in the audience retaining some of the content in the covert video clips. In other words, the unconscious mind saw what the conscious mind could not," said Kristian.

"Correct," said The Guardian. "Find has taken the concept of subliminal suggestion to a much higher level. They are able to not only suggest behavior to the human mind, but they are also close to being able to deliver suggestions to the human mind via telecommunications, namely cellular communications."

"Guardian, what is the threat to the timeline should Find deploy this technology to the masses?" asked Aaron.

"In the altered timeline, Find, along with its sponsors in the US Government, successfully deploy Find's technology. The US

Government is sponsoring the technology as a potential weapon that could be utilized to effectively disarm the enemy by controlling the minds of its military and political assets. But the naivete of the Government is unaware that The Find Corporation, whose top echelon of leaders, is intent on using the technology to control the masses in favor of establishing a totalitarian regime that completes the goal of the force you call Evil. The masses are economically enslaved at a minimal level of existence where they are overseen by robotic machines under control of the State."

"This sounds like what we saw in the altered timelines where the United States was conquered by the Nazis and Japanese in the 1940s. In that timeline most of the US. was subjected to a totalitarian regime," said Kristian.

"Yes, but with Find's technology, the entire world will be overcome with no hope of recovery," said The Guardian.

"So how does Find influence the masses to coerce them to subjugate themselves to the Find elites?" asked Aaron.

"First, let's look at how Find delivers its influence on the human mind by viewing a laboratory test of the technology. We are now positioned above two separate rooms in the lab, looking down at a control center and a test subject. The test subject has no knowledge of what is being tested and has been told he is testing a new smartphone. Watch what happens closely," said The Guardian.

The test subject was seated in an office, behind a desk. To his left was a computer workstation. The office was furnished nicely with a glass desk and a small conference table. A window provided a view of a courtyard with a garden and fountain where Find employees went to relax and enjoy the Southern California weather. On the desk, a smartphone rested just to the right of center. At rest, the smartphone resembled an oblong piece of transparent glass.

In the control center, a white-coated technician could be seen reviewing what appeared to be a script on a high-resolution, clear screen. The technician issued a verbal command, "initiate test script A-1." In the office, the smartphone buzzed on the desk. Its screen activated and showed a female wearing a white lab coat and Find badge on the lapel. The test subject verbally answered the phone while leaving it lying on the desk. A voice emanating from the phone said, "Hello, are you feeling good today?"

The test subject responded, "Yes."

"Good, please look out of the window behind you and tell me the weather conditions you see," said the voice from the phone.

Turning around while remaining seated, the test subject looked out the window and said, "It is raining."

"Is there anyone in the garden sitting in the rain?" asked the voice from the phone.

"No," said the test subject. "Why would people be sitting in the rain?"

The true weather was sunny, and people were sitting on benches and appeared to be enjoying the garden. Something was controlling the mind's eye of the test subject.

"So, Guardian, how was the message delivered that altered the test subject's reality? We didn't' see or hear anything that would have altered his reality?" said Aaron.

"You both are here with me because your minds were scanned and downloaded to artificial bodies. The technology that scanned your minds was adapted to implanting thoughts into the minds of humans. And the delivery mechanism was the wireless technology that carries voice, video, and messages enhanced to deliver subliminal content."

"So, anyone with one of the mobile phones like that used in the test can be persuaded to think, say, or do anything?" asked an incredulous Aaron.

"Essentially, yes."

"So, how is the technology used to ultimately subject the world to one of elite rulers and slaves?" asked Kristian.

The Guardian closed his eyes and lowered his head. In both Aaron's and Kristian's minds a series of visions begin to unfold. Seen first, is what appears to be a meeting of high-level military and government officials viewing a test like that they just witnessed. The test demonstration was successful. The next vision appears to be a video advertisement advertising a new mobile smartphone like that seen in the test at Find's laboratory. Like virtually every new version of mobile phone since Apple's 2008 iPhone, the public scoops up the new phone like manna from Heaven. Find makes the phone one of the most affordable smart devices in decades which results in a huge increase in market share over the next four years.

Then, in the year 2056, the United States enters its Presidential election cycle. One party is still espousing the evils of the rich, the long-extinct racial persecution of the non-white races, gender identity politics, and the benefits of Socialism under strict government control, which has been rejected repeatedly by a growing majority for over thirty years by American voters. Four years after its introduction in 2052, approximately 70-percent of American voters possessed the Find mobile phone. Using the technology to deliver subliminal orders, the Presidential and down-party candidates advocating Socialism are elected in a landslide. The Socialist Party now controls both the Presidency and The House of Representatives and has a super-majority in the Senate of seventy-two senators. Retirements and deaths of Supreme Court Justices now threaten the conservative majority enjoyed for the past thirty years. Further, the United States immediately begins support of Socialist states throughout the world. In the Middle East, support in the form of military equipment is provided to Iranian and Saudi dictators. Support for Israel is discontinued. A new alliance with Russia is struck and The United States withdraws from NATO, effectively gutting the only unified force standing in the way of a Russian- Iranian-Saudi takeover of Germany, France, Italy, and the Nordic countries. The US – Russian alliance provides military support for the removal of European governments.

Because the Find technology is now in the possession of approximately 75-percent of the global public, there is minimal and ineffective resistance to the new world government. Visions of masses of people living in poverty but failing to protest their conditions are seen by Aaron and Kristian. Visions of elites living in opulence in Washington, D.C., New York City, Paris, Dubai, St.

Petersburg, Russia, and other governing capitols and major cities are seen. Their servants being selected from the poor, have been relocated from the cities to rural areas and are living in squalor.

The visions cease and Aaron and Kristian awaken from their dream. After a few moments of silence, reflecting the shock of what they had just seen, Aaron asks The Guardian, "How do we prevent this disaster? It would seem that there is nothing that could control the eventual deployment of this technology."

"Unlike the previous threats to the timeline that you both averted, this threat will need to be stopped in multiple ways. We can set it back years, perhaps decades, but the only way to eradicate this threat is to educate the masses of its existence and threat to human existence," said The Guardian. "But we must do all we can to thwart it and delay it so the masses can be educated."

Chapter 34

A black SUV with US. Government tags pulled up to the entrance to DARPA. The Secretary of Defense, Katherine Hodges, and Chairman of the Joint Chiefs of Staff, General Jeffrey Holland, exited the vehicle and proceeded up the steps to the security checkpoint. Facial recognition scanners in front of the security screening stations identify the two officials, who are told by a faceless voice emanating from the scanner to proceed to their left and bypass the security checkpoint. On the other side of the checkpoint, Colonel John Matheson saluted the visitors and escorted them to an elevator. They entered the elevator and Colonel Matheson said, "L5". The elevator scanner confirmed the Colonel's identity and the elevator descended to basement Level 5, five stories below the main floor, where the group exited into a large room. In the room was a large oblong conference table. On the walls on either side of the table were large video screens running a video promoting DARPA projects.

Already seated in the conference room are the CEO of Find Corporation, the CEOs of two prominent smartphone manufacturers, and the CEOs of two dominant telecommunications companies. Present, but unseen by the rest, are The Guardian, Kristian, and Aaron.

"Gentlemen," begins The Guardian. "A demonstration of the telepathic control of a subject's mind will be displayed to these high-ranking officials. You will use your abilities to take temporary control of the Secretary of Defense, and the test subject. Aaron, you will be working with the test subject, located on the third floor of this building. Kristian, you will work with SecDef." "Aaron, the test subject will be in a room overlooking the street. The weather is clear and bright, with a slight breeze from the south, a temperature of sixty-three degrees and humidity at forty-seven-percent. There are moderate traffic and pedestrians walking on the sidewalks on both sides of the street. When the smartphone sitting on the desk is activated, the voice on the smartphone will ask the subject to look out the window and describe the current weather conditions. At this point, you will enter and take control of the test subject's mind. If you fail, the subliminal commands delivered by the smartphone will result in the test subject standing and looking out the window to reply that the weather is currently raining, that pedestrians appear to be chilled and walking with umbrellas, and that traffic is apparently snarled. Since you enter the subject's mind after the subliminal commands have been delivered, your mind will not have received the commands and you will reply with the actual conditions I just described, rendering the test a failure."

Back in the DARPA conference room on basement Level 5, the test is presented to the audience using the large monitors on the walls surrounding the table. The test fails. There is a mixture of shock and embarrassment on the part of the CEOs at the table. There is a level of irritation seen on the expressions of the government and military personnel, which is especially visible on SecDef's face.

"Gentlemen," begins SecDef, "It appears that your technology needs work. It is obviously not dependable at this point. How do you explain this abject failure here today?"

"Madame Secretary," said the CEO of Find Corporation. This test has been conducted literally hundreds of times in our laboratories. It has experienced a 99-percent-plus success rate. I suggest we run it one more time."

"Very well," said SecDef. "But if it fails a second time, this meeting is over."

"Yes, Ma'am."

The CEO turns to his assistant and orders the test be rerun

using the backup test subject. In less than five minutes the assistant whispers in the CEO's ear, indicating the test is ready.

"Aaron, are you prepared to perform the procedure a second time with a different test subject?" asks The Guardian.

"Yes, definitely," replied Aaron.

The second test commences following the same script as the first test. The result is the same.

"Kristian, you will now take control of SecDef's mind. Although she is highly irritated, she will condescend to the CEO of Find to give them an opportunity to go back and research their failure here today. You must reply for her that she is not interested in failed exhibitions of mumbo jumbo and waste of taxpayer dollars on supernatural folly. Scold the Director of DARPA to ensure that programs that fail are discarded and ones that are brought forward are sound. This way the program will be set back, possibly for years until the next administration assumes control of the government."

Back in the conference room, SecDef, her neck and face visibly red with anger, says with irritation in her voice, "Gentlemen, it appears this demonstration, this technology, is a failure. This meeting is over."

"Madame Secretary," said the Find CEO, "please, at least give us an opportunity to investigate the reasons for the failed tests today. This technology has performed flawlessly in our labs."

At this point, Kristian takes control of Katherine Hodges' mind. The SecDef looks pointedly at the CEO. "We have invested hundreds of millions of dollars in your technology at DARPA's recommendation and this is all you have to show? No, sir, this program is defunded immediately. Director Hanson, this failure also reflects poorly on DARPA's ability to supervise programs that will provide iron proof reliability to the US military. Please exercise greater discretion regarding the programs you bring to us. We must have programs that enhance the safety of our soldiers and our citizens."

With that, Secretary of Defense Katherine Hodges and General

Holland rise to leave. The remaining attendees also rise as the Secretary and General exit the room.

The CEO of Find addresses the remaining attendees. "I don't know what happened here today, but I will fund an investigation into this failure. I know of no reason why the tests crashed and burned today. I am confident we can regroup and get the program resurrected from the ashes. Director Hanson, we will keep you apprised of our findings and progress."

"Sounds like mission accomplished," said Aaron.

"We won this battle, but we are a long way from winning the war. Find and the other companies here today have unlimited resources to resurrect this program. Do not forget their real intentions of world domination using this technology."

"Well, Guardian, it has been a privilege working with you to save the world, once again," said Kristian. "I am sure that this will not be the end of our work together."

"You are correct, Kristian. We may have won this battle, but the war is far from over."

Chapter 35

It is September 2041. A cyborg body lies on a stainless-steel table in the operating room at the Barnett Center for Neurological Restoration. Surrounding the operating table are Dr. Ansley Barnett, Chief Scientist of DARPA's Robotics Division, Dr. Savannah Richards, Director of the Barnett Center for Neurological Restoration, Captain Jeffrey Barnes of the United States Naval Space Command, and several technical specialists. High definition video monitors, hanging at strategic viewing points around the operating table, monitor the cyborg's internal systems as well as the status of the communications network and software programs used to download Commander Erik Richard's consciousness to the cyborg body.

"OK, people, let's do this," said Dr. Barnett. "Network status?"

"Network running at maximum capacity," replied a technician watching a video screen showing a graphical representation of download speeds.

"Programs status?" asked Dr. Barnett.

"Programs ready to execute," replied another technician observing another video screen. "All programs showing green."

"Cyborg systems?" barked Dr. Barnett. "Batteries charged and ready."

"Cyborg electrical systems all green."

"Nerves active and communicating with cyborg brain."

"Download test files," ordered Dr. Barnett.

After about ten seconds, a technician said, "Test files downloaded successfully. Download speed optimum."

"Execute full download and data distribution," commands Dr. Barnett.

Ninety-seven seconds later a technician said, "Download complete. Initiating data distribution."

Thirty-three minutes later, "Data distribution complete." The blue eyes, a perfect match to Erik's corporeal eyes, fluttered open and scanned the OR. Dr. Barnett said, "Erik, can you hear me?"

Erik's eyes turned towards Dr. Barnett's voice and blinked slowly.

"Erik, are you able to speak? Do you know where you are?"

At first, Erik simply stared at Dr. Barnett for what seemed like several minutes but actually was only a few seconds. Then, the corners of his mouth rose slightly in what appeared to be the beginning of a smile. "I'm on Mars," he said in a somewhat gravelly voice.

Dr. Savannah Richards, Erik's sister, standing opposite Ansley Barnett at Erik's shoulder let out a gasp. "Erik! Are you OK? Can you hear me?"

"Hi, Sis," replied Erik, now visibly smiling, his voice clearing and sounding remarkably like the voice from his corporeal body. "I didn't know you came to Mars."

Knowing her brother was a frequent practical joker, Savannah responded, "OK, wise guy, joking around at a critical time like this. I should smack you!"

"Enough screwing around," said Ansley. "Erik, we need to begin testing your simulated nervous system to see if all your parts are working. Please move the fingers on your right hand." Testing continued successfully until Ansley asked Erik to move the toes on his right foot. "Are you fooling around again, Erik? Please move the toes on your right foot."

"I am moving them," Erik replied.

Ansley adjusted the OR table so Erik could see his feet. "Move your toes, Erik."

"I ... I can't," said a disturbed Erik. "I can't move my toes, my feet, or my legs!"

"Erik, you need to concentrate. Your mind will need to learn how to control your new body. You're like a newborn baby," said Savannah.

"Let's try some sensitivity tests," said Ansley. Using what appeared to be similar to an acupuncture needle, Ansley said, "Erik, I will lay you back down. Then I will be sticking your lower extremities with this needle. I need you to tell me if you feel anything."

Ansley stuck Erik on several points on his legs, ankles, and feet. At first Erik showed no response. He wasn't feeling the needle. Then, as Ansley stuck the needle into the big toe on his right foot, Erik said, "I felt that! Do it again so I can be sure." Ansley stuck the needle into his toe and Erik said, "I definitely felt that." "Erik, try moving your toe again," said Savannah. At first nothing, then the toe appeared to twitch slightly. "Erik, I think I saw movement.

Try again!" said Ansley.

Erik's toe moved back and forth.

Testing continued as Erik slowly gained motion control of his lower extremities. Within two weeks, he was learning to walk in his new body. Drs. Barnett and Richards concluded that Erik's mind retained the belief that his lower limbs were paralyzed and that had temporarily blocked his ability to move his limbs.

Chapter 36

Lying on the recharging bed in his suite at the Barnett Mansion, Kristian's mind kept returning to the recent event with Aaron Adams and The Guardian. With guidance from The Guardian, Aaron and he had successfully disrupted the use of advanced communications technology to control the mind of an unknowing subject. But this event was not supposed to happen for another ten years. "Since we know what may be happening in the future, could we take steps now to prevent the technology from ever being developed?" he thought. "Or, if the technology was developed, could they take steps to educate key government leaders regarding the threat it presented?" Kristian then closed his eyes and concentrated on summoning The Guardian. He had never attempted to summon The Guardian. The Guardian had only come to him when he needed him for an assignment.

Several hours passed when Kristian's mind saw a white mist begin to form. Becoming visible within the cloud was a human shape. The cloud began to evaporate until standing before him was The Guardian, still dressed in a white T-shirt, blue jeans, motorcycle boots, long leather coat and a Stetson. "You summoned me?" asked The Guardian.

"Y … yes," said Kristian. "I have questions regarding our last assignment."

"You wish to know if the timeline associated with the development of mind control communications technology can be changed," said The Guardian.

"I guess you could put it that way," said Kristian. "Since we know that the technology will be developed, is there any way we can stop it now, in a more … conventional way?"

"From your experience with me, you know that timelines are alterable. Although timelines are pre-destined, they can be changed through human free will."

"So, we, Aaron and I, could begin work now to either derail the development of the technology or begin the process of educating key government officials regarding the threat it presents. I have nearly unlimited resources to invest in attempting this."

"Yes," replied The Guardian. "But be aware that you are attempting to alter a timeline that is pre-destined. It will not be easy, and you will need to tread carefully. Your enemies will present a constant threat." The Guardian then began to fade and disappeared within a few seconds.

"I am prepared to take the risk," said Kristian.

Aaron Adams was immersed in a software project when his smartphone buzzed. Seeing that Kristian Barnett's name scrolled across his smartphone screen, he picked it up immediately. "Kristian, how are you? Great to hear from you."

"Hello, Aaron," said Kristian. "Would you be able to come to the mansion this weekend? I have some important ideas we need to discuss."

"Kristian, yes, definitely. I can be there Friday evening about 7 PM."

"Great. We'll plan dinner on the pool deck. Miguel will have a pitcher of margaritas waiting." Miguel, Director of Security and General Manager of Barnett Mansion operations, was also Kristian's parents' long-time bartender. He was known for his masterful libations. His margaritas were legendary due to a secret ingredient he employed. Rumors, never confirmed, were that he used only Gold Patron tequila which gave the unique flavor to his recipe.

Aaron exited the driverless Uber and bound up the steps to the mansion's main entrance. Shortly after ringing the bell, Kristian opened the door. "How are you, Aaron?" said Kristian as the two men shook hands and exchanged a brief man-hug.

"I am fine, great," said Aaron, smiling.

"Hello, Aaron," said a subdued Ansley, standing behind Kristian. It was obvious by her tone that Ansley still did not fully approve of the growing friendship between Kristian and Aaron. Her memory of their sexual encounter still haunted her every time she saw him. Whenever Aaron started to say something, she felt herself grow tense as she feared he would slip and make Kristian aware of their tryst. She was glad that alcohol could not loosen the cyborg's tongue.

"Hello, Ansley," said Aaron. "Great to see you again. How is Savannah?"

"Dr. Richards is doing quite well," replied Ansley. "She will be joining us for a game of doubles in the morning, and then lunch."

"Excellent," said Aaron. "I do need to warn you that my tennis game is a bit rusty."

"Let's go see about those margaritas," said Kristian, putting his arm around Aaron's shoulder as they walked toward the glass enclosed elevator in the foyer rotunda.

Margaritas on the pool deck were followed by dinner served under the beauty of a California sunset. Blue, green, yellow and orange hues could be seen from the setting sun's reflection off the wispy clouds in the distance. A light breeze from the southwest added a slight chill to the air. After seafood appetizers that included freshly peeled shrimp and King Crab legs, served with a lovely Chardonnay, a prime rib main course was served with roasted potatoes. Kristian's favorite dessert, crème brulee, was served with coffee.

As the meal concluded, Ansley stood, followed by Kristian and Aaron, and said "I am feeling chilled and will leave this beautiful evening with you guys. Good night."

"Good night," they replied and sat back down.

"Aaron, I've been giving some thought to our last mission with The Guardian," said Kristian. "Those events happened more than ten years in the future. There may be a way we can stop the development of the technology, or at least educate key people as to the threat it presents."

"I tend to agree with you, Kristian," said Aaron. "But how do we go up against the billionaires who will develop the mind control technology? They have literally unlimited financial resources to throw at this effort."

"Well, I did something the other day that I wasn't sure would work. While resting on my charging bed I summoned The Guardian. After what seemed like quite a long time, he appeared to me. I asked him if it was possible to alter the timeline that we experienced ten years in the future. He said that although it would be difficult, it is possible."

"So how do we go about a mission to derail the timeline where the mind control technology is developed and deployed?" asked Aaron. "Do we pop into some CEO's head, take control, and cancel the project?"

"I believe it may be possible to derail the mind control project in a more conventional manner, or at least influence key government officials against the project. We know too well if it falls into the wrong hands that it could very well mean enslavement for humankind. The Guardian has already shown us the outcome should the technology be deployed."

"I know you understand that executives at Find Corporation and their associates in the telecommunications industry can exert strong influence on high level government officials and members of Congress. How can we get them to reject the lobbying efforts of these companies who often contribute huge amounts to election campaigns and regularly deliver perquisites like exclusive travel and very expensive gifts?" questioned Aaron.

"We will need an intensive effort to formulate a plan. The plan will need to include research into technologies that could block the mind control element in their technology. As the time grows closer to their smartphone deployment, we will also need a plan to present the nature of the threat and its possible outcomes to the government. And should that not work, we will need a plan to educate the masses regarding the danger of the technology. Educating the masses may help us gain credence with elected officials reacting to the demands of voters."

"What you are describing will be quite a large effort, involving money and people. I believe you probably have the money, but who will be able to dedicate their careers to this on a full-time basis?"

"I'm glad you asked that question, Aaron. I would like to offer you an executive position with Barnett Industries as Senior Vice President of Research. The title is vague enough to allow you to go in virtually any direction to develop and execute these plans. You will be reporting to Noel Donovan, CEO of Barnett Industries, ... on paper. Actually, you will be working directly with me. We will offer you a salary and executive benefits commensurate with your position. Your offices will be located at the Barnett Center for Neurological Restoration so you will be close to me here at the mansion. We can offer you temporary housing here on mansion property at our VIP guest house until you find permanent accommodations. How soon could you start?"

"Whoa!" exclaimed Aaron. "Can I have a moment to digest what you just said? Do you not need board approval for an executive-level position? Does anyone at Barnett Industries even know you're ... back?"

"Noel Donovan knows I am back, as you put it. She had to know as CEO. Also, Ansley is Chairman of the Board of both Industries and the Center. I will have Ansley speak to the other board members individually to clear a favorable vote for creating the position," said Kristian.

"Ansley?" questioned Aaron. "I get the impression that she is not too favorable towards me, especially since I crashed the mansion to meet you."

"I will deal with Ansley," Kristian replied. "Now, how soon can you start?"

Chapter 37

It is mid-April 2042, approximately nine months after the transfer of Commander Erik Richards consciousness to a synthetic body. Erik was the third mind transfer to a synthetic body and the first transfer for an active-duty military officer.

It is a beautiful spring day in Washington, D.C. The cherry blossoms are still in bloom as the black government SUV containing Drs. Ansley Barnett and Savannah Richards, Commander Erik Richards, and Captain Jeffrey Barnes sped along just northwest of the Lincoln Memorial on their way to DARPA Headquarters. Meeting with them today are William Bonner, Secretary of Defense, Admiral Max (Tomcat) Tucker, Chairman of the Joint Chiefs of Staff, Earnest Spellman, Admiral (Ret.) and Secretary of the Navy, Rear Admiral Richard Hampton, Commanding Officer of the U.S. Naval Space Command, and James Hanson, Director of DARPA. Drs. Barnett and Richards exited the SUV, followed by the others in their party and entered DARPA headquarters.

Waiting there for them was a tall, dark gentleman in a blue suit with a wireless earpiece only slightly visible when he turned his left ear towards them. "Good Morning, I am Secret Service Agent Jeremy Anton. Please follow me." The group followed Agent Anton to a bank of elevators. After boarding the elevator, the agent said, "Fifth Floor, LL". The elevator descended five stories down and opened onto a large conference room. An oblong stainless steel and glass table was in the center of the room surrounded by padded, high-back black leather conference chairs. Clear video screens hung from the ceiling arranged to enable viewing a single presentation or broadcast from any seat at the table.

As Ansley, Savannah, Erik and Captain Barnes entered the conference room and began to take their seats, Director Hanson entered the room. "Commander Richards, welcome to DARPA," said Hanson, extending his hand to shake Erik's. "I am Jim Hanson, DARPA Director. Please follow me."

Erik followed Hanson through a single door at the west end of the room and returned in a few moments. "I have asked Commander Richards to wait in the office adjacent to this room. I want to introduce him to the military brass … in a dramatic moment." Hanson then took a seat next to Ansley at the table.

A few moments later the Secretary of Defense (SecDef) appeared at the conference room double doors accompanied by Admirals Tucker and Hampton, and the Secretary of the Navy (SecNav). Flanking these gentlemen were Agent Anton and one other who appeared to be a second Secret Service agent.

"Good morning, Jim," said SecDef as the gentlemen took their seats. "I trust you have good news for us."

"Good morning, Secretary Bonner," replied Hanson. "I believe you will be astounded at what we have to show you today." Hanson waved his hand over the display on the table by his seat and said, "Commander Richards, please enter the conference room."

As Erik entered the room, erect and smiling in his Naval service dress uniform, audible sounds of surprise and amazement could be heard coming from several of the attendees. The last pictures any of the government dignitaries had seen were of Erik unconscious in a hospital bed surrounded by medical machines connected to his body by tubes and wires monitoring every area of his body. A nasogastric tube from which nourishment was fed entered his left nostril and endotracheal tube entered his mouth to facilitate breathing. Seeing a seemingly healthy, smiling individual come through the door and enter the room was quite a shock for some in the room.

"May I be seated?" Erik asked no one in particular.

"Please," replied SecDef, pointing to a chair at the head of the table directly opposite him.

"Commander, how do you feel?" asked Admiral Hampton. "Great, Sir," replied Erik. "Never better. Ready to return to space."

"Gentlemen," interjected Director Hanson. "Dr. Barnett has some video clips showing Commander Richard's recovery as well as clips showing his physical ability. With your permission, Secretary Bonner, I will turn the floor over to Dr. Barnett."

SecDef nodded and Hanson turned to Ansley and said, "You're on."

Approximately ten minutes of video showed more of Erik prior to the cyborg transformation followed by Erik awakening in his cyborg body. Video of his physical therapy ensued, showing Erik gaining control of his new artificial body. Then video was shown of Erik performing physically, which astounded the meeting attendees. Erik was clocked running one hundred meters in 5.2 seconds, half the current world record. He was seen deadlifting one thousand kilograms, more than two thousand pounds, without straining. He then achieved a 21.5 meters Long Jump, nearly three times the current world record. Finally, Erik reached over four meters in the high jump, over fourteen feet.

At the conclusion of the videos, Ansley said, "As you can see, gentlemen, the cyborg body is capable of physical performance that is significantly greater than the most capable human. We believe this level of performance meets the requirements set forth by the U.S. Military at the initiation of this program. With the cyborg body controlled by the mind of a trained operative, the opportunity for unexpected displays of this performance is minimized."

The room was silent for what seemed like several minutes. SecDef then asked Ansley, "I understand the process to transform Commander Richards into a cyborg took approximately nine months. Doctor Barnett, how can we speed up the process? If we go into battle, we could have many soldiers who would benefit from this process."

"Mr. Secretary," Ansley replied. "Several human-cyborg

transformations could occur simultaneously given the necessary equipment, facilities, and trained staff to successfully accomplish the tasks. Of course, the necessary funding would be required."

Admiral Hampton then turned to Erik. "Commander Richards, now that your recovery is complete, there is the matter of a Board of Inquiry to determine if there are any charges associated with the accident on the USS Elon Musk."

A Military Board of Inquiry (BOI) is made up of officers who must be senior in grade to the officer who is the subject of the BOI. Board of Inquiry is an administrative process reserved for officers when looking into alleged sub-standard performance or misconduct. If allegations are substantiated, then this Board of Inquiry can go further and make a determination of whether the circumstances justify the officer's' separation from the service. A Board of Inquiry may be convened after an incident occurs that damages the reputation of the officer or the military such as a friendly-fire incident, an aircraft crash, or other such occurrence. "Yes, Sir," replied Erik. "You will have the full cooperation of both my crew and I for any administrative procedures deemed necessary."

"In the meantime, I am assigning you to Naval Space Command Intelligence until any and all charges have been satisfactorily addressed. You will serve under Captain Barnes here and be based at the Pentagon."

"Thank you, Sir. With your permission I would like to request thirty-days leave to take care of some personal business before I return to active duty."

"Captain Barnes, your call," said Admiral Hampton.

"I see no problem with the request, Commander. Please complete the routine paperwork for your leave request and route it to my attention," said the captain.

Chapter 38

Sunday evening, following Aaron's departure from the mansion, Kristian invited Ansley up to the pool deck for a glass of wine. The weather was once again perfect with a temperature of seventy-three degrees and humidity a low twenty-one percent. "Ansley, I have something very important to discuss with you. I need to make you aware of something that has happened to me since my brain went into that stasis bottle."

"Kris, are you OK? Are you experiencing issues?" replied Ansley, becoming visibly concerned for what Kristian may be going to tell her.

"I am perfectly fine, better than ever," said Kristian. "What I have to tell you is … not anything you could imagine on your own. Believe me when I say you will be astonished, to say the least."

"OK, go ahead," Ansley said, hesitantly.

"Apparently, when the human mind is separated from the body, the normal occurrence is for the consciousness, the spirit if you will, to move on to the next level of existence. Downloading the consciousness, the spirit, to an artificial body in this level of existence prevents the consciousness from rising to that next level. When I use the term 'consciousness' it may be clearer to think of it as 'spirit'."

"Let me try to understand," said Ansley, with a suspicious tone in her voice. "You are saying that because you did not fully die when your brain was extracted that your spirit is blocked from moving into some sort of afterlife?"

"Yes, but not completely," said Kristian. "There are times when I am able to experience ... supernatural abilities."

"Oh, Kristian, you are beginning to frighten me. I think I need to have you speak with Dr. McKensey. How long do you believe you've been aware of this?"

"I can assure you I do not need to speak with Dr. McKensey. My first experience with this phenomenon occurred when my brain was in stasis, before my consciousness was downloaded to the cyborg." Kristian then went on to explain his encounters with The Guardian. He described The Guardian and the supernatural powers he experienced under The Guardian's guidance. He described the nature of timelines and how they can go awry, threatening humanity. He recalled his time spent in the Nineteenth Century in the U.S. Civil War, his role and actions which were critical to maintaining the timeline in which the Union won the war.

"Kristian, please give me a moment to comprehend what you are telling me," said Ansley, her voice reflecting her heightened emotional state. "Am I to understand that you, your spirit as you call it, guided the outcome of the U.S. Civil War? My God, Kris, I'm a scientist! I can't just accept such a wild statement like that without some evidence. And I'm sorry, from a person whose brain was extracted, maintained in stasis, and downloaded to an artificial body! How do I know this isn't some wild hallucination resulting from the trauma you've experienced?"

"Ansley, this was no hallucination," Kristian said, calmly. "Would you like me to describe, in detail, my experiences existing in the mid-19th Century United States for three years? Or the moment when I had to give the order to kill Stonewall Jackson through the mind of Major John Decatur Barry of the Confederate Army?"

"Describing your... experience does not constitute scientific evidence," said Ansley, becoming visibly irritated with the discussion.

"You're right," replied Kristian. "I cannot prove these events occurred. Have you ever had to have faith in someone, something? You must have had faith in me when you married me. There was no scientific proof that I would be good to you, treat you kindly, remain loyal. I'm asking that you at least give me the benefit of the doubt here."

After a few moments of Ansley just staring at Kristian, tears welling up in her eyes, she said, "OK. So why are you telling me this now? Why did you wait so long after regaining consciousness?"

"Let me first add that Aaron has also experienced contact by The Guardian. And his first assignment also resulted in changing a timeline that would have resulted in the destruction of the United States during World War II. I can give you more details if you like."

Ansley just continued staring at Kristian and said, "No, no, perhaps another time."

"Aaron and I, together in our latest encounter with The Guardian, were transported ten years into the future. A technology will be developed that will enable control of a human mind using advanced communications technology with a smartphone. We were able to disrupt a demonstration of the technology to high- level US government officials. But I believe, and Aaron concurs, that we must attempt to derail the development of the technology beginning now."

"So, you time-traveled to the future with this … Guardian … to save humankind from permanent destruction?"

"Yes," said Kristian. "The sponsors of the technology are multi-billionaires and are developing the technology under the guise of use by the U.S. Military to control the actions of an enemy. DARPA is involved. Their true intentions are to gain control of the human race and subjugate it to slavery, serving them and their elite colleagues."

"I am struggling to have faith in you with all of this, Kristian. You are telling me all of this because you must envision a role for me."

"Ansley, I intend to bring Aaron on-board to help me plan and conduct the effort to derail the development of this technology. I would like to offer him the position of Senior Vice President of Research for Barnett Industries. He would report to Noel on paper, but actually be working with me here at Barnett Center. What I need for you to do, as Board Chairperson, is clear the position with our board of directors."

Ansley continued to stare, expressionless, at Kristian. Her mind was racing with the concern that somehow Aaron would reveal her tryst with him. But Aaron and Savannah had hit it off well on the tennis court this afternoon. Lots of friendly flirting and such. Perhaps there may be something there that would distract Aaron away from his feelings for her. "You know that I have mixed feelings regarding Aaron. He's a bit of a … wild card. Recall how he accosted you in the mansion lobby! I don't know, Kristian, if I can support this."

"Ansley, think about what I just told you. We are talking about the destiny of humanity," said Kristian, his passion visible in his face and body language. I can't emphasize enough the importance of the program I've described. Believe me when I say the force of evil is real and extraordinarily strong in the universe. It wants nothing less than the complete destruction of humanity."

"OK, please give me a general description of Aaron's position and responsibilities. As soon as I have it, I will contact the board members individually for their approval. At the next board meeting, the position will be included in the list of ratifications and likely go unnoticed."

Chapter 39

Following the presentation of Erik at the meeting at DARPA, Erik returned to Barnett Center with Ansley and Savannah. DARPA needed a few days to set up the charging station and network connection in Erik's apartment in Arlington, Virginia, near the Pentagon. Since the initial two cyborgs, Aaron and Kristian, were created, DARPA had been developing a portable, combined charging station/backup storage device that could fit in a carry-on bag to facilitate ease of travel for the cyborgs. The portable charging station operated off a standard 110/120- volt outlet. The portable data storage unit provided backup by downloading the human mind to the available 100 terabytes of light-based computer chips, built with a material called black phosphorous which enabled a form of light-based computing. Using a biotechnology called optogenetics, the ultra-thin chips' electrical resistance changes based on different wave lengths of light. From there, the device adds or deletes data in a manner similar to neurons in the human brain. The portable backup device could then be connected to an ultra-high-speed network connection, encrypted and transmitted via the internet to a secure data center. Like the permanent backup stations used by the cyborgs, the portable unit only transmits changes made to the data from the previous download, significantly reducing the amount of data transmitted.

"Erik, this is your portable charging and backup station," said technician Janice. "You simply plug in the cables as you currently do with the charging and backup unit in your room here at Barnett Center."

"Got it," replied Erik, smiling. "So, when I travel, I will be carrying my mind in a box."

"I guess that's true," said Janice, who caught herself staring dreamily at Erik's blue eyes and quickly looked away.

That evening Erik lay down on his charging bed. He had been coached by Kristian to let his mind wander as he rested since the cyborg doesn't sleep like a human. He began thinking about the Board of Inquiry he would face upon return from his approved leave. As he reviewed the events from the horrible accident that claimed four of his crew, including the beautiful Arya, he wondered what else he could have done to save them. They were warned of space debris in the area. Perhaps he should have requested a different course to Space Dock. As ship's captain, should he have ordered his executive officer to handle the emergency? But he knew his training as a fighter pilot would never have allowed him to hand off a life-or-death emergency to a subordinate. You have no subordinate in an F-35.

As he continued to dwell on the events of the accident he began to see, in his mind, a mist beginning to form. Then, still with his eyes closed, his mind saw a figure begin to form in the mist. Out of the mist stepped the figure of a man dressed in an open, long leather coat. Underneath the coat the figure was dressed in a white T-shirt and blue jeans. On his head was a Stetson. The figure continued to approach Erik.

"Hello, Erik," said the figure. "I have come to you while you are in a dream state. You will be unable to awaken from the dream state until I release you. I am here to tell you about myself and describe your role in an assignment you will soon be given."

Erik tried unsuccessfully to open his eyes and abandon the dream state he was in. "Who ... who are you? What do you want with me? Are you ... a ghost, an angel?"

"Do not be concerned," replied the figure. "I bear you no harm. The figure you see before you is not my natural appearance. You would likely go insane if you saw my real appearance. Your fellow cyborgs, Kristian and Aaron, refer to me as Guardian."

"So … Guardian, why are you contacting cyborgs? As far as I know there are only three of us right now. What is it we can do for …" he paused, and then added, "a supernatural being?"

"Let me first describe the unique situation in which you exist. When the physical human body dies, the consciousness or spirit elevates to the next level of existence. That level is one of pure energy. There is no physical body. There is no suffering, no disease. There is no concept of time as you know it. Recall that energy cannot be destroyed, so its existence is infinite. But since your consciousness, your spirit, has been downloaded into an electronic brain, you cannot fully elevate to that level. However, it is possible, with my guidance, to temporarily separate your spirit from your artificial body while the body is inactive. While your spirit is separated you are able to instantly travel to any moment in time. In this unique state you are also able to control the thoughts and actions of human beings. Those that have fully elevated do not have this ability and my being is too foreign to the human mind to exert control over it. Cyborgs like you and the others are the only beings with this ability."

"So, when we die, we, our consciousness, moves to an … afterlife?" said Erik.

"Yes, that is correct." said The Guardian.

"Why would we ever need to control another human being?" asked Erik.

"Allow me to finish and your question will be answered. Every event in the Universe is a part of a timeline that has been set in motion by the Creator. But the Creator has endowed humans with free will, which gives humans the ability to change a timeline. Timelines are altered thousands of times every day with no impact on humanity. However, evil forces in the Universe determined to destroy humankind sometimes can persuade humans, through their actions, to change timelines in a manner that is destructive to human existence. It is in these situations that we need to intervene and keep a timeline on its predestined course."

"Can you enlighten me by giving an example where a timeline was corrected? Have either of the two cyborgs created before me actually participated in correcting a timeline?" asked Erik.

"Both Kristian and Aaron have used their abilities to correct timelines that, had they not been corrected, would have led to the destruction of the United States and the enslavement of humanity. You will also use your abilities to save humankind."

"Do you have an … assignment for me now, Guardian?" "Soon," said The Guardian as he began to fade into the mist.

Erik began to slowly awaken from the dream. When he opened his eyes, he wondered whether what he, his mind, had seen was real. The Guardian seemed very real. The dream was very vivid, not like any dream he had ever experienced. As he lay on the charging bed he wondered if he should contact Kristian regarding the dream. But he was hesitant to raise the question fearing that he may be seen as losing his sanity.

Later that day, Erik met Kristian for lunch in Kristian's office in the mansion. Pulled pork barbeque served on a bun with coleslaw and steak fries were on the menu. "Erik, how is your life as a cyborg going?" asked Kristian, barbeque sauce dribbling down his chin.

"So far, it's been pretty amazing. Being able to perform physically like a superman has been incredible. But Ansley, Dr. Barnett, mentioned that those abilities will be adjusted to be that of a normal human. The superman act may be over, at least for a while."

"Yes, neither Aaron nor I were able to test the physical limits of these bodies. Ansley was intent on keeping a tight rein on that aspect of the cyber body. Have you felt anything unusual since you awoke as a cyborg?" Kristian was intent on finding out whether Erik had had an encounter with The Guardian yet.

"Well, uh, no, not really, that I recall," replied Erik, remaining hesitant to mention his encounter with The Guardian. "Have you experienced anything unusual, especially since you had the lengthy step where your brain was kept in stasis?"

"Have you had any dreams while you're charging yet?" asked Kristian.

"Funny you should ask. I had one very odd dream last night. I dreamed that a dude showed up looking like something out of an old western movie. Told me I was going to receive an … assignment that could save humanity."

"Erik, that was no dream, at least in the conventional sense. Aaron and I both have had several assignments with The Guardian. It seems people like us, cyborgs whose human mind controls an artificial body, have some unique abilities that The Guardian needs in order to keep things on track," said Kristian. Kristian went on to describe his assignments with The Guardian for over an hour. When he was finished, Erik just sat silent, in awe of what he had just heard.

Then, after a few long moments, "So, if Stonewall Jackson had not been killed, the South would have won the Civil War?" Erik asked.

"Yes, according to The Guardian. Not only would the South have won but the timeline would have resulted in the United States losing World War II and would have been conquered by the Axis powers."

"I wonder what my assignment will be. It must be something incredible based on what you've just told me."

"According to The Guardian, there are numerous timelines that will need to be guided with our help. As more cyborgs are created, there will be more like The Guardian overseeing their own teams.

Chapter 40

About two weeks had passed since Kristian had asked Ansley to clear a path to hire Aaron with the Board of Directors of Barnett Industries. As Kristian and Ansley dined on the pool deck, Ansley said, "Kristian, I have spoken with each of the Board members regarding the position for Aaron. You were clever to make the job description vague and tie it to the potential development of new business opportunities leveraging advanced technologies now under development. I used the analogy of the railroad companies in the Nineteenth Century failing to view themselves as transportation companies, resulting in their diminished role in global business development." That failure is why there never was a B&O or Union Pacific airline or auto manufacturer. "I told them to look at companies like General Electric which developed several lines of business. The members generally agreed with few questions. You are free to negotiate the position with Aaron. I just hope you've given this careful consideration."

"Thank you, Ansley. I know hiring Aaron makes you somewhat uncomfortable. But based on what I told you regarding The Guardian and the opportunity, we have to derail Find Corporation and its mind control project, I feel Aaron is the right man, the only man for the job. I will call him first thing in the morning."

Aaron was on his way to the office, riding in his Uber driverless auto when his smartphone buzzed. Kristian's face popped up on the screen. "Good morning, Kristian, what can I do for you?"

"Good morning, Aaron, I have some good news for you. The board approved your position with Barnett Industries. I need to connect you with our human resources attorney so he can formally present the offer and contract to you. What's a good time for you?"

"Wow, that's great news!" said Aaron. I can be available at 4 PM today if that's not too soon."

Kristian was pleased Aaron did not mention engaging an attorney to represent him. "We'll make it happen, Aaron. When do you think you could start?"

"I really should give the traditional two-week notice. These folks have been particularly good to me. Today is Wednesday. Tentatively, two weeks from Monday?"

"Sounds good, Aaron. Be thinking of ways we can derail those monsters at Find Corporation."

Find Corporation was created after the U.S. Department of Justice successfully led the suit that resulted in the breakup of Google in the late-2020s. In building services outside their core web search business — Google Maps, Chrome, Android, YouTube, Google Hotels, the ill-fated Google+, Project Fi, and dozens more — there was strong evidence the company leveraged its monopoly position in search technology to illegally influence U.S. elections. Find was the successor to the original search function that had grown to be the biggest part of Google.

Aaron's smartphone buzzed at 4:07 PM. The screen showed Barnett Industries. "Hello, this is Phil Preston," said Aaron, using his witness protection identity.

"Hello," a pause, then, "This is Timothy Banks. I am an attorney with Barnett Industries calling Aaron Adams."

"This is Aaron. I see you know my true identity."

"Yes, and I've executed the necessary non-disclosures. I have an offer in front of me. Do you have time to discuss it?"

"Yes," replied Aaron. "Let's do this face-to-face, electronically." Aaron pressed a key on the smartphone and a holographic image of Banks appeared in the chair across from him.

Attorney Banks went over the terms of the offer which included the job title, salary, stock options, deferred income savings plan, and fully paid, non-deductible health insurance, including supplemental that provided extensive care options that exceeded the standard federal government Universal Healthcare Plan. Terms of the employment contract were then reviewed, whereby items including the term of the contract, severance pay for involuntary termination without cause, and non-disclosure of any and all of Barnett Industries intellectual property were discussed. At the end of the one-sided conversation, which took thirty-five minutes, Aaron was silent for several moments. "Do you have any questions, Mr. Adams?" asked Banks.

"I … it all sounds incredibly good, Mr. Banks," said Aaron. "Can you send me the documents for my review? I'd like to go over them before I sign on the dotted line."

"Check your email, Mr. Adams. I believe you will find the documents waiting for you."

Aaron opened the email app on his smartphone. The documents were in his inbox. "Ah, yes, I see them. I'll review these and get back to you before the end of the day tomorrow. But, from what I've heard, you have my acceptance pending my review and any questions I may have."

"Thanks, Mr. Adams. I look forward to meeting you in person soon.

"Please call me Aaron."

Chapter 41

The morning following his lunch with Kristian, Erik rolled out of his charging bed and picked up his smartphone. Checking his email, he saw the message from Captain Jeffrey Barnes' office in the Pentagon approving his request for thirty-days leave. He immediately dictated a message to Arya Anderson's sister, Ksenia, with whom he had been communicating for the past six months while he was recovering and training in the functions and use of his cyber body. In the message he again reiterated his sorrow and regret at Arya's passing in the accident aboard the USS Elon Musk. He then requested that he be invited to visit Ksenia, as well as the rest of Arya's family in Norway, to express his condolences in person and provide more insight as to the cause of the accident. Erik stepped into the shower which was modified for cleansing cyborg bodies, delivering a high-pressure flow of chemicals and steam.

After his shower, Erik was dressing in his tan Naval service khaki uniform when his smartphone buzzed, indicating an incoming message. Grabbing the phone off the dresser he saw the message was from Ksenia. "Hello, Erik. I would be pleased to meet you in person and I believe my parents would as well. However, my brother, Thor, is still angry over Arya's death and is looking to place blame. We will have to use caution when you meet him. In the meantime, I continue to work with him trying to dissuade his anger. When can you come to Norway?"

Erik dictated a reply to his smartphone, "I am on thirty-days leave from the Navy and would like to come as soon as I can arrange a flight. If I can get a flight later today, that would put me in Bergen by mid-day tomorrow. Would that be OK with your schedule?" Erik than instructed the digital assistant app to begin searching for flights from California to Bergen, Norway.

Erik's smartphone buzzed again, "Erik, if you can get over here tomorrow that would be great. My ship docks early in the morning and we'll spend the rest of the day in Bergen and then head to Flåm, to my parents' farm."

Erik's phone then emitted a sonar ping, indicating a message from the digital assistant. Erik said, "play message," and the digital assistant read aloud a flight itinerary that would put him in Bergen at 1330 hours (1:30 PM), local time, the next day. The assistant than asked if it should book the flights.

"Yes, please book and arrange transportation from my current location to the airport allowing plenty of time to catch the flight. Also, please send the itinerary to Ksenia Anderson."

In a few moments the phone again emitted the familiar sonar ping. "Erik, you have been booked on Icelandic Airways Flight 444, from LAX to Reykjavik, Iceland. The aircraft is a Boeing 977-SST which departs SFO at 21:59 local time and arrives at Reykjavik at 07:14 local time. Flying time is three hours, fifteen minutes. Flight 444 then continues to Bergen at 08:44 and arrives at 12:30 local time." Sonic booms resulting from aircraft flying at supersonic speeds were eliminated by the mid-2020s, which led to significant reductions in flight times over populated areas. By 2040, most long distance transcontinental and overseas flights were utilizing supersonic transport (SST) aircraft.

Chapter 42

As Aaron Adams descended on the escalator to the baggage claim at LAX, a gentleman dressed in a black chauffer's uniform approached him. "Hello, Mr. Preston, welcome to Barnett Industries. I am Neil Grayson. I will be taking you to Barnett Center after we claim your baggage. There will be a representative from Barnett Human Resources there to get you started with your on-boarding. May I assist you in gathering your baggage?"

"Hello, Neil," said Aaron. "Yes, I see my two large bags over there on the carousel. I'll grab them and join you outside." Neil then moved quickly to the carousel and gathered the two bags containing most of Aaron's clothing and personal items. "Neil seems to be on top of his game," thought Aaron.

"Please follow me, Mr. Preston," said Neil, continuing to use Aaron's witness protection name as he walked towards the exit doors to Ground Transportation.

Arriving at Barnett Center, the black limo stopped on the circular drive in front of the main entrance. "Mr. Preston, I will see that your baggage is delivered to your suite," said Neil.

"Thank you, Neil," said Aaron just as a young woman dressed in a bright blue blouse, black skirt, and one-inch black heels opened the limo door.

"Hello, Mr. Preston, I am Sandra Fleming, from HR. If you will come with me, I will get you started with your on-boarding and executive orientation."

"Right," said Aaron as he climbed out of the limo. "Pleased to meet you, Sandra," he said, while thinking that Sandra was quite attractive. "What do you do for Barnett HR?" he asked, attempting to make conversation.

"I am Director of Recruitment," said Sandra, glancing back at Aaron.

Following a morning of reviewing company polices, watching security videos, and signing the requisite employment documents including non-disclosure agreements, Aaron met Ansley and Savannah for lunch in the Barnett Center's executive dining room. While Ansley and Savannah dined on salads with a side of fruit and a cup of green tea, Aaron enjoyed his cheeseburger, fries, and chocolate milkshake.

"You cyborgs are disgusting," said Ansley, half-smiling. "Here Savannah and I are forced to eat bunny food while you gulp down whatever fat-laden, sugar-spiked food you want with no ill effects. You should be ashamed."

"Hey, I'm just a product of your genius, so don't blame me," said Aaron.

"What is it you will be doing for Barnett Industries, Aaron?" asked Savannah. Aaron was unsure how much Ansley had shared with Savannah regarding the real reasons that Kristian wanted Aaron hired.

"Research and development," he replied, trying to think of a way to change the subject.

"Research and development of what?" asked Savannah.

"Er, … new business investment opportunities. Kristian is intent on seeing Barnett Industries expand into new markets. There are many new technologies on the drawing board, some with potential to change our culture, that we will be researching." "Sounds interesting," said Savannah. "You will be based here at the Center?"

"Yes, Kristian wanted me in close proximity as he and I will be working closely on this effort."

As the conversation continued, Ansley could sense that Aaron and Savannah were hitting it off quite well, which helped quell her fear that Aaron would divulge her tryst with Aaron while Kristian was still in stasis.

Kristian returned to HR after lunch to continue his executive orientation to Barnett Industries. The afternoon wrapped up with a holographic meeting with Barnett's CEO, Noel Donovan, and the Barnett division heads. Noel introduced Aaron using his acquired witness protection name of Philip Preston and had each division head describe his or her division's role, goals and objectives in order to give Aaron a view of the corporation's operations. Having studied the last three annual reports in detail provided Aaron with the necessary background for both fielding and asking questions from the group.

Aaron's background as Philip Geoffrey Preston had been created to show that he had attended Stanford for both graduate and postgraduate work, obtaining a bachelor's degree in Computer Science and a master's degree in International Business. The appropriate supporting documents had been created and filed by Stanford verifying Preston's degree programs complete with transcripts as part of the witness protection program at Kristian's request, submitted by Ansley. This was apparently enough to satisfy the senior executives of Barnett Industries that he was an excellent recruitment.

The next day, Aaron met Kristian in his office at the mansion for a day-long meeting regarding strategies for taking on Find Corporation's mind control project. "Good morning, Aaron, I hope you didn't find our orientation process too boring. Unfortunately, since the dawn of the 21st Century, the lawyers have turned hiring into a quagmire of paperwork that only they truly understand."

"Good morning," Aaron replied. "It was a long day, but I did learn quite a lot about Barnett Industries. The meeting with Noel and the senior execs was quite valuable. Hopefully, I came across as competent to them."

"I've been doing a bit of research on the issue of Big Tech exerting control over the populace in order to sway elections and support their ideologies," said Aaron. "Studies of the 2016 and 2020 elections have revealed that Tech's influence, particularly with social media, swayed several million votes towards the progressive candidates that supported Tech's agenda. The result was victories in the popular vote over the conservative candidate, Donald Trump, in both elections. Fortunately, the effect of the Electoral College overcame the popular vote for those elections. Controls and corporate breakups of the largest tech firms in the mid and late 2020s, as well as an extensive education campaign of the public regarding the fallacies of social media, diminished the effects of social media on swaying voters."

"Therefore, the bottom line is Tech corporations have, and still are, trying to establish their ideologies and agenda by any means possible," said Kristian.

"Exactly. I believe we can leverage the public education of people regarding the egregious danger and evil intent of Find Corporation's mind control program by leveraging the techniques used in the early 2020s, following the 2020 election." "Good thoughts, Aaron," said Kristian. "Please consider drafting a white paper detailing what we've discussed here today. This definitely needs to be a key element in our plan for derailing Find."

"Will do, Kristian. Incidentally, have you given any thought as to how you will reenter public life? I believe that direct communication between you and key political and corporate figures would significantly enhance our efforts. Your name is well known, whereas mine, both of them, are unknown."

"I have some ideas that I need to discuss with Ansley, and perhaps, Savannah. Since the world believes that I have been completely incapacitated since 2037 we will need a viable story supporting my return to full health. The problem is that any story will involve serious scrutiny by the press and the medical community. Perhaps we consider abandoning the diagnosis of ALS and go with a strange, previously unheard of, virus that caused ALS-like physical deterioration and symptoms. In order to prevent further deterioration of my nervous system I was put in a low-temperature sleep state until a means to control the virus was determined. But then again, the scientific community will be very suspicious and be demanding explanations."

"I believe that line of thought does have merit. Could you shut down the scientific community using Ansley's relationship with DARPA? Sorry, folks, the cure is classified...," said Aaron.

"Possibly, but that will take some serious discussions with DARPA to get them to play along."

Chapter 43

Erik's flight to Bergen, Norway landed on time at 11:30 AM. Erik immediately messaged Ksenia advising of his arrival. Ksenia replied and said she would be waiting for him right outside of the immigration hall at Bergen Airport. Erik walked from the arrival gate, rode down the escalator to baggage claim. Shortly his checked bag appeared on carousel number two and he proceeded through the immigration/customs exit admiring how easily that process was compared to entering the United States. In fact, he didn't even see a Norwegian immigration officer at the exit. As he exited the baggage hall, he saw Ksenia to his right and headed toward her, thinking how lovely she appeared. While quite a contrast to her sister, the tall, blue-eyed, blond Arya, Ksenia was shorter with light brown hair and green eyes.

"Erik, how lovely to finally meet you in person," said Ksenia, still wearing her cruise ship officer's black uniform with the two gold stripes on the sleeve reflecting her position as a Second Mate. Her hair was pulled back in a bun, according to uniform regulations. Ksenia had attended the U.S. Merchant Marine Academy at Kings Point, New York as a foreign student. Subsequently she interned with Viking Cruise Lines as a Deck (navigation) Cadet and was hired by Viking as a Third Mate upon her graduation.

"Hello Ksenia," said Erik, smiling. He was immediately struck by Ksenia's lovely smile, which was possibly the one thing she shared with her deceased sister. "I didn't expect to see you in uniform. Perhaps I should've worn mine."

"I just got off duty about an hour ago and rushed to the airport to meet you. I didn't have time to change," she said, admiring how handsome Erik was with his blond hair, blue eyes and boyish features. He hardly had the appearance of a spaceship captain. "I would like to run by my apartment to change clothes and grab a bag. Then we can have lunch before we drive up to my parents' farm near Flåm."

"Oh, I wasn't aware we were going to your parents' home today, so I booked a room at the Hotel Norge," said Erik.

"Oh, sorry, I should have discussed this with you before just assuming," said Ksenia. If going to Flåm today is a concern for you I can call mother and change the plan. When do you think you would like to go?"

"No, no. I will cancel the hotel room. I am looking forward to meeting your family."

"Are you sure?" said Ksenia. "I don't want to seem forward or push you before you're ready. I expect meeting them will be emotional for them… and for you."

"No, I'm ready, and I want to meet them as soon as possible."

Ksenia changed into casual clothes and packed a bag to take to her parents' home near Flåm and the two headed for lunch at the Daily Pot, a lunch café that was just around the block from her apartment.

"So, what do Norwegians eat for lunch?" asked Erik, perusing the menu.

"Do you like Asian food?" replied Ksenia. This café has excellent soups, two of which are Asian-based."

"I'm easy to please when it comes to food," said Erik, thinking it didn't matter much what he ate unless, of course, it was octopus. "I'll try the Asian Pot. Seems to be one of the few that actually have meat in the recipe."

"I'm going to have the Thai Pot," said Ksenia.

In an attempt at making conversation and getting to know Ksenia, Erik asked, "What made you choose a seagoing career, and how did you end up at Kings Point? I'm sure there are similar maritime schools in Europe."

"We moved to Flåm from Sweden when I was twelve years old. From the farm we can look down at the fjord and see the cruise ships coming and going during the summer months. Seeing those beautiful, large ships gave me a desire to someday be on one of them. In my third year of high school I began looking at the requirements for gaining employment on one of the cruise lines. I found that navigation and engineering candidates were usually either hired from merchant vessels or from maritime schools. I did consider a couple of European schools but Kings Point really held an attraction for me. So, I applied through our foreign education program and was accepted."

"It sure looks like you've done very well and achieved your career goals. You must be an incredibly determined person to go to a foreign country to pursue your dreams," said Erik.

"Well, I feel that I am making progress, but I won't be satisfied until I become the captain of a Viking cruise ship," she said, smiling and admiring Erik's azure blue eyes. "Now what about you, how did you become the captain of a spaceship?"

"Well, that's a bit dramatic, you know, the captain thing. As you know, my rank is commander. But I knew I wanted to fly since I was about eight years old when my grandfather used to bring over toy drones for me to fly. Actually, he did most of the flying and regularly lost the drones in our large magnolia trees and in the nearby lake. But as I grew older my interest in flying continued until I took flying lessons when I was fifteen. I soloed on my sixteenth birthday and then, being so excited, promptly failed my driver's license test to my father's great embarrassment." "Oh, my," said Ksenia, laughing. "How could you solo in an airplane and fail a simple driving test?"

"Just a crazy teenager, I guess," said Erik, also laughing. "I originally wanted to go to the Air Force Academy and my parents took me to Colorado Springs in my junior year of high school. It is a beautiful school and I would have been honored to go there. But when I applied for the Congressional appointment, my congressman asked me in my interview if I would be interested in applying to the Naval Academy. He, being a Naval Academy graduate, may have had something to do with it but I told him I would be honored to attend Navy. The next thing I knew, I received a phone call from the congressman telling me I had received an appointment to the Naval Academy."

"Right after graduation I was able to get a slot in Naval flight school. From there I was assigned to an F-35 squadron on the USS Enterprise. I spent the requisite six months at sea in the Pacific flying sorties up and down the Chinese coast, occasionally mixing it up with Chinese patrols. When I returned, the U.S. was commissioning the Naval Space Command and I immediately applied for a pilot spot. But the NSC turned me down saying I needed more flight time in the F-35 before I could qualify. So, back to sea I went for another six-month tour. At four months into the tour I was summoned to the CAG's, Captain of the Air Group's, office and told I was being assigned to Top Gun. Top Gun is the unofficial moniker of the Naval Strike and Air Warfare Center at Naval Air Station Fallon, Nevada. You may recall the hit movies starring Tom Cruise as Maverick. After graduating from Top Gun, I again applied to the NSC and was ultimately awarded one of the four pilot positions on the USS Elon Musk. After three roundtrips to Mars on the Musk, with the third as XO, I was promoted to commander and given command of the Musk."

After lunch, Ksenia called a rental car using the Avis app on her smartphone to meet them outside of her apartment for their drive to Flåm. The self-driving rental appeared outside of her apartment in fifteen minutes and they departed for Flåm. While in Bergen, the car was self-driving but as they approached the city limit the video screen on the dash began flashing red letters on a blue background "Self-driving terminating in 5 kilometers." The screen stopped flashing, but the message remained with the distance decreasing in one-half kilometer increments. If a driver did not take control of the vehicle at the one-half kilometer mark the car would pull over and stop. When the driver acknowledged taking control of the vehicle it could continue its route. The technology supporting self-driving vehicles in Norway was provided by Barnett Industries. All passenger cars in Norway, and in most other countries in Europe were electric by law.

Chapter 44

Kristian and Ansley met for lunch in Kristian's office in the mansion. "Thanks for coming up for lunch, Ansley. I have something important to discuss with you."

"Oh, is this another revelation of your life as a cyborg that will cause me to faint?" asked Ansley, giving Kristian a stern raised eyebrow.

"I hope not. I'm just spit-balling at this point, but I believe it is time we consider bringing me back into the world. I am growing tired of being a recluse and I am needed for the project to stop Find Corporation's mind control program."

"Kristian, the world still thinks you are suffering from advanced ALS for which there is no cure yet. How do you propose we get past that without bringing the medical community down on our heads demanding that we reveal the cure?"

"I've got some ideas. I've done a little research and it seems that there are ailments, Lyme Disease being one, that mimic the symptoms of ALS that can be cured. Perhaps we go public with the story that I was misdiagnosed with ALS and I was suffering from one of the ALS mimics."

"Kristian, you were first diagnosed with ALS fourteen years ago, in 2028. Trying to use a misdiagnosis as the basis for your return as a completely healthy man in his forties would certainly draw a lot of questions. And most of these questions would fall on Savannah since she oversaw your treatment plan."

"Where is Savannah with a cure for ALS? She seemed to believe she'd have a way to at least stop the progression of the disease by the mid-2030s."

"I know she is making progress using nanotechnology to inject nano particles directly into the brain, but that has not even gotten past Phase One trials."

"I believe we need Savannah, and also Tyler and Aidan, to put their medical minds together and see if we can come up with a viable plan that won't inundate Savannah and the Center with demands from the medical community."

"Tyler and Aidan? You haven't seen them in fourteen years. I've spoken to them on the phone several times over the years when they were checking up on your condition." Tyler and Aidan Sullivan were Kristian's personal physicians.

"Tyler and Aidan were mentioned in the press releases when my diagnosis was revealed to the public. They may be able to contribute to my 'coming out party' depending on the story we develop."

"If we bring them in, we will need them to sign non-disclosure agreements. When they see you, they will be shocked at your excellent condition. If you like, I will contact them and speak to Savannah. Hopefully, we can set up a meeting in the next week." "Yes, please see if you can set up a meeting. I see this a must do rather than a nice to do. Also, please attend the meeting yourself.

We may need some … cooperation from DARPA to give the plan credibility … or to protect us from enquiring minds."

"Hello, this is Dr. Ansley Barnett, may I please speak with Tyler Sullivan?" said Ansley to Dr. Tyler Sullivan's digital assistant." Telephones answered by human office assistants were quite rare, and unexpected in 2042.

"Dr. Sullivan is with a patient. May I take a message?" answered the assistant.

"Yes, please have him call me at his earliest convenience," said Ansley, hanging up and beginning her walk down the hallway of the fourth floor of the Barnett Center to Savannah Richard's office.

Savannah's door was open, and Ansley stuck her head just inside the doorway. "Hi Savannah, have you got a few moments?

I have been speaking with Kristian and he has asked me to set up some time with you."

"OK, what's on his mind? Come in and have a seat," said Savannah.

Taking her seat in one of the teal leather and polished aluminum desk chairs at Savannah's glass desk, Ansley said, "Well it seems he has decided he does not want to live the life of a recluse much longer. He is looking for help from us in determining a way he can reenter public life without raising suspicion in the medical and scientific communities."

Just then, Ansley's smartphone buzzed indicating an incoming call. Dr. Tyler Sullivan's image appeared on the face of the smartphone and Ansley answered, "Hello, Tyler, thanks for returning my call. I am sitting here with Dr. Savannah Richards. May I put you on speaker?"

"Certainly, Ansley," said Tyler. Ansley's smartphone clicked and a holographic image of Tyler appeared in the chair adjacent to Ansley's. "Hello, Dr. Richards, nice to see you again. It's been awhile."

"Yes, it has. Please call me Savannah."

"Now that I've got you both here, I was just telling Savannah that Kristian has a somewhat … unusual request. Without divulging Kristian's condition, which I will get to in a moment, Kristian would like to re-enter public life. He has grown weary of living life as a recluse. What is quite unusual about his request is that Kristian has returned to full health and suffers no lingering ill effects from his bout with ALS."

"Ansley, how is this possible?" asked a stunned Tyler Sullivan. "The last time we spoke he was in the final stages of the disease." "I can't go into that without properly … preparing you and Aidan, legally," said Ansley. "How Kristian was cured is classified as Top Secret."

"Ansley, does this have something to do with the work you're doing for DARPA?" asked Tyler.

"I am not at liberty to discuss this until we meet in person, Tyler. When will you and Aidan be available?" said Ansley.

"We will be available at whatever time you decide, Ansley. This is much too important to delay discussions further."

Chapter 45

The drive from Bergen to Flåm included beautiful scenery as Ksenia and Erik passed near several of the fjords visible from the road. The water was a dark shade of green contrasting with the still- snowcapped mountains. The weather was sunny and mostly clear with a temperature hovering just below sixty degrees Fahrenheit.

"How are your parents dealing with Arya's passing? It must have been extremely hard on them," said Erik.

"It was awfully hard on them, especially at first. But time has a way of muting the pain although it can never be completely erased. The last time I was home, about ten weeks ago, Mother told me that Father still suffers periods when he is unable to sleep. He sometimes lies awake in bed or sits up all night and she has seen tears silently running down his cheeks."

"I can only imagine the pain they must have felt losing their beautiful and talented daughter," said Erik. "Arya and I were growing close during our twelve-month mission at the Mars outpost. I miss her terribly and still lie awake at night wondering what I could've done differently ... to prevent the accident or save my crew." Of course, Erik no longer slept like a human sleeps. Nevertheless, he often experienced memories of the accident during his recharging periods.

Erik and Ksenia completed the three-hour drive from Bergen to Flåm at approximately 5 PM. Flåm was a lovely small town that sits at the end of Aurlandsfjord, a branch of the vast Sognefjord. As they began to climb the hills around Flåm on the E16 Highway they could see a Viking cruise ship anchored in the harbor. It was just past the beginning of cruise season in May.

"That's the Viking Sky on its summer schedule," said Ksenia. "It just returned from its Caribbean schedule a few weeks ago. I served on that ship last summer for ten weeks, sailing to four ports in Norway, to the Faroe Islands, and then to four ports in Iceland. It is an older ship, but it has been maintained beautifully by Viking, as are all of their ships."

They turned off the E16 with its multiple hairpin turns onto an even narrower road. After a couple of miles, they turned again and drove up an unpaved, tree-lined gravel drive to the house. It was immediately obvious to Erik that Arya had downplayed her description of the house. It appeared to be much larger than she described. The house sat on what appeared to be an above-ground basement. The main center section was two stories, with single story wings on either side. A two-sided staircase rose from the ground to the front entrance on the first floor. Its roof was red tile. "That is quite an estate," said Erik. "I can see why your family moved here from Sweden."

"Yes, it has been in mother's family for over three hundred years. The original house was built in 1733. It was last renovated in 1954 by my great grandfather, Baron Carl Bergland."

"Wow, Arya never shared that you are nobility. Should I bow and kiss your ring when I greet you?" said Erik, smiling.

"Perhaps you should," said Ksenia, laughing.

"Seriously, is there anything special I should do when I meet your parents, you being royalty and all."

"No, my father will greet you as he does all guests, with a handshake. Just give my mother a very slight bow. Let her come to you for either a handshake or a hug if she chooses."

"Got it. Now that I have been briefed on the proper etiquette for meeting the lord and lady of the manner, I shall behave accordingly. What about your brother?"

"Let him take the lead. Do not be offended if he does not offer to shake your hand. He still harbors much resentment towards you for the accident."

As Erik and Ksenia climbed one side of the steps that led to the front entry, Ksenia's parents stepped outside. "Ksenia, Erik, very nice to see you," said Ksenia's mother, Ebba, as she hugged her daughter and gave her a kiss on the cheek. Ebba was nearly the same height as Ksenia, about five-foot- -six inches, blonde with touches of gray, and green eyes. He could see a resemblance to both Arya and Ksenia. "Erik, so glad you could come to our home," Ebba said as she extended her hand to shake his.

"Thank you, Mrs. Anderson," said Erik. "Very nice to finally meet you."

Ksenia's father, Carl Anderson, was tall, over six feet, and thin. His hair was mostly gray and thinning. He extended his hand to shake Erik's. "Welcome to our home, Erik."

"Thank you, sir," replied Erik.

"Let's go inside and then out to the lysthus," said Ebba. "Gazebo," whispered Ksenia to Erik, who nodded slightly to indicate he understood.

Walking in through the double doorway, Erik saw an immense chandelier hanging from the second-story ceiling and a wide stairway to the second floor to his right. They proceeded through the center of the house, down a long hallway to the back. As they exited through double doors at the back of the hallway, they followed a slate path to the gazebo about thirty meters away from the house.

As they sat down around a low, round cocktail table, Ebba said, "We have refreshments. Traditional Scandinavian hors d'oeuvres of pickled herring and vodka."

Carl Anderson, Ksenia's father, was describing the estate and farming operations when a tall figure appeared at the mansion's back door. He stood just outside the doorway but did not approach the gazebo. "Thor, please join us," said Carl, waving.

Thor did not move for a few seconds. He then turned around and went back inside the house.

"As I told you, Thor still harbors strong feelings over Arya's death," said Ksenia.

"I understand," said Erik. "I can't say that I would react differently if the situation were reversed."

Carl, Ebba, Ksenia and Erik walked back towards the house as they finished their cocktails. "Thank you, Mrs. Anderson, for the delicious appetizers," said Erik.

"Come, Erik, I will show you to your room so you can freshen up for dinner," said Ksenia. As they began to climb the stairway to the second floor Thor appeared at the top of the stairway.

"Ksenia, I need to speak with you. Please come into my room." "Certainly, right after I show Erik to his room."

"Ksenia, what is the meaning of bringing our sister's murderer into our home?" demanded Thor. "I don't know if I can keep from killing him!"

"Thor, we've discussed this. The incident on the USS Musk was an accident! Erik did everything he could to save Arya and his crew. Please, do not embarrass our parents by acting badly. They've been through quite enough!"

"He survived. She did not. That is the only thought that dominates my mind."

"And he was severely injured attempting to save her. He was in a hospital and rehabilitation for over a year."

"It was his command and his decision to fly through a debris field that he had been warned about! Had he changed his approach to the space station this would not have happened!" Thor said, his voice loud and face red.

"There is no point discussing this with you while you are this angry," she said, as she turned and walked out of Thor's room.

Ebba and Ksenia brought the food in from the kitchen and set it on the table. The meal was a Norwegian spring delicacy of cured trout and spruce tips, served with spring mashed potatoes and peas. A light white wine was served with the meal.

"Mrs. Anderson, this looks delicious," said Erik, as they sat at the table. Carl sat at the head with Ebba opposite him. Ksenia and Erik sat together on one side leaving an empty place setting across from them.

"The trout takes about three days to properly cure and is eaten cold," said Ksenia, just as Thor appeared in the dining room arched doorway, scowling.

"Thor, please sit and join us. This is one of your favorite meals," said Ebba.

With respect for his mother, Thor sat silently at the table facing Ksenia and Erik, intermittently glaring at Erik. The food was passed among them in silence and they began to eat.

"The trout is amazing, Mrs. Anderson. Your mom is quite the chef, Ksenia," said Erik attempting to break the silence and lighten the dark mood brought to the table by Thor.

"Thank you, Erik," said Ebba, smiling. "I am pleased that you like it. Thor, how do you like it?"

Thor just cleared his throat and nodded without saying anything.

The remainder of the main course was completed mostly in silence.

"Ksenia, help me clear the table for dessert," said Ebba. Erik began to rise to clear his plate from the table when Ksenia grabbed his arm. "Sit, I will clear your plate," she said as he noticed the other two men made no effort to rise and assist with table duties.

"Thor, Ksenia tells me you run the farming operations," said Erik, still trying to break the silence and engage Thor in conversation. "That must keep you very busy during the spring and summer months."

"Yes, very busy," said Thor, staring at Erik and making no effort to contribute to the conversation.

"Thor studied and received his college degree in agriculture from the Swedish University of Agricultural Sciences," said Carl.

"Quite an accomplishment, Thor," said Erik. "Several of our state universities offer agricultural programs."

Ksenia and Ebba returned to the dining room, Ksenia carrying an almond cake for dessert. After they had finished eating, Carl said, "Gentlemen, let us retire to the parlor to enjoy a drink while the women clean up."

Erik glanced at Ksenia, smirking at her father's suggestion, while Ksenia glared at her father but remained speechless.

Carl poured the drink into three shot glasses. As Erik and Thor each took their glass, they all sat. Carl sat in the largest chair between Erik and Thor. "Linje Aquavit is named after the tradition of sending oak barrels of aquavit with ships from Norway to Australia and back again, thereby passing the equator ("linje") twice before being bottled. The constant movement, high humidity and fluctuating temperatures cause the spirit to extract more flavor and contributes to accelerated maturation. Therefore, Norwegian aquavit is darker than Swedish or Danish aquavit."

"Erik, will you be returning to space?" asked Carl.

"I hope to," replied Erik. "There remains the manner of the investigation of the accident by a Naval Board of Inquiry. Unfortunately, it is rare that a Board of Inquiry results in the complete exoneration of a commanding officer whose ship is involved in a serious incident. There are those in the Navy that will discourage giving me command of another ship. I will probably be assigned to a desk job with Navy Space Command at the Pentagon when I return."

In a few moments, Ebba and Ksenia joined the men in the parlor. "Erik, please tell us what happened on your ship. How did the accident happen?" asked Carl, with emotion detected by the others in his voice.

Silent until now, Thor said, "Yes, please tell us what happened. Be sure to include just how your ship came to be in a debris field after you were warned."

"Thor!" said Ksenia.

"It's OK," said Erik. I fully understand how Arya's passing may have devastated you."

"Do you, now?" said Thor, his voice rising in anger. "Have you had a beloved and beautiful sister taken from you due to gross carelessness of another?"

Carl said, "That's enough, Thor. If you cannot be civil, please excuse yourself."

"Father, how can you tolerate this ... man, whose actions caused our Arya's death, in your home and remain civil?" Thor yelled.

"Thor! Please leave now!" said Carl, his voice raised and face red with anger and embarrassment. "Erik, Ksenia, let us all retire for the evening. Things are too emotional to continue this discussion now."

Chapter 46

Aaron jumped on the transporter, a short hyperloop designed by Barnett Industries, located on the basement floor of Barnett Center and was in the mansion transporter lobby in five seconds. He rode the escalator up to the main floor foyer and then climbed the circular steps to Kristian's office on the second floor.

"Morning, Aaron, how is your research into Find Corporation's activities dealing with mind manipulation?"

"Morning. Apparently, the idea of using electromagnetic technology for behavior control has been around quite a while. The CIA was investigating the technology as early as the middle of the Twentieth Century. Experimentation has been going on for at least twenty years. The Loughborough University Sleep Research Centre in England devised an experiment to test the effects of cellular technology on behavior. Early results were surprising. Not only could the cell phone signals alter a person's behavior during the call, the effects of the disrupted brain-wave patterns continued long after the phone was switched off. The significance of the research is that, although cell phone power is low, electromagnetic radiation can nevertheless influence mental behavior when transmitted at the proper frequency and strength."

"So, what Find has or will be able to do is to fine-tune the frequency and strength of their smartphone to specifically control the behavior of a user," said Kristian.

"Exactly. As early as 1998, scientists had warned that the control and manipulation of a human brain was a terrifying possibility.

Lieutenant Colonel Timothy L. Thomas, U.S. Army (ret), published an article in the military journal Parameters which likened the mind to a new battlefield. He quoted a Russian army major in relation to weapons that affected the mind, "It is completely clear that the state which is the first to create such weapons will achieve incomparable superiority. There was no doubt that, notwithstanding that governments still covered-up the development and research of mind control technologies, which could read human thoughts remotely and subvert an individual's sense of control over their own thinking, behavior, emotions or decision making by attacking the brain and nervous system with electromagnetic frequencies."

"Do we know what the current state of the science is? If this information is twenty years old, certainly someone is making progress towards turning smartphone technology into a weapon for influencing behavior," said Kristian.

"I am working on getting that answer. I think our best bet would be to approach the government regarding the work in this area. However, my personal contacts in the government are extremely limited. Do you suppose Ansley would be able to assist in getting to the people who may know where the government is currently with this?"

"I'm not sure Ansley could do much, but I will ask her. She is well established with the Director of DARPA, Jim Hanson. Jim would probably be the best source regarding DARPA projects. The problem I see is that the project we may be discussing is highly classified, top secret."

"What about your contacts in industry? Or should I say former contacts?"

"I am working towards resurrecting myself but that may take some time. I've got a meeting coming up with Ansley, Savannah, and my personal physicians to devise a plan that won't bring the medical community down on our heads demanding answers," said Kristian. "This must be done prior to me contacting any CEOs or politicians who may be able to help. What about the Chinese? Surely, if anyone is delving into mind control, it would be the Chinese, or maybe the Russians."

Chapter 47

Drs. Tyler and Aidan Sullivan arrived at Barnett Center a few minutes before their scheduled appointment with Ansley and Savannah. A young man dressed in a lab coat over a golf shirt, blue jeans and sneakers met their car in front of the steps to the Center and introduced himself as a bioscience technician on Dr. Barnett's staff. "Good morning, Doctors. If you will follow me, I will take you to Dr. Barnett's office."

Once inside the main entrance to the building, they stopped at a desk where their photographs were taken which would then be used by the facial recognition system in the building for security purposes. They then proceeded to a bank of elevators. Once inside an elevator the tech said, "Level Four." They exited the elevator on Level Four and were led to a conference room.

"Good morning, gentlemen. Thank you for meeting with us on short notice," said Ansley as the doctors entered the conference room. The room was furnished with a long oval glass table. The conference chairs were Ansley's favorite teal leather and polished aluminum.

"Good morning, Ansley, so good to see you again," said Tyler. "We are quite intrigued with the subject of today's meeting. Will we be able to see Kristian today?"

"Definitely," replied Ansley. "But we need to complete some paperwork to keep me out of jail before Kristian arrives." Ansley then handed Tyler and Aidan a non-disclosure agreement that stated that the meeting which was about to commence was considered

Top Secret. Should they disclose any information gained during the meeting to an unapproved source, they would be criminally prosecuted.

"Wow! This is pretty strong stuff," said Aidan. "We could actually go to jail for an innocent slip of the tongue?"

"I'm afraid so," said Ansley, as the two gentlemen returned the signed documents to her.

"Good morning, doctors," said Savannah as she entered the conference room. Great to see you both again. You don't seem to have aged a bit."

"And neither have you, Savannah," said Tyler, extending his hand to shake hers.

"Good morning, folks," said Kristian as he entered the conference room. Tyler's and Aidan's jaws dropped when they saw Kristian, in perfect health and looking like he was ten years younger than when they last saw him.

"My God," said Aidan. "How can this be? The last time we saw you, you were confined to a wheelchair with a terminal disease."

"Ansley, perhaps now would be a good time to bring Tyler and Aidan up to speed on what has been accomplished since they last saw me," said Kristian.

"Tyler, Aidan, what you see before you is perhaps the greatest medical miracle in human history. Using top-secret technologies developed by DARPA beginning in the mid-2020s, we have created a near-perfect vessel to house the human mind. Kristian is, for lack of a better term, a cyborg. His body is completely artificial and houses his mind, his thoughts, memories, emotions, and ideas in an electronic brain."

"Ansley, how…?" said Tyler, at a complete loss for words. "The how is top secret, but it originated with … foreign sources," said Ansley, knowing that the foreign sources were not from Planet Earth, a fact known only to a very few individuals within the federal government.

"Ladies and gentlemen, can we now get on with the purpose of this meeting? After my … transformation, I have been forced to live the life of a recluse, and frankly I'm growing tired of it. In addition, a threat to the future of humankind on this planet requires that I re-enter public life. The question is how I do this when the media made it clear that I was rapidly becoming a vegetable many years ago. Unfortunately, a cure for ALS has not yet been discovered despite Savannah's great work."

"What if we go aggressive with the idea that Savannah has indeed been making progress towards the cure for ALS?" said Aidan.

Tyler continued, "Or if we can get DARPA to play along with us, we can say that the experimental cure was developed under a top-secret government program. Further, that the program did not have FDA involvement or approval. For all they know, DARPA developed a machine that broke down Kristian into molecules and then reassembled him disease-free."

"Gentlemen, I do not believe DARPA will 'play along' in wild fantasies," said Ansley. "A question for the other three doctors in the room: would it be plausible to stretch the truth a bit and simply state that Barnett Center has been developing a possible cure for ALS, and that Kristian's current condition is the result of testing the cure? Barnett Center is known worldwide for its work in advanced neurological restoration."

Silence fell on the room as the attendees pondered Ansley's idea. After a few moments, Savannah said, "I suppose that would be possible. Testing a cure for a disease as complex as ALS requires years, which we could use to diffuse the onslaught of the medical community's inquiries. At the current point in our testing, we do not know if the cure is stable, or if it is permanent or merely temporary. As more testing is completed and the cure is found to be viable, we will present it for FDA approval for testing, which takes several more years before it can be approved for the public. In the meantime, Barnett Center has no obligation to reveal the science behind the cure."

"Sounds reasonable to me," said Kristian. "I suggest we don't go with a press release announcing my return to public life, though.

Just let me move about in the circles I need to quietly and remain out of the spotlight as long as possible."

"You have another problem, dear," said Ansley. "You have the looks of a thirty-year-old, but your biological age is forty-two. I think we need to age you a bit. After all, you've been through a harrowing experience and have been near death. A little gray hair around the temples and a few wrinkles would help the credibility of this story."

"Do I detect a bit of jealousy in that recommendation, Dear?" said Kristian, grinning.

"Careful, Dear, I can give you the face of an eighty-year-old," said Ansley, glaring at her husband.

Chapter 48

At approximately 5 AM, Erik completed the charging and backup cycle for his cyborg body using his portable charging and storage device. He disconnected the cable from the back of his neck and then lay on the bed for another thirty minutes. He then decided to get up and go outside and perhaps enjoy the sunrise. He dressed in a golf shirt and jeans, exited his room, and descended the steps carrying his shoes so as not to disturb the others who were still sleeping. He walked quietly down the hallway to the rear entrance that led to the gazebo and bent over to put on his shoes. He stepped outside and immediately felt the brisk spring morning air and saw the sun shining through the trees. He then saw a figure sitting at the gazebo. Walking closer, Erik saw that the figure was Carl Anderson.

"Good morning, Mr. Anderson," said Erik. "A beautiful morning, yes?"

"Good morning, Erik, indeed it is a beautiful morning," his voice carrying an element of sadness as he spoke. "Please, join me. The women will be up soon making breakfast."

"You asked me last night to give you more detail regarding the accident aboard my ship. Would now be a good time for you to hear this?" asked Erik.

"Yes, I would like that. I need to know what happened to Arya, aside from all of the press reports," said Carl. "One can rarely get accurate reporting from the press since they report to sell content and not necessarily to tell the facts."

"Arya and I were on the Mars team developing techniques for growing crops on Mars. She was on my ship for the five-month trip to Mars. The team had been on Mars about six months when Arya and I had developed … an attraction for each other. By the time we were nearing time to return to Earth we had grown quite close. During the return trip, we spent time together when we had breaks from our on-board duties."

Erik paused as he could feel his emotions begin to well up, although not yet noticeable to Carl. Fortunately, he had been practicing describing what had happened on the Elon Musk for his upcoming Board of Inquiry. "We were entering Earth's orbit on our way to Space Dock when Dock Control issued a warning for debris in the area. Space Dock also vectored us in, programmed the path, for us to reach Space Dock. Once the vector is established, control of the ship is automatically given to Space Dock. It is essentially like a harbor pilot coming aboard a ship to guide the ship to port. But, of course, it is all automated on a spaceship. The captain does have the ability to override Space Dock control in the event of an emergency or unforeseen navigational correction."

Erik continued, "After control of the Musk was taken over by Space Dock, we on the bridge of the ship heard a noise, a bang, that seemed to come from the lower decks. Alarms indicating a hull breach began clanging immediately and the ship yawed about fifteen degrees to port. We, my XO, Jim Spaulding, and I scanned the cameras in the sections below and saw that the passenger cabin was venting air rapidly. It appeared on the video screen that the passengers were unconscious from low oxygen. I then ordered Jim to take the con, unstrapped from my seat and proceeded down the ladder to Deck Two where the passenger cabin is located. Reaching the bottom of the ladder I saw that the bulkhead hatch had closed on the passenger cabin, further indicating that a hull breach had occurred. I punched in the captain's override code on the hatch and was able to pull it open with great difficulty as the atmosphere above the hatch rushed into the cabin. I bent down to look into the cabin and as I did, the hull breach opened further. This had the effect of causing a catastrophic decompression of the cabin and forcing the hatch door down on my back so hard it knocked me out immediately. The next thing I remembered was several weeks later when I was awakened from the coma I had been kept in while my body tried to survive serious injuries."

"What I was told later was that all four crew members in the passenger cabin died as a result of the accident. That, except for Arya, they probably died from asphyxiation. I was then told by my XO that Arya had been returning to the passenger cabin from the head, the bathroom, when the breach expanded after the initial contact of debris with the ship. She was not strapped in and was sucked out into space."

"Did Arya suffer, feel pain, when she went out into space?" asked Carl.

"During astronaut training for emergencies in space, we are told to exhale immediately if we are exposed unprotected to a zero-atmosphere condition. The reason for this is if you inhale and hold your breath the air in your lungs will expand and rupture. Arya's autopsy did not reveal that her lungs were ruptured so she followed her training. We may have been able to revive her had we gotten to her in less than two minutes. Unfortunately, that was not possible. In any event, Arya likely would have passed out within fifteen seconds after exposure. After that she would not have felt anything."

"How long did it take to recover Arya's body from space?" asked Carl.

"I was told that it took about three days. In the deep cold of space, the body does not deteriorate like it does here on Earth," said Erik.

"How is it that you were able to survive the decompression? Why were you not also sucked out into space?"

"Two reasons. First, I was trapped between the hatch and the entrance to the passenger cabin. Second, my XO, Jim, assigned control of the ship to one of our pilots almost immediately and got to the ship's engineering department where he activated the force field on the lower deck, sealing the breach. Then he came to me and was able to lift the hatch off me and move me to the ship's sick bay. Jim saved my life that day."

By now, Carl could hear the emotion in Erik's voice as he recounted the details of that terrible accident. Both men wiped at their eyes as they sat in silence for a few moments.

"Why could the force field not be activated automatically in the event of a breach?" asked Carl.

"As you might imagine, the force field exerts a very strong electrical field. Activating it in the presence of people could kill them. Activating it is considered only when the survival of the ship is at stake. Looking at the passengers still strapped into their seats after the catastrophic decompression confirmed that they were dead, so Jim made the decision to activate the force field."

"Hey, you two, would you like some coffee?" yelled Ksenia, standing at the back entrance to the house. "Shall I bring it to you?"

Erik stood and said, "Coffee would be great. I'll come get it.

Mr. Anderson, how do you take your coffee?"

"Black with a little sugar," said Carl.

Chapter 49

A couple of days later, Erik and Ksenia were walking about the estate in the middle of the afternoon. The May weather in Norway that year was quite beautiful. The temperature was in the low sixties and the sky was partly cloudy with a light breeze from the west. Erik hadn't made much progress reaching out to Thor. Thor had calmed down and was not as volatile as he had been, but he was visibly angry whenever Erik was nearby.

"Ksenia, perhaps it would be best if I leave," said Erik. "I don't know if Thor will be able to get over his anger towards me while I am here."

"Erik, no," said Ksenia. "Thor is not the only member of this family. Father seems to have lost any animosity he may have had. I think he's actually enjoying your company at the gazebo early in the morning. His mood has elevated since you arrived. You two seem to be hitting it off quite well given the circumstances. And I believe Mother thinks the world of you. Were she young and single, I believe she would be trying to woo you."

"Woo me?" Eric laughed. "I guess I could continue to try to talk to Thor if I could just get him to sit down and listen. I mean, I almost lost my life trying to save Arya and the others. I would hope that would count for something with him."

As they continued their walk, Erik reached down and touched, then took Ksenia's hand. Ksenia responded by holding his hand. Still on the estate, they came upon the shore of a lake. The water reflected the sunlight as it rippled from the breeze. Erik and Ksenia turned to face each other. "Ksenia, I must admit that I can feel myself growing closer to you. Ever since I first saw you in the Bergen airport, I could sense someone or something within me whispering 'she is beautiful, go with her'."

Ksenia blushed a little and smiled, looking straight into Erik's azure-blue eyes, "I think I am growing closer to you, Erik. I have so admired how respectful you have been to my parents and your efforts to engage Thor. And I ..."

Erik bent slightly and slowly moved towards Ksenia until their lips met. They continued to embrace, gently at first, and then with more passion. They then heard a branch break and the rustling of leaves. Turning, they expected to see a deer or fox but instead saw Thor's back walking rapidly through the woods away from them.

"Oh, that can't be good," said Erik.

"Do you suppose he saw us?" said Ksenia.

"I'm sure he saw us. I know he will be more furious than ever with me now. He'll probably go straight to your parents and berate them all over again for allowing me to stay."

"If he does that it may just backfire on him. But perhaps we should try to catch up with him before he does get to them and twists what he saw into something ... bad."

"Perhaps it would be better for us to just go to straight to your parents and explain that we have ... feelings for each other," said Erik. "We may be able to diffuse whatever story he concocts to turn them against me."

"I think you may be right. If we try to chase him down now while he's enraged, he may just try to turn violent with you. My parents should be out at the gazebo soon. Come, I know a shortcut back to the house that may get us there before Thor."

Ebba and Carl sat down at the table in the gazebo as the late afternoon sun, still high in the sky, shown through the trees.

"So, what do you think of Erik?" asked Ebba?

"I think he is a fine young man, dedicated to his work. He would have made a fine husband for Arya," said Carl. "Erik explained how the accident aboard his spaceship happened and what he did to try to save Arya and his crew. Had she or any of the others survived, Erik would be getting a medal instead of a Board of Inquiry."

"I agree," said Ebba. "He certainly is a fine-looking young man."

"Mother, Father," shouted Ksenia from about thirty meters away from the gazebo. "We, Erik and I need to talk with you." They continued approaching the gazebo, holding hands, just as Thor opened the back door of the main house.

"Sit," said Carl. "What can we do for you?" Thor stopped and held the door open and glared at the four at the gazebo.

"Erik and I are … developing feelings for each other…beyond just friendship. We wanted to tell you …"

"I'm not at all surprised," smiled Ebba. "I could see that soon after he arrived."

"We will support you in whatever way you wish, daughter," said Carl.

They then heard the rear door of the house slam shut as Thor reentered the house.

"I think it is time we, Ebba and I, had a talk with Thor.

Especially with this … new development," said Carl. "Would you like us, Erik and I, to join you?" said Ksenia. "Let us approach him first," said Carl. "Ebba, shall we?"

Ebba and Carl climbed the steps to Thor's second story room and knocked.

"Yes?" said Thor.

"Thor, we need to talk," said Carl. "May we enter?" "Talk about what?" demanded Thor.

"Our family. May we come in?"

The door opened and Thor stood in the doorway briefly, then backed up a couple of steps to allow his parents to enter his room. All three sat, Ebba and Carl on a duvet across from Thor's bed, and Thor on his bed.

"We understand how upset you are due to Arya's death, Thor. We were all completely devastated by our loss," said Ebba. "It has been over a year since the accident, and it is time we all got on with our lives. Arya would have wanted that for us."

"I'm getting on with my life just fine," said Thor. His voice rising, "But I want justice for Arya's death. Her murderer is living in my house, your house, our home! How am I supposed to accept that? How am I supposed to tolerate my sister embracing, kissing the very devil that killed our beloved Arya?"

"Thor, there was no murder. The tragedy on the spaceship was an accident. Erik and Arya had feelings for each other, and Erik was also devasted by her death. Erik told me all the details of the accident. He was severely injured trying to rescue her and the others. It is amazing that he has returned to good health and his career. And he still faces a Board of Inquiry from the U.S. Navy regarding the accident."

"Thor, carrying these feelings of resentment, hatred even, in your heart cannot be good for your health," said Ebba. "Erik has offered to sit with you and share the true events of the accident, which were not reflected truthfully in the media. Why don't you at least give him that courtesy, especially since you saw that Erik and Ksenia have developed a romantic relationship. Don't make Ksenia choose between you and Erik."

"You both know that I have tremendous respect for you and that I love my only living sister dearly," said Thor. "For that reason, I will honor your request and sit with Erik. But I cannot guarantee that my feelings towards him will change."

"All we ask is that you try. When would you like to sit with him? We will inform him of your preference," said Carl.

Erik and Ksenia were still sitting in the gazebo when Carl exited the rear door of the main house and began walking towards them. It had been about thirty minutes since Carl and Ebba went inside to talk to Thor.

"Erik, Thor has agreed to meet you here on the gazebo at 5:30 AM, tomorrow. We asked him to give you a chance to explain to him what actually happened on your spaceship. Tell him what you told me. I think he will listen, but I cannot guarantee it will change his feelings."

"Thank you, Mr. Anderson," said Erik. I will do my best to help him see the truth regarding what happened."

"Shall I come too?" asked Ksenia.

"No, I think it will be best if it is only he and I," said Erik. Carl nodded in agreement as he turned to return to the house.

Erik rose from his bed at 5 AM and stowed his backup and charging device in the bedroom closet. He didn't want to have to explain to anyone what the device was, but if necessary, he would say it was needed for his ongoing rehabilitation from the accident. He dressed and went downstairs, carrying his shoes to avoid unnecessary noise. Once at the rear entry of the house, he donned his shoes and opened the door. He could see Thor standing in the gazebo some thirty meters away and walked towards him.

As he got close to the gazebo, he raised his right hand and said, "Good morning, Thor. Thank you for agreeing to talk this morning." "Father and Mother asked that I allow you to explain the events on your spaceship that led to Arya's death. Father has given you his endorsement for your actions. I cannot until you convince me, until you change my mind that you are guilty of negligence in Arya's death. From everything I've read, negligence was the cause."

"Can we sit?" asked Erik. As they both sat at the table, Erik said, "I know what was reported in much of the media, but I can assure you that what was reported was not entirely accurate." Erik went on to explain the events of the accident that occurred aboard the USS Elon Musk just as he had a few days earlier with Carl. He displayed his emotions which were reflective of his feelings for Arya carefully, but he didn't hide them either.

Thor sat silently for the twenty minutes while Erik spoke. When Erik finished, Thor remained silent for what seemed like minutes but was actually only several seconds.

"So, the ship was not under your direct control when the debris struck?" said Thor.

"Technically, responsibility for the ship is always that of its captain. However, as with a harbor pilot aboard a sea vessel, Space Dock Control is in direct navigational control of the ship during approach and docking. The ship's captain can take command back from Space Dock in an emergency. But the ship was damaged before I could reassume direct control."

"If what you say is true, why is your navy conducting a formal Board of Inquiry?" asked Thor.

"Any time a serious incident occurs aboard a naval vessel, especially an incident where lives are lost, a Naval Board of Inquiry will conduct an investigation to determine if any policies or procedures were violated. If criminal activities are suspected, the Naval Criminal Investigative Service, NCIS, also investigates. As far as I know, NCIS is not involved here."

"What would happen should the board of inquiry determine that you were responsible for the deaths of the crew?" said Thor. "Should the Board of Inquiry deem that I should be charged with a violation, they can recommend a full court martial. I would be tried as a defendant and judged by a panel of naval officers appointed by the court. If the Board of Inquiry determines that regulations were followed, they can still make recommendations regarding my career. It is rare that a ship's captain is not … punished in some way for an incident."

"Your naval career, your career in space, then is dependent upon the recommendations of your board of inquiry?"

"Very much so, I'm afraid," said Erik.

"Why are you afraid, if you know you did everything you just described?" asked Thor.

"Naval tradition deals harshly with a ship's captain who has brought down negative attention on the service, even if he or she followed all the rules and regulations. This is especially true when a highly visible, and political arm of the service is involved. There is constant pressure from Congress to abandon the space program."

"What are your feelings towards Ksenia?" asked Thor, changing the subject.

"I know you saw us embracing in the woods yesterday. To be

honest, I am very fond of her, and I believe she is of me. I hope you will be able to accept our relationship, Thor."

Thor stood. His six-foot three-inch frame, lean and muscular from years of farm work would have intimidated most men. Erik stood as well and looked up at Thor from his five-foot-nine-inch frame. The two men stood inches apart, looking each other eye-to-eye for several seconds, when Thor extended his hand to Erik in friendship. "I hope we get to know each other better," said Erik. Thor seemed to flash the briefest of smiles, said nothing, and turned to walk back to the house. Erik waited a few moments and then saw Ksenia come bouncing out of the house coming quickly towards him.

"How did it go?" she gushed. "Did he listen to you? Is he still angry?"

"We shook hands at the end."

Chapter 50

Kristian Barnett exited the transporter in the basement level of Barnett Center and took the nearby elevator to Aaron Adam's office on the third floor. As he walked out of the elevator a long- time assistant to Dr. Savannah Richards did a double-take when she saw him. Her jaw dropped and she stared at him as he walked past her, not noticing the attention she was giving him. "Was that Kristian Barnett?" she thought. The last time she had seen him he had been confined to a motorized wheelchair, barely able to speak using a special implant on his vocal cords. She stepped into the elevator and said "Level Four" to go directly to Dr. Richards' office to inquire about Mr. Barnett.

"Good afternoon, Aaron, how are things going with you?" said Kristian.

"Hi Kristian, I am trying to organize the research I've done on the mind control technologies and sort out those that may be viable and discard those that have been disproven. One thing I believe we should investigate further is what is going on regarding these technologies in our federal government. If China and Russia have funded secret research, then the U.S. must be actively funding it as well."

"I tend to agree with you, Aaron. I am putting together a list of people I know that are still in Congress or federal agencies that I will be contacting. I will need you to put together a brief of the technologies and which countries are involved or suspected to be involved with each. If my contacts do not know about any programs being developed, perhaps I can persuade them to start asking some questions."

"What about DARPA?" asked Aaron, knowing Ansley's involvement. "It would seem that if any agency is involved in this technology, it would be the one developing advanced systems for the military."

"I've been thinking of DARPA for a while," said Kristian. "I will discuss it with Ansley to see if perhaps she and I could meet with Jim Hanson. At least Jim knows the truth behind my recovery from ALS so it wouldn't be a shock for him to see me in person."

Later that evening over dinner on the mansion pool deck with Ansley, Kristian raised the possibility of approaching DARPA regarding mind control technologies. "Ansley, Aaron has been investigating the state of mind control using various technologies. We are certain that both China and Russia have active research and development in this area. One important question that remains unanswered is what the United States is doing with mind control. Do you suppose DARPA has a program?"

"I wouldn't be surprised if we have a program developing a means to control human thought and action, especially if our enemies are exploring this science," said Ansley. "But I wouldn't know how you would find out for sure. DARPA research and development is compartmentalized by its projects. My department is the Biological Technologies and Robotics Office. Those outside of the projects essentially know nothing of their existence. Consider my specific project area, no one outside of it even knows it exists. The consequences of leaks to the wrong sources, the press, or our enemies, could be catastrophic. I suspect that you need to contact the Defense Sciences Office."

"I understand. But isn't there at least one person in the chain of command that has knowledge of all the projects? I'm thinking specifically of Jim Hanson. As director, should he not have knowledge of all of the active projects going on at DARPA?"

"Oh, I'm sure he does. But if he were to reveal any of the projects to unauthorized sources, he would lose his job or worse, go to prison. Even if he revealed information to me about another project, he would be breaching protocol."

"Then who can authorize Hanson to speak to me, to us?" "Well, I suppose the President could authorize it," said Ansley, smiling.

"What about a senator or representative?"

"Perhaps, if the congressman were on a committee providing pertinent oversight for DARPA. In fact, an inquiry from a congressman with proper security clearance would be the way to get Jim's and/or the director of Defense Sciences cooperation, rather than trying to do it directly."

"DARPA is under the Department of Defense so I will need to contact a member of an Armed Services Committee whom we can trust with our concerns. I'll do some checking to see if either of our senators or our representative is on one of those committees," said Kristian.

The next day, Kristian found that Senator Bradley Richards of California, whom he knew and supported personally, and through the Barnett Corporation since his affliction with ALS, was still a member of the Senate Armed Services Committee. In fact, Senator Richards was the ranking member on the committee. Another point of interest is that Senator Richards is Savannah and Erik Richards' uncle. Although a member of the liberal party, Senator Richards, a retired captain from the United States Navy, was focused more on military accountability than on the headline politics of the day.

"KB," said Kristian to his digital assistant. "Please contact Senator Bradley Richards' office and arrange a time when the two of us can speak. Better to have this first conversation remotely, so meeting face-to-face with the senator is not necessary. The conversation will be an informal catch-up on issues," said Kristian.

"Yes, sir, Mr. Barnett. I will advise when I have a time set up with the senator."

"Good. If necessary, you can move items on my calendar to accommodate the senator's schedule. Also include Aaron Adams on the appointment. Now, take a message to be sent to Aaron Adams. "Aaron, we may have a breakthrough in gaining knowledge regarding what DARPA is doing with mind control. More later, but in the meantime, be looking for an appointment from KB. Kristian.""

Chapter 51

Erik remained a guest of the Andersons at their estate near Flåm, Norway for another week when he received a confidential text message dated May 16, 2042, 0900 hours from his commanding officer, Captain Jeffrey Barnes. "Commander Richards, sorry to cut short your shore leave, but the Board of Inquiry has reached its conclusion in your case. You are to report to the Washington Navy Yard at 1000 hours on Thursday, May 22nd. Please acknowledge receipt of this message." Erik pressed the "ACK" button on the screen at the bottom of the message which immediately transmitted his acknowledgement while thinking, "damn, that only gives me a few more days with Ksenia."

After informing Ksenia of his new orders, she responded by saying, "Why don't I come with you? I still have over another month off on my schedule rotation."

Hesitating because he was a bit surprised at her response, he said, "I … think it would be best if I went back first, received the results from the inquiry, and received my new orders before you join me. Who knows, they could order me to Space Dock for a thirteen-month rotation."

"I suppose you're right, Erik," said Ksenia, saddened as the thought of Erik leaving indefinitely struck her. "Let's make the most of our last few days together. I suppose you will be leaving Monday or Tuesday to return to the United States."

"Yes, I will need to arrange and book my flight itinerary. Will you be able to take me back to Bergen?"

"Of course, I want to be with you as much as possible before you leave. We can stay a night or two at my apartment."

Erik booked an itinerary that departed Bergen at noon on Tuesday, May 20th. Ksenia informed her parents of their plans to depart the Anderson home on Sunday, May 18th. As they were packing their car Sunday morning, Thor appeared at the front door of the house. "So, you are leaving us," he said to both.

"Yes, Erik has orders to return to the United States," said Ksenia.

"Those orders were unexpected?" asked Thor.

"Yes, The Board of Inquiry has reached its conclusion in my case and will issue their findings on Thursday," said Erik.

Thor descended the steps and walked to the car and said, "I hope all goes well for you, Erik. I hope you receive a fair verdict." Thor extended his hand to shake Erik's.

Taking Thor's hand, Erik said, "Thank you, Thor. It has been a pleasure getting to know you."

"Likewise," said Thor, finally smiling genuinely. "Ksenia, will you be returning home after Erik's departure?"

"Not immediately, but perhaps in a few days," she replied, still hoping she would get to join Erik in the States.

Just then, Ksenia's parents, Carl and Ebba, appeared at the front door and descended the steps to the driveway. "Erik, it has been a pleasure getting to know you. Thank you so much for coming all this way," said Ebba.

"Mr. and Mrs. Anderson, the pleasure has been all mine. You have a beautiful home, ... and a beautiful daughter," he said smiling at Ksenia. "I truly enjoyed my stay here and have appreciated your hospitality. I hope I will see you again soon."

Erik and Ksenia arrived back in Bergen at approximately 1 PM Sunday, turned in the rental car and grabbed an Uber to Ksenia's apartment. The excellent weather that they had enjoyed since Erik arrived in Bergen continued as it was sixty-two degrees Fahrenheit with a light breeze out of the west. While they were driving, Erik wondered how he would be able to attach his portable charger and backup device in the tight space of Ksenia's one-bedroom flat. He knew he was able to go several days without recharging but wasn't comfortable getting on a long flight not having recharged since Saturday night. He may have to get creative to come up with a believable story why he must attach the device as he thought it much too soon to reveal his …'condition' to her. Later Sunday evening, after dining at a waterfront restaurant, they walked back to Ksenia's apartment. Although after 8PM, it was still quite bright but getting cooler. Walking together, talking and laughing about their stay at the Anderson home, laughing at the way Thor had come around to Erik, Erik stopped and said, "Ksenia, I hope you know that I am falling in love with you. I've never felt the way I do, even for Arya, as I feel for you. Arya and I were growing closer but not … like this."

Ksenia, blushing, said, "Erik, I too have never felt this way for another." She then put her arms around his neck and kissed him. They embraced until they realized passersby were beginning to stare, then continued walking.

They reached Ksenia's apartment, stepped inside and closed the door, and immediately embraced again. Erik had no idea how his cyborg body would react but that did not stop him from the foreplay that would ultimately lead to making love to Ksenia for the first time. While at the Anderson's home, Erik and Ksenia agreed to not attempt to go beyond minor displays of affection out of respect for Carl, Ebba, and Thor. But the result of that restraint was a building desire to ravish the other as soon as they could. In just a few moments they were both naked and had lay down on Ksenia's bed. At first Ksenia climbed on top of Erik, kissing him from the lips to his neck to his chest and his navel as he caressed her back and thighs. At that point Erik, his cyborg body still tuned for combat, flipped Ksenia over on her back like she was a twig. She was startled enough to let out a small cry. Erik said, "Are…are you all right?"

She replied, "Oh yes, I didn't expect you to be so strong." "Excitement of the moment," he said as he kissed her, first on the lips and then slowly moved down her neck to her breasts and nipples, then down her belly to the light brown patch of hair. They grew more and more excited until he entered her and began carefully thrusting so as not to exert his full cyborg strength on her. After several more minutes, they climaxed together, her moaning and him uttering what sounded like a guttural animal groan. Afterward, he fell off her onto his back. She simply lay there, breathing hard, unable to move. Eventually, she fell into a deep sleep. "Now," he thought, "would be the time to connect his charging and back-up device."

After he was fully recharged, he disconnected the device and stowed it in its briefcase. Thankfully, she was still sound asleep. But soon she began to stir, and he took her in his arms. Soon, he felt himself getting aroused again and they performed another round of lovemaking that was every bit as sexual as the first.

Erik and Ksenia spent Monday sightseeing in Bergen. They started the day with a late breakfast followed by visiting a tiny museum room in Old Bryggen which had housed a resistance unit in World War II. A gentleman with a strong accent gave a history of the museum, so it was difficult for Erik to understand him. He talked for about thirty minutes straight and it was a struggle to pay attention, even though what he said was very interesting. Next, they spent several hours at the KODE Art Museums of Bergen where masterpieces by Edvard Munch, Nikolai Astrup, Pablo Picasso, Paul Klee, J. C. Dahl and "the Silver Treasure" can be viewed. In Building 2 they viewed the Edvard Munch exhibition, a large, well-curated collection from all facets of his oeuvre, including lithographs, portraits, impressionism, and expressionism. In Building 4 they dined at Lysverket, a restaurant specializing in seafood. Their last stop before returning to Ksenia's apartment was the Magic Ice Bar. For an entrance fee of forty-four U.S. dollars each got a free wine with a cloudberry. There were many fascinating ice sculptures to admire, and the bar, chairs, and tables were carved of ice.

Shortly after returning home, Erik stripped down to his T-shirt and shorts. Ksenia emerged from the bathroom wearing a semi-shear, short shift. It wasn't long before they engaged in passionate love making, she falling asleep afterward and he recharging while she slept. As the early morning light filtered through the curtains, they made love one more time before it was time for him to dress and prepare to leave for the airport.

They said their goodbyes at the airport before the entrance to Passport Control, pledging their love for each other and embracing passionately. He then turned and walked towards the departure gates. She watched until he was out of sight.

Chapter 52

Erik Richards' flight, a Boeing 797 SST from Bergen to Washington - Dulles Airport took just under four hours. Due to the six-hour time change between Bergen and Washington, D.C. he arrived two hours before he departed. Erik deplaned and completed the mandatory stop at the Global Entry immigration kiosk where his passport and fingerprints were scanned to confirm his identity, and then proceeded to baggage claim. One thing the airlines had not improved much was the time it took to retrieve one's bag. Erik waited twenty-five minutes for his luggage to arrive on the inbound baggage carousel. While waiting, he told his smartphone digital assistant to call a driverless Uber to take him to his Arlington, Virginia apartment.

Erik's Board of Inquiry hearing had been on his mind since he boarded the plane in Bergen. His first concern was that he would never again be given the command of a spaceship. If his space career was over, could he stand sitting at a desk in the Pentagon until he qualified for retirement. Then his thoughts got more positive as he thought that the government had just spent more than one hundred million dollars giving him his cyborg body. Would they really throw that away putting him in a desk job?

Erik arrived at his apartment at 4:30 PM Eastern Time and immediately texted Ksenia to let her know he had arrived in D.C. "Arrived in D.C. Missing you. Worried about hearing tomorrow," said the text.

In a few minutes he received a response. "Miss u 2. You will do fine at the hearing. Get some rest tonight so you are fresh in the morning."

Erik replied, "Yes, planning on an early evening. The Nationals game tonight is at 7, so should be over by 10."

The Nationals beat the Atlanta Braves by a score of 7-2 and the game ended at 10:20 PM. Erik did not bother eating. The cyborg eats for pleasure or to socialize, not nourishment, and he was in no mood for pleasure or socializing. He connected the backup and charging cable to the port just below the base of his neck by lifting the flap of artificial skin and lay down. Closing his eyes, he was able to shut off his thoughts regarding the hearing, Ksenia, his future, and everything else after about twenty minutes. While not sleeping like a human, his mind could enter a state of rest.

After an indeterminable amount of time, he began to detect a mist forming across the room. Then, he could see two figures in the mist that was beginning to clear. The first was the being that called himself The Guardian. The second surprised him even more. It was Kristian Barnett.

"Greetings, Erik," said The Guardian. "Remember when I told you that I would return with an assignment for you? Well, that is why I, or we, glancing at Kristian, are here. There is a timeline in jeopardy that, should it go astray from its predestined course, could result in the likely destruction of humanity as well as a large percentage of the animal kingdom. The best-case is that humanity is thrown back into a dark age after millions perish from the Earth. I will need both you and Kristian to correct this deviation and ensure the timeline is restored to its rightful path." "Oh-OK," said Erik. "How will … we set the timeline back on its correct path?"

"Recall the abilities you have with your mind existing between the earthly realm and the next level, often referred to as the afterlife or heaven? I will guide you to the proper time and place where you will begin by observing the negotiations of the two world leaders threatening armed escalation. At a specific point in the escalation, you will, if necessary, use your powers to enter the mind of one of the key participants and steer him towards a peaceful outcome. Kristian will be prepared to influence another key official."

"So, where and when will this occur?"

"The events I am referring to are the Cuban Missile Crisis that occurred in October of 1962."

"I recall studying that at the Academy. It was probably the closest we have ever come to annihilation. Fortunately, Kennedy and Khrushchev came to their senses and negotiated a peaceful outcome."

"Yes, a peaceful outcome was achieved, but not without our … involvement," said The Guardian. Erik then began to view visions of what could have happened. He saw rockets launching that had both the U.S. flag and the Soviet Red Star emblazoned on their fuselages. He saw images of Washington, New York, Norfolk, Jacksonville, Miami and Tampa – all key military installations on the East Coast - crumble in the nuclear fire. He saw people running in the streets literally wiped off the face of the Earth as the incredible force generated by the bombs devastated the cities. He saw people by the thousands dying in hospitals, burned by radiation and facing certain death. Not only both the United States and Russia were destroyed, but the huge amount of radiation generated from the nuclear bombs wiped out eighty percent of the population of the planet. 2.5 billion lives were lost. An equal percentage of animal and plant life was destroyed. The nuclear winter following the devastation plunged Earth into an ice age not seen for ten thousand years. Humans that survived the holocaust were seen living as their ancestors did eons ago, as hunter-gatherers living in caves. Most technology advancements developed in the past two-thousand years no longer existed.

"OK, I get it," said Erik. "I've seen films of the devastation our bombs caused in Hiroshima and Nagasaki. We must do all we can to avoid another nuclear catastrophe. How do we proceed?" "Both of you grab hold of my sleeve," said The Guardian, extending both of his arms to Erik and Kristian. In an instant, they found themselves standing, undetectable in spirit form, in the White House Oval Office on the morning of October 16, 1962 shortly after 9

AM. Present were President John F. Kennedy, McGeorge Bundy – National Security Advisor, and Kenneth O'Donnell, Presidential Advisor.

"Mr. President," said Bundy, "here are the photos from U2 reconnaissance of the suspicious activities in Cuba. It is clear that medium-range nuclear missiles are being deployed."

Erik and Kristian, with The Guardian, then found themselves in the White House Cabinet room at approximately noon the same day. Present were President Kennedy, Attorney General Robert Kennedy, Secretary of State Dean Rusk, Secretary of Defense Robert McNamara, McGeorge Bundy, General Maxwell Taylor, Chairman of the Joint Chiefs of Staff, Vice President Lyndon Johnson, Adlai Stevenson, Ambassador to the United Nations, Kenneth O'Donnell, and several other high-ranking officials. Representatives of the Central Intelligence Agency then gave a briefing on the situation in Cuba and the threat of nuclear missiles being deployed ninety miles off the U.S. coast. The missiles had the potential to erase eighty million American lives in a timespan of only five minutes. General Taylor stated that placing the missiles indicated a change in Soviet doctoral thinking to a first-strike policy.

"This is completely unacceptable. We must see that the missiles are removed," said the President. Immediately after the meeting, the President confided in Robert Kennedy and O'Donnell that he saw no other option than a military strike on Cuba. "Bobby, I need you to get a consensus from those in the room regarding our plan of action."

"I can do that, Jack," said Bobby. "I will formalize the group naming them the Executive Committee of the National Security Council, EXCOMM."

"So how do we intervene in these decisions?" asked Kristian. "The opportunities will be revealed soon," replied The Guardian.

That same evening at approximately 9 PM the EXCOMM group returned to the White House cabinet room. Kristian, Erik and The Guardian were present. General Taylor spoke for the group and recommended not only a strike against the Cuban missile sites, but a full-scale invasion of Cuba. Dean Acheson, Secretary of State under President Harry Truman, supported the Joint Chiefs recommendation and provided further details including a likely scenario of Soviet response to the invasion.

Erik, Kristian, and The Guardian then followed the President, Robert Kennedy, and O'Donnell to the Oval Office where JFK expressed his doubts regarding the option to invade Cuba. "If we invade, we know what the response will be from the Soviet Union. Nuclear war, which is not acceptable. Bobby, get the group back together and continue to explore other options."

Chapter 53

On Saturday, October 22, 1962, while visiting Mayor Richard Daley in Chicago, JFK received word that EXCOMM had indeed arrived at a consensus for responding to the Soviet threat and that he needed to return to Washington as soon as possible. In a meeting at the White House between JFK, RFK and EXCOMM, the consensus recommendation was to establish a blockade, technically a quarantine, preventing ships carrying arms from arriving at Cuba. A blockade is considered an act of war whereas the term quarantine avoids that connotation.

Robert McNamara went on to explain that there are between twenty and thirty Soviet ships steaming for Cuba. The U.S. Navy, positioned eight-hundred miles off Cuba, will intercept the ships and inspect them for weapons. If weapons are found, the ship will be turned back. Further, this will provide the Soviets with an opportunity to remove the missiles already in Cuba. If they refuse, the U.S. will retain the option for a military strike.

However, there was still contention in the EXCOMM group regarding the best response. RFK was still adamantly opposed to a surprise attack on the island. He stressed that a surprise attack will provoke the Russians into launching the missiles, starting a nuclear holocaust. John McCone, Director of the CIA, stated that there are those in the group who prefer a military strike. The Russians may decide that they should use the missiles before they lose most of them in an attack from the U.S. Adlai Stevenson then raised the option of a negotiated settlement where the Russians withdraw the missiles from Cuba in exchange for the US withdrawing missiles from Turkey and closing Guantanamo Naval Base. JFK dismissed Stevenson's suggestion and stated that he had not reached a decision regarding the action the U.S. will take. He stated that he will address the nation on Monday, October 22nd and instructed Pierre Salinger to prepare speeches for both the quarantine and a military strike.

Congressional leaders were called to the White House on Monday, October 22nd at 5:30 PM to brief them in advance on the President's 7 PM speech to the nation. Present were President Kennedy, Vice President Lyndon Johnson, J. William Fulbright, the chairman of the Senate Foreign Relations Committee. Also, in attendance were Representative Carl Vinson, Senator Minority Leader Everett Dirksen, Senator Richard Russell, Chairman of the Armed Services Committee, Senate Majority Leader Mike Mansfield, and House Minority Leader Representative Charlie Halleck. Senators Fulbright and Russell argued emphatically in favor of an invasion of Cuba rather than the quarantine of Cuba. However, Congressional negative opinions did not alter JFK's intent to announce the quarantine as the first-step response to the Soviet incursion.

At 7 PM Eastern Time, The Guardian together with Kristian and Erik watched JFK give his speech announcing the quarantine prohibiting ships carrying weapons to Cuba would begin at 7AM the next day.

Early Tuesday, October 23rd in a meeting of EXCOMM with the President and Robert Kennedy, the group was briefed on the situation by Admiral George Whelan Anderson. Twenty- six Russian ships were steaming towards Cuba. American Navy warships were positioned to intercept the Russian ships and inspect their cargo. Should a ship refuse to stop for inspection, the Navy was prepared to take steps, escalating to firing upon and disabling the Russian ship if necessary. This appears to raise the eyebrows of JFK and he stressed there will be no firing on Russian ships without his expressed approval. General Taylor then stated that low-level surveillance flights will commence immediately to capture the latest and improved photographs of the missile installations. JFK stared at Taylor, then ended the meeting by silently leaving the cabinet room.

Following the meeting, JFK and Kenneth O'Donnell discussed what was just said by General Taylor. "Do you see what they are trying to do, Jack?" said O'Donnell. "They are trying to bypass your orders and set up for an attack. You know damn well the Cubans will fire on our reconnaissance aircraft flying at low level and very vulnerable to attack. They will not know if our planes are carrying bombs or cameras. The Joint Chiefs will use any attack on our planes as their excuse for ordering retaliatory air strikes. They want a war, Jack, and they're arranging things to get one!"

"Yes, Kenny, I can see that very plainly. But I will protect our pilots! Tomorrow morning, I am taking command of the quarantine operation from the Situation Room. McNamara will be over at the Pentagon."

A few minutes later, O'Donnell was on the phone with Commander William Ecker, commanding officer of Photo Reconnaissance Squadron 62 (VFP-62), located at Key West Naval Air Station, while Erik, Kristian and The Guardian watched and listened. Commander Ecker will lead the photo reconnaissance mission over Cuban missile sites. "Good morning, Commander. I am Kenneth O'Donnell, special assistant to the President. I am relaying an order directly from the President to you that you are not to get shot down this morning."

After hearing the order and a brief hesitation Commander Ecker responded, "we will do our best, sir."

"I don't believe you understand, Commander. The President has ordered you not to get shot down. A mechanical problem or crashing into a mountain is OK. But you are not to get shot down."

"What the hell is this about, Mr. O'Donnell?"

"Commander, listen up because this is critical. If you or your men get shot down today, the President will try to protect you. And he doesn't want to do that. You see, if he does try to protect you it could involve using the Bomb. Do you understand me?"

"We will do our best, sir," replied Ecker.

"We know you will, Commander," said O'Donnell, and hangs up the phone.

"Erik, take my hand," said The Guardian. In the next moment Erik and The Guardian were standing in the ready room of NAS Key West. Commander Ecker was briefing his wingman Lieutenant Bruce Wilhelmy on their reconnaissance mission.

"Erik, since you are a fighter pilot you will be perfect for this assignment. You will fly with Commander Ecker this morning on the reconnaissance mission. You will experience what he experiences so that we can be assured that events happen to avoid a deviation in the timeline."

Erik climbed aboard the jeep to ride out to the flight line with Ecker and Wilhelmy. He noticed the aircraft are RF-8A Crusaders and thought flying in one of these antique fighters will be fun. He then noticed that the RF-8A is a single seat aircraft and wondered how he is supposed to ride along. Then he recalled that he is essentially a ghost that will not take up any space on the aircraft. He will essentially sit, in spirit form, with Ecker in the cockpit of the RF-8A Crusader.

Commander Ecker gave the signal to start his engine and he and Wilhelmy taxied out to the runway. Cleared for takeoff, they blasted down the runway and climbed vertically. In a few moments Ecker gave the hand signal to Wilhelmy to descend to one-hundred feet where they will remain through the reconnaissance portion of the mission. Erik was quite impressed with their flying skills. As they approach Cuba, Ecker gave the hand signal to start their cameras. As they approached the first missile sight, a Cuban soldier heard the approaching aircraft and soldiers scrambled to prepare to fire machine guns and anti- aircraft missiles at the approaching aircraft. Ecker's aircraft was struck on the starboard wing with machine gun fire but was able to continue and complete the reconnaissance mission. "Wow, that was close," thinks Erik. The two aircraft then returned to NAS Key West.

The pilots descended from their cockpits and walked to Ecker's starboard wing. "Looks like you took some fire, Commander," said the chief mechanic.

"Those were bird strikes, Chief. Sparrows," replied Ecker. "Ah, were those twenty caliber bird strikes, sir?" said the chief. "Bird strikes, Chief. That's the way it is," said Ecker, turning and walking towards base headquarters.

As Ecker entered headquarters, a corpsman said, "Commander, the Pentagon is on the phone for you."

Ecker said nothing, sighed and proceeded to his office to take the call. "Yes, sir, I will grab a flight immediately and be at your office this afternoon," Ecker is heard saying by Erik and The Guardian. "Corpsman, inform the Chief I will need an aircraft readied immediately for a flight to Washington D. C. Wheels up in thirty minutes!"

"Yes, sir," replies the corpsman as he scurried out of Ecker's office to inform the chief mechanic.

"What's that all about?" asks Erik.

"Commander Ecker has been summoned to Washington to personally deliver the photos and to brief the Joint Chiefs of Staff on the mission this morning. This is where you will fulfill your mission to keep the timeline on its predestined track and avoid a nuclear war. You will accompany Commander Ecker to Washington. When he is met by General Taylor you will take control of his mind. When asked if you were fired on in any way on this morning's mission, you will say that you were not. What occurred causing the timeline to go askew resulting in a nuclear holocaust was Ecker told the Joint Chief's that he indeed had been fired upon but that no significant damage was done. The result of his honesty was the Joint Chief's immediately contacted President Kennedy who gave the order to initiate retaliatory air strikes on the Cuban missile sites. The conflict quickly escalated to Russia launching nuclear missiles towards the United States and the U.S. launching its missiles at Russia. It is critical that Ecker be stopped from telling the truth this afternoon. Are we clear, Erik?"

"Yes, I am clear on what must be done. However, I am unclear as to how I take control of Ecker's mind. I have never done that, how does that work, Guardian?"

"You simply see yourself as Commander Ecker and you will assume control of him."

"OK. I hope I can pull this off. I feel like I've been handed control of a completely alien spacecraft and expected to fly it in battle."

"Good afternoon, Commander Ecker," said General Maxwell Taylor, Chairman of the Joint Chiefs of Staff. "Please put your flight gear in the chair to your right and join us in the conference room." Taylor then proceeded ahead of Ecker to the conference room.

As they were walking, Ecker said, "Thank you, sir, it's a pleasure to be here."

The Pentagon conference room was furnished with a long oak table and leather chairs that appeared to accommodate twenty people. Erik had never seen a military conference room that did not have any high-definition screens or other audio- visual equipment. Taylor and Ecker took their seats near the other attendees, Joint Chiefs General Curtis Lemay, and Admiral George Whelan Anderson at one end of the table.

Erik then concentrated on Commander Ecker and immediately was looking out of Ecker's eyes at the officers facing him. He blinked, noticeably.

"Commander Ecker, are you OK?" asked Admiral Anderson. "Yes…yes," replied Erik as Ecker. "Lot of flying today. Guess I'm a little tired."

"Commander Ecker," began General Lemay, looking eye-to- eye at Ecker. "There is just one thing I want your honest answer for. Were you or your wingman shot at by so much as a BB gun over Cuba this morning?"

Erik stared at Lemay then glanced at the other officers. "The mission was a walk in the park, sir."

Silence fell on the room for what felt like minutes but was really only a few seconds. Lemay stared, unblinking, into Ecker's (Erik's) eyes. Then said, "Thank you, Commander, for your bravery and duty." To General Taylor, Lemay said, "General, I believe this meeting is over," and got up to leave the conference room.

"Commander Ecker," said Taylor, "thank you for coming all this way. Have a safe flight home."

Erik then left Commander Ecker. Ecker again seemed to blink hard, unnoticed by the other meeting attendees. Ecker rose and exited the conference room, gathered his flight gear and proceeded to return to Andrews Airforce Base to return to Key West. Riding to Andrews in the staff car, Ecker kept returning to the moment in the meeting with the Joint Chiefs when he said the mission had been a walk in the park. He knew that he had never used that phrase to describe a mission and wondered where he had picked it up. What he didn't know was that the phrase was commonly used by Naval aviators up to six decades in the future.

Chapter 54

Erik awoke from his adventure with The Guardian and was quite amazed at what he had just experienced. It took him a few minutes to come back to the reality that he would face the Board of Inquiry later this morning. He stepped into the shower, modified for synthetic body cleaning, then dressed in his Navy Service Dress Blue uniform. He noticed that his smartphone had a message waiting.

"Good luck, today," said the message from Ksenia. "Please call me when it's over."

Erik smiled and replied, "Thank you. I will."

Erik called an Uber automated car for transportation to the Washington Navy Yard, Building 200, the location of the Board of Inquiry for his case. The Washington Navy Yard is the former shipyard and ordnance plant of the United States Navy in Southeast Washington, D.C. It is the oldest shore establishment of the U.S. Navy. The Yard currently serves as a ceremonial and administrative center for the U.S. Navy and is the home of The Judge Advocate General's Corps, also known as the "JAG Corps" or "JAG," which is the legal arm of the United States Navy. The Washington Navy Yard often functions as a ceremonial gateway to the nation's capital.

The six-mile route from his apartment to the Navy Yard took him past the Pentagon, across the Potomac River with the Jefferson Memorial visible to his left. He rehashed the events that happened aboard the USS Elon Musk the day of the accident. He recalled the accident claimed the lives of four of his crew and dwelled on what might he have done differently to mitigate the damage caused by space debris. He concluded by realizing that his actions were guided by years of training for catastrophic events and that he reacted instinctively to the conditions presented by the accident.

Erik entered the small hearing room in Building 200 at the Washington Navy Yard. There were three rows of bench seats divided by a walkway down the middle. There was a podium at the end of the walkway that faced the bench behind which the panel members sat. As he entered the hearing room, he saw his Executive Officer from the USS Elon Musk, Lt. Commander Jim Spaulding sitting in the second-row bench to his left. "Jim, great to see you," said Erik extending his hand to shake Spaulding's.

"What brings you here?"

"Hello, Erik," replied Spaulding, smiling. "I was interviewed extensively by the panel. Just want to see that they provide a ruling that lines up with what I told them."

"Thanks, Jim. I'm sure I'll need all the help I can get with this. These things generally don't go well for a ship's captain."

In the front row to his right he saw his commanding officer, Captain Jeffrey Barnes.

"Captain Barnes, thank you for coming to the hearing today," said Erik extending his hand to shake Barnes'.

"I hope we get good news here today, Erik. I need you back on duty."

The Board of Inquiry panel members filed into the hearing room from a door located behind and to the right of the bench. A captain took the center seat behind the bench and was flanked by two commanders, one on each side.

"Commander Erik Richards, please stand before the panel," said the captain.

Erik rose from his seat and stood at attention at the podium about ten feet directly in front of the captain.

The captain then read the findings. "We find that the incident aboard the USS Elon Musk, resulting in the deaths of four of her crew, was accidental and could not be avoided. The crew cabin was severely damaged from a collision with unmapped space debris resulting in an explosive decompression of atmosphere. Commander Richards and the Elon Musk were following the flight plan loaded by the International Space Station, Naval Space Dock, and did not deviate from that plan. We therefore find Commander Richards not at fault for this incident. Further, this panel commends Commander Richards for his bravery, risking life and limb attempting to save his crew and his ship. Commander Richards is returned to flight status immediately. These proceedings are closed."

"Congratulations, Erik," said Captain Jeffrey Barnes, extending his hand to shake Erik's, as Erik hesitated briefly before turning to leave the hearing room. "Please come by my office after lunch today and we'll discuss your next assignment. In the meantime, I have a staff car if you'd like a ride back to the Pentagon."

"Yes, sir. Thank you, sir," said Erik as they exited the room and prepared to leave the Navy Yard.

Erik returned to his office adjacent to that of Captain Barnes office at the Pentagon. He closed the door and withdrew his smartphone from his jacket's pocket. "Send the following message to Ksenia," he started. "BOI is over. I was exonerated and returned to flight status. Speaking with Captain Barnes on next assignment this afternoon."

Within a few seconds the reply came from Ksenia, "Excellent! I knew you would do fine! I am returning home this afternoon for the remainder of my shore leave. Unless, of course, you want me to join you."

"Better wait to see what my new orders will involve but I hope you are able to join me," replied Erik

Chapter 55

Saturday, October 27, 1962. Kristian and The Guardian were observing a meeting in the Oval Office between JFK, Bobby Kennedy, Kenneth O'Donnell, McGeorge Bundy and Secretary of State Dean Rusk. What had transpired was that a letter was received from Premier Khrushchev offering to withdraw the Soviet missiles from Cuba in exchange for a commitment by the United States that Cuba would not be invaded. The letter was then followed with another letter the next day adding that U.S. missiles located in Turkey must be removed.

EXCOMM had met with the President earlier and convinced him to put U.S. forces on alert for invasion following the shooting down of a U.S. U2 spy plane over Cuba. This discussion centered around how to respond to the Soviets.

"So, we reject the second letter?" questioned the President. "No, we need to respond positively to Khrushchev's first letter," said Bundy. "Do not acknowledge the second letter."

RFK agreed, "We accept the first letter and pretend the second letter doesn't exist!"

In a meeting at 9 PM, following the earlier Oval Office discussion, EXCOMM members voiced their opinions of the plan to accept the terms in Khrushchev's first letter.

"It won't work! It's wishful thinking!" exclaimed CIA Director John McCone.

"It can work IF the Soviets believe we will attack, hit them hard!" said Secretary of Defense McNamara. "We have time for one more round of diplomacy before we strike!"

"We also need to offer them something additional," said JFK. "We need to tell them we'll remove the missiles from Turkey."

Negative comments and groans were heard from several members. JFK cut them off, "Wait a minute! We'll tell them we'll remove the missiles from Turkey in six months so there is no linkage with their withdrawal of missiles from Cuba. If they go public with our offer now, we'll deny it and the deal is off."

"So how do we deliver this message to them and get a response in the twenty-eight hours remaining until we strike?" said Rusk. "Whoever carries this message must hit the nail on the head."

"Bobby, you know (Russian ambassador) Dobrynin best. You will need to make them understand that we need an answer because on Monday, we go to war," said the President.

Kenneth O'Donnell and Robert Kennedy drive from The White House to RFK's office at the Justice Department where Ambassador Dobrynin is waiting. Kristian and The Guardian are riding with them.

"I'm not sure I can do this," said RFK, visibly nervous. "There's no one I trust more going in there than you," said O'Donnell, sincerely.

"Kristian, you will ensure that the message to Ambassador Dobrynin is delivered. As Robert Kennedy delivers the message and terms you will be prepared to take control of his mind. You will enter RFK's mind when he sits down with the ambassador. But you will only take control if Kennedy falters. Do you understand?"

"I...I think so. But why not take control outright and deliver the message to avoid any chance of … slippage?"

"We never take control in situations like this when the subjects are fully capable of taking the correct action," said The Guardian. "Kennedy is fully capable of delivering the message. The concern is that he may succumb to the importance and pressure of this event. Also, if you do take control there will remain lingering doubt in his mind that he can make the right decision and take appropriate action in tense situations, which could impact future decisions he will make."

"Greetings, Mr. Ambassador, thank you for coming on short notice," said Robert Kennedy as he entered his office and extended his hand to shake Dobrynin's. "I believe we can avoid a serious confrontation on the issue of your missiles being deployed in Cuba. First, please know that my colleagues, my friends, my brother and I cannot tolerate the presence of these missiles so close to our shores."

"For us to remove the missiles we must have your government's promise that Cuba will never be invaded by the United States or any of her allies. Additionally, your missiles based in Turkey must be removed concurrent with the removal of our missiles in Cuba," said Dobrynin.

"I am able to guarantee that the U.S. will not invade Cuba. However, I cannot grant your second condition regarding missiles in Turkey."

This last statement alerts Kristian that he may need to take control of RFK's mind.

"Then I am afraid that we face war," said Dobrynin bending over to pick up his briefcase, preparing to leave.

Bobby rises out of his chair, turning his back to Dobrynin momentarily. He then turns to face Dobrynin, "We are prepared to offer the removal of our missiles from Turkey in six months. We cannot risk agreeing to more and more conditions. What then is to stop you from demanding more?"

Kristian relaxes as he hears Bobby Kennedy deliver the message the President approved.

Dobrynin puts down his briefcase and sits back in his chair and said, "This may be acceptable, but I will need to seek agreement from my superiors."

"One more thing, Mr. Ambassador," said Kennedy. "We will need an answer tomorrow morning. I cannot stress this enough." Kristian then leaves RFK's mind.

"Then it seems I have work to do," said Dobrynin.

"The crisis is over. The timeline is restored," said The Guardian.

Kristian, lying in his recharging bed at the mansion, awakens as his spirit returns to his cyborg body at the exact moment it had left to join The Guardian

Chapter 56

"Come in, Erik," said Captain Jeffrey Barnes. "Have a seat. We have some big plans for you."

"Thank you, sir," said Erik, sitting across from Barnes at his desk in the Pentagon. "Am I to return to command the Elon Musk?"

"No, Erik, you are not returning to the Musk."

"But, sir, didn't the Board of Inquiry just reinstate my flight status?"

"Yes, they did. But we have bigger plans for you than flying around in a spaceship. You are being assigned command of an elite group of space-aviators, scientists, and engineers to develop our first starship."

"St…starship, sir?" said Erik, his eyebrows visibly raised.

"Yes, you see, Erik, the source behind the reason you are sitting here this afternoon is also the source for our accelerated development of other advanced technologies. In this case, it is the development of inter-stellar space travel."

"Where will I be based?" asked Erik.

"Initially, during the design phase of the project, you will be located at Space Base Alpha, near what is commonly known as Area 51. During the construction phase you will be working between a new, for now top secret, space station currently under construction in orbit and Space Base Alpha."

"What is the timeframe for the design and construction of the starship?"

"Five years. Design is anticipated to take two years, construction to take two years, then flight testing to take one year. The schedule will be refined once we develop the detailed requirements in a phased approach."

"So, this … source for advanced technologies. Does it have anything to do with the still unidentified objects that have been spotted and recorded by Navy pilots repeatedly?"

"Erik, the U.S. government successfully denied the existence of extraterrestrial aircraft in our skies until it no longer could. Video from Navy F-14 Tomcats of aircraft that were defying known laws of physics early in this century could no longer be denied and was released to the public by the Pentagon in 2020. In fact, the purported crash of an alien spacecraft in the Arizona desert in 1947 was real. The government is still officially denying that event, but it was indeed real. Technological advancements gained from reverse-engineering that craft, and its occupants, include how you are sitting here today in perfect health."

"The spacecraft recovered in that incident completely baffled our top scientists for decades," continued Barnes. "But enough progress was made early in the 21st Century to develop and fly a craft similar in appearance but without all of the technology now known to be in the alien craft. The craft that flew in 2004, known as the Black Manta, was a joint effort between the U.S. government, McDonnell Douglas, and Northrop. In 2019 the U.S. Navy took out a patent for a design based on that ship. The abstract for the patent states, and I quote: "A craft using an inertial mass-reduction device comprised of an inner resonant cavity wall, an outer resonant cavity, and microwave emitters. The electrically charged outer resonant cavity wall and the electrically insulated inner resonant cavity wall form a resonant cavity. The microwave emitters create high frequency electromagnetic waves throughout the resonant cavity causing the resonant cavity to vibrate in an accelerated mode and create a local polarized vacuum outside the outer resonant cavity wall." In other words, the ship will bend space-time in order to attain the speeds needed for interstellar travel. Indeed, many believe a ship of this design will enable faster-than-light speeds."

"Fascinating," said Erik. "Given that a patent for this craft has existed for over twenty years, why hasn't there been attempts to build it before now?"

"The short answer is politics," replied Barnes. "You can imagine that getting politicians to invest millions, perhaps billions, in a starship project at the expense of those receiving entitlements is a tough hill to climb. One senator, your uncle Bradley Richards, took it upon himself to lead a following sufficient to gain approval for the funding. Senator Richards is the ranking member of the Senate Armed Services Committee, one of the most powerful committees in the Senate. He is also known as one of the few truly bipartisan members of Congress. He has campaigned on putting country above party and has a lot of support from the conservative party. Essentially, in that role, when Senator Richards speaks, people listen. It is rumored that he is contemplating a run for the White House in 2048. That a member of the minority liberal party speaks in favor of funding for a starship project over other entitlement- oriented projects normally promoted by that party doubled the influence he was able to exert. So, here we are today, fully funded."

"The ... other technologies you mentioned. The occupants of the alien craft were cyborgs? So, Ansley Barnett didn't create the synthetic body that saved or restored Kristian, Aaron, and me?"

"Dr. Barnett did indeed create the cyborg using technologies found in that alien craft and her crew. You see, the ship's crew were cyborgs that appeared to have been designed for inter-stellar space travel. Dr. Barnett reverse-engineered them in order to adapt them to human physiology." "It took what, seventy years to reverse-engineer the alien cyborgs?" questioned Erik.

"We didn't have the necessary equipment or even a basic understanding of what we had, until we achieved an advanced degree of artificial intelligence, AI, in the 2020s."

"Has anyone else been selected for this project? You mentioned scientists, engineers, aviators. Will I be able to have input regarding the selections?"

"You, along with me, other Naval personnel, and senior

representatives from the corporations that will be selected to partner with the government will have input on the selection of team members. We will also include team members from friendly allies as this is to be an international endeavor. However, in the case of Naval Aviators and other service branch pilots of high- performance aircraft, we will prioritize selections from those like yourself, who have been restored from injury using the synthetic technology."

"When do you anticipate we will be relocating to Space Base Alpha?" asked Erik.

"The facility is still under construction with a ready date of late Spring 2043. In the meantime, we will be working here at the Pentagon. This will be more convenient for building the team, conducting interviews and background checks on candidates. We'll have my staff to handle the routine work."

"One more thing, Erik, this project is classified top secret. Your security clearance has been upgraded to the highest level to accommodate this project. Do not take this lightly."

"Yes, sir," said Erik, thinking the ruling by the Board of Inquiry had to have been known, even arranged, for this to happen so quickly.

Handing Erik a sealed manilla envelope Captain Barnes said, "Here are the resumes of several candidates for the project. Please review them carefully and use my staff as needed to run down answers to questions you may have regarding the candidates. Let's get back together on Monday to discuss them. My digital assistant will update your calendar."

Back in his office Erik ordered his smartphone to dial Ksenia. As her image appeared on its screen he said, "Hello Ksenia, I have some news regarding my next assignment."

"Oh, will we be able to see each other or are you going back into space?" she replied.

"I will be mostly earthbound for the next five years working on a special, top-secret project for the Naval Space Command. I will be based at the Pentagon for about a year, then relocating to Arizona." "Fantastic!" Ksenia replied, making no effort to conceal her enthusiasm. "Are you happy about this new assignment? I know how much you loved flying in outer space."

"Yes, Ksenia, I am very excited about this new project. It is top secret so I cannot divulge what it is, but I will say it has the potential to be a factor for the future of this planet."

"Wow! It sounds like an opportunity you could not pass up, even for space travel."

"Ksenia, why don't you plan on coming here for the remainder of your shore leave? How much time remains before your next cruise?" asked Erik.

"I have about two weeks until my next cruise. I already have a ticket on hold for tomorrow's flight from Bergen to Washington. I just had a feeling that I would be hearing good news from you, so I reserved the flight earlier today. I hope that's not too soon."

"Perfect," said Erik. I'll meet you at the airport."

The next day, having completed the resume review and background check information provided for three engineering and computer science candidates, one from MIT and two from Caltech, Erik departed the Pentagon in a driverless Uber for Dulles Airport at approximately 1430 hours (2:30 PM). Ksenia's flight was scheduled to arrive at 1605 hours and Erik's digital assistant was showing the flight slightly ahead of schedule with an estimated time of arrival of 1542 (3:42 PM). Erik planned to meet Ksenia in the international arrivals area just outside of U.S. Customs.

Erik arrived at Dulles at 1535 hours and headed directly to the international arrivals' hall. Shortly, his digital assistant chirped and said, "United Airlines Flight 2231 has arrived," indicating the aircraft was beginning to deplane its passengers. Erik knew it would probably be at least thirty minutes before Ksenia cleared U.S. Immigration and Customs. While waiting, Erik checked his email and saw a message from Captain Barnes.

"Commander, please make plans to join me on Wednesday June 4th. We will be traveling to Groom Lake, Arizona. You will have a chance to spread your recently restored wings and will fly an F/A-18 Super Hornet to and from the destination. I will be your WSO

(Weapons System Officer – occupying the rear seat). Wheels-up at 0630."

"Wow!" thought Erik. "I'm finally going to fly again! Groom Lake, Arizona. Hmmm – oh, of course. That's the airfield at Area 51. It's been over five years since I flew the F-18. I'd better get a check ride in a simulator and soon."

Erik acknowledged Captain Barnes' message and looked up to see Ksenia exiting the Immigration and Customs area. She was wearing her hair down, the way he liked it, and he was mesmerized by her beautiful smile. They embraced and kissed like they had been separated for months instead of hours.

"You got through Immigration pretty fast," said Erik.

"I've been through so many immigration halls throughout Europe and the U.S. traveling on Viking, I know which lines to avoid. Also, I seem to have much better luck with male border guards than with female. I smile and make eye contact with them and it usually causes them to be less suspicious of me, although sometimes that backfires as they want to flirt with me," she said, laughing. "Most females, however, give me a look that says, 'I know you must be guilty of something.'"

Erik and Ksenia arrived at Erik's apartment near the Pentagon in Arlington a little after 5 PM and wasted no time embracing each other which led quickly to heated love making. Ksenia was fascinated with Erik's near- perfect physique. And, of course, he was passionately probing her body while reminding himself to use caution with his cyborg strength. He didn't want to repeat what he'd done in Bergen when he had nearly put her up on the ceiling while flipping her over.

Afterwards, lying next to each other, while she was still breathing hard, Erik said, "You know that we have a three-day weekend coming up. The Memorial Day Holiday. How would you like to go to the Eastern Shore of Maryland and spend a couple of days at the beach? We could leave after I get off work tomorrow and return Monday evening."

"I think that would be lovely," said Ksenia. "Do you think we could still get reservations this close to the holiday?"

"Let's try right now," said Erik, getting up from the bed and pulling on his briefs to get his smartphone. To his digital assistant he said, "Find us a beachfront hotel in Ocean City, Maryland, or Fenwick Island, Delaware, check-in May 23rd, late evening, check-out May 26th."

Shortly, Erik received a response, "I have found just one room available for the dates requested. It is at Hyatt Place, Ocean City, Maryland. The hotel is oceanfront and located directly behind the Ocean City Boardwalk at 16th Street. The one remaining room is an oceanfront penthouse. The rate for Memorial Day Weekend is $1,735.00 per night."

"Book it," said Erik, not hesitating at all after hearing the rate.

"Erik!" exclaimed Ksenia. That rate is exorbitant, even for a penthouse!"

"Not to worry, my dear," said Erik as he jumped back in bed. Remember that I recently collected my back pay for the year I was recuperating from the accident."

Chapter 57

On Friday, Erik ordered a Hertz rental Terrafugia Model T-5 flying car to be readied for their flight to Ocean City. The T-5, designed for urban areas, is a vertical takeoff and landing vehicle featuring four passenger seats and a luggage compartment. It can be used as a conventional car as well as an aircraft. The all-electric T-5 features a range of five hundred miles and a top speed of two- hundred miles per hour. It is completely computer driven with emergency controls available if needed. They would pick up the flying car at the Pentagon Hertz office where they would safely take off for the one-hour trip to the landing point, just west of Ocean City on Route 50. From there they would drive the T-5 to their hotel.

"Ksenia, are you ready to go?" asked Erik as he entered his apartment. "I've got the Hertz car parked downstairs. I just need to change out of my uniform and grab my bag and briefcase." The briefcase housed Erik's portable charging and backup equipment for his cyborg body. He could likely go without it for three days but preferred to keep the equipment near him when he traveled. "Yes, I'm ready. My bag is next to the front door," said Ksenia. She wore her hair in a ponytail, and wore a sleeveless top, short skort and flip flops. She carried a red Viking Cruise Lines windbreaker for after sundown.

Erik carried their bags down the single flight of stairs from his apartment to the parking lot and walked towards the Hertz self-driving car. "Will this car take us to Ocean City?" said Ksenia.

"Yes, I thought it was fitting for a trip to the beach," said Erik.

"Climb in while I load our bags in the trunk." Erik then got into the driver's seat and connected his smartphone to the vehicle. "Take us to our destination," he ordered, having pre- programmed the car to take them to the Pentagon Hertz office so he could surprise Ksenia with the flying car. The self-driving vehicle then took control, backed them out of the parking space, exited the parking lot, and then took them to the entrance of the Hertz office at the Pentagon.

As they entered the Hertz office parking lot Ksenia asked, "Why are we going to Hertz? I thought we were taking this car to the beach."

"Patience, my dear," said Erik, smirking. "In a moment we will board our chariot to the beach." The Hertz car pulled into a parking space facing several T-5 rentals about fifty feet in front of them. "Shall we board our chariot?" said Erik.

"We're going to fly to the beach?" said Ksenia.

"Would you expect anything less from the captain of a spaceship?" said Erik, grinning.

Erik loaded their bags in the luggage compartment of the T-5 and they climbed aboard. Erik gave the T-5 the destination and the order to take off. The craft's twin rotors, housed in nacelles, extended from beneath the vehicle to their vertical takeoff position. The twin electric engines revved, the fan blades extended from the nacelles, and they lifted off, quickly reaching an altitude of twelve-hundred feet. The vehicle's wheels were retracted. The engines then rotated forward, and the propeller blades were tucked. The ducted fan at the rear of the craft propelled it forward and the craft quickly attained an altitude of three-thousand feet and a cruising speed of one-hundred fifty miles per hour. Flying the craft was accomplished entirely by the onboard computer which was connected to FAA Drone and Light Aircraft Control. The FAA system was designed to manage the air traffic and, using advanced artificial intelligence software, navigate around bad weather and negate any chance of collision. Even so, Erik had to exercise restraint to avoid taking control of the craft and flying it himself.

As they approached the Chesapeake Bay Bridge, they saw the

long backup of vehicles below heading to the beaches for a long weekend. "Looks like it will be a busy weekend at the beach," said Erik. "Glad we're not down there in that mess."

"These flying cars are a godsend in heavy city traffic," said Ksenia. "Can you imagine having to drive a car manually through that congestion? I wonder how our parents ever tolerated it."

After just over an hour, they began their descent to the Ocean City Municipal Airport, just three miles southwest from the beach resort on Route 611. After their vertical touchdown, the T-5's engine nacelles folded back underneath the vehicle, the short wings folded back and tucked into the rear sides of the vehicle, and rear-view mirrors that complemented the rear view screen in the T-5's dashboard appeared on the left and right fenders.

"I'm getting hungry," said Erik. "Let's grab dinner before we go to the hotel. Captain Barnes recommended the Delmarva Boil Company. Said they make the best seafood boil in town."

"What's a seafood boil?" asked Ksenia, hesitantly.

"Well you throw a bunch of crab legs, shrimp, mussels, some sausage into a pot with red potatoes and corn on the cob. It is usually served in a bucket."

"OK, that sounds … interesting. Let's go!"

"It's in north Ocean City so will probably take about forty- five minutes to get there by surface street. But it'll be worth it. Plus, we can see most of Ocean City, except the boardwalk. T-5, take us to the Delmarva Boil Company in Ocean City."

Shortly after they were seated, a young waitress wearing a light blue blouse with the Delmarva Boil Company logo on the left breast pocket and a short denim skirt approached their table. "Hi, my name is Angie. Can I take your drink order?"

"Just water with lemon for me," said Ksenia.

"Same for me, but also a glass of Devil's Backbone Lager," said Erik. "Ksenia, a good beer goes great with the seafood boil. Sure you don't want one?"

"Can you drink that and drive legally?" asked Ksenia. "We have zero-tolerance laws against driving after drinking in Norway, and in most of Europe except the United Kingdom."

"Still point .08 in the good ole' USA," said Erik, thinking he could drink a gallon and it would have no effect on his synthetic body. He would also blow 0.00 in a breathalyzer test no matter how much he drank. He did miss an occasional buzz from a strong drink but that was a small price to pay for his incredible body.

"OK, then. I'll have what he's having," Ksenia said to the waitress. "I thought I might have to drive if he drank any alcohol." Their boil appeared shortly after ordering and they fully enjoyed the variety of seafood, the sausage, and the corn and potatoes. Ksenia had some difficulty using her hands as primary utensils but eventually adjusted and matched Erik's messy hands and face by the time they finished. They both laughed looking at each other near the end of the meal. "I think I'll need a shower after this meal," joked Ksenia.

Erik decided against another beer fearing Ksenia would fuss if he attempted to drive afterward.

Erik and Ksenia arrived at the Hyatt around 8:30 PM and checked in after unloading their bags and handing the key fob to the female attendant at valet parking. The attendant was visibly astounded at the thought of driving the flying car, if only to a parking space. "Don't engage flight mode," said Erik, smiling.

"No, sir," said the attendant. "But I have always wanted to park one of these … in my driveway!" she said, returning his smile. Their penthouse suite was on the top floor. It was 1,435 square feet, had three private balconies, two overlooking the boardwalk below and a third on the bay side where one could watch boats sailing in the bay. They stripped down shortly after entering the suite and stepped into the clear glass enclosed shower which also featured steam jets. After soaping and rinsing they turned to each other and made slow and passionate love while the warm water and steam embraced them. However, when they climaxed together, Erik momentarily forgot his strength and snapped the metal towel rack he had been gripping in two. He recovered immediately by smiling saying, "Oops! Must have been a cheap towel rack."

Ksenia bent down and picked up a piece of the broken towel rack. Looking at the broken end she said, "Erik, this looks like pretty thick metal, like that on Viking ship bathroom towel racks."

Looking at the broken towel rack, Erik said, grinning, "I guess there's no limit to how much you are able excite me."

They returned to the luxurious shower several more times over the weekend and enjoyed the Ocean City Boardwalk and beach. Erik introduced Ksenia to Thrasher's French fries, a staple of Ocean City since 1929. They had cocktails in the evenings on the balconies of the suite before going out to a different restaurant for dinner each day. The weather was perfect with temperatures hovering about eighty degrees during the day and dropping into the low sixties at night. The Atlantic Ocean temperature was a cool sixty-two degrees, but Ksenia found it bearable thanks to her Nordic background. And, of course, Erik's synthetic body could withstand temperatures close to freezing.

On Sunday afternoon, as they lay on their beach towels, a woman nearby screamed and pointed towards the surf. The weather was cool, clear, and quite breezy. Warning flags indicated that a strong undertow was present. Erik turned to face the water and saw a young teenage girl struggling in the surf. She was caught in an undertow. The lifeguard had just jumped down from his observation stand and began running towards the surf. Erik jumped up and also began running. Not thinking about his cyborg strength, he quickly passed the lifeguard and dove into the surf. He swam and reached the struggling girl in just a few seconds, before the lifeguard could enter the surf himself with his buoy slung over his shoulder.

Erik grabbed the girl, calmed her, and quickly returned to shore. He had no problem swimming against the strong undertow and reached knee deep water in a matter of seconds. He then aided the girl walking the rest of the way up to the beach where her mother was still sobbing. Then it seemed that everyone on the beach, including Ksenia, was staring at Erik.

"Man, where'd you learn to swim like that?" asked the lifeguard.

"Uh…, I'm in the Navy," replied Erik, seeing all the faces staring and some mouths dropping in shock. Erik turned and walked back to his towel where he feigned exhaustion for Ksenia's benefit. "I'm spent," he said, breathing hard for effect.

"You looked like…Superman!" exclaimed a still surprised Ksenia. "How did you do that?"

"I… I don't know. Adrenaline, I guess. You've heard of people lifting thousands of pounds to free someone trapped, haven't you? They always say it was an adrenaline rush," said Erik, thinking that he must do a better job of controlling his cyborg body.

After their near-perfect weekend Ksenia and Erik returned to Arlington, Virginia, Monday evening, again watching the Bay Bridge congestion from their altitude of 3,500 feet. Later that evening, as they were lying in bed in Erik's apartment, Ksenia recalled the moment during their passionate lovemaking back in Bergen when Erik nearly planted her on the ceiling while flipping her over. Then she recalled him breaking the thick stainless-steel towel rack in the hotel in Ocean City. Finally, she remembered the incident on the beach where Erik saved that girl caught in the surf. "Just how strong is he?" she wondered.

Erik and Ksenia spent their last week together as much as possible given Erik's schedule. They continued to learn more about each other and fall deeper in love. By the time Ksenia flew to Barcelona to join her next ship, The Viking Star, on Monday, June 1, they had developed a close relationship. Now the true test of their love would come at living a part-time, long-distance romance while she was at sea. Her next scheduled time off would not occur until August.

Chapter 58

I t was now Tuesday, May 27th, 2042. Aaron Adams boarded the transporter tube system to take him from the Barnett Center for Neurological Restoration to the Barnett mansion. Aaron will be attending a meeting with Kristian and Senator Bradley Richards. After introductions, the discussion will focus on mind control technologies, strategies, and development by the United States.

"Senator Richards, thank you for allowing us to meet with you today. I believe you will find the topic interesting, if not quite concerning," said Kristian as Senator Richard's full-size holographic image appeared in the chair across the leather sofa upon which Kristian and Aaron were seated. "With me today is Phillip Preston (Aaron Adams), my senior vice president of research."

"Good morning, gentlemen," said Senator Richards. "A pleasure to meet you Mr. Preston. Kristian, you certainly look well given your medical condition."

"Thank you, Senator. We are making particularly good progress on developing a cure for this horrible affliction," replied Kristian, sitting in a wheelchair so as not to arouse excitement regarding his condition. "My condition today is wholly the result of medical technology that is much too soon to release to the public. It is not stable, and the effects are far from known. I am the first human guinea pig for Dr. Savannah Richards' treatment for ALS, and I am excited to be in this condition regardless of how long it lasts."

"But, in order to maximize our time with you this morning, I will dive right into why we contacted you. We have it on good authority that there is an effort to develop a mind control technology that would enable control of the thoughts and actions of masses of people. This technology may be used to control the outcome of national elections, support for legislation that would otherwise be rejected, and ultimately could lead to enslavement of a large portion of humanity. Now, before you conclude that we are a couple of lunatics, we have researched the state of mind control technology and found that it is indeed being funded by unfriendly nations including Russia and China. We also have some information indicating the results of experimentation of this technology on human subjects by these countries. What we have been unable to crack so far is where the United States is on this technology. There has been no documentation of any kind that we have been able to find."

After a brief period of silence, Senator Richards said, "Kristian, isn't your wife one of the higher-ups at DARPA. Would she not be a possible source for finding out where we are with this technology?"

"I approached Ansley on this issue, and she said that, even if she did know something, she could not reveal it to anyone without explicit approval. Apparently, the only persons at DARPA who would know anything are Jim Hanson and the project team working on this technology. Hanson would not reveal anything about any project unless authorized by someone above his paygrade."

"Well, I am able to say that activity in the field of mind control technologies has been ongoing for some time. I'm not able to reveal specifics due to the nature of the security classification associated with it," said Richards.

"Sir, are there any partners from the private sector involved with the U.S. Government?"

"The short answer is yes. However, I am not at liberty to reveal who they are."

"Sir, is Find Corporation involved in the project?" "Kristian," the Senator began after a brief pause. "I told you I am not at liberty to reveal any details regarding the activity associated with this technology."

"Then would it be possible for Barnett Industries to become a partner with the federal government on this? I doubt that there was a conventional bidding process for partners on this project given its secrecy."

"Kristian, you probably know that Find is a major supporter for me."

"Yes, I do. But so is Barnett Industries."

"What could Barnett bring to the table, Kristian? I would need some pretty good justification to raise the possibility of Barnett joining the project with the Secretary of Defense and Director of DARPA."

"Barnett Industries is at the forefront of technologies supporting wireless transmission of critical signals. Our traffic systems manage millions of vehicles globally as they traverse roads and highways with antennas wired to transmit control signals to individual vehicles. It would seem that wireless technologies would be critical to the transmission of signals used to control the human mind. Barnett has wireless infrastructure installed in many cities, both domestic and international."

"Hmmm," started the Senator as he contemplated Kristian's response. "Wasn't Barnett Industries a partner with the DOD (Department of Defense) for wireless technologies used on the battlefield?"

"Yes, sir," replied Kristian. "Our wireless technologies have been applied in urban situations and used to guide several models of unmanned high mobility, multi-purpose land-based drone vehicles."

"Let me get with my contacts at DOD and DARPA. I think we may be able to find a spot for Barnett on the project," said Senator Richards.

Kristian ended the call and said to Aaron, "It looks like we got the Senator to admit that the U.S. is highly involved in mind control research. Note he referred to the research as a project, which means it is funded and likely under the direction of DARPA."

"And he never denied Find's involvement on the project," said Aaron. "Do you have anything else for me? I'm meeting Savannah for lunch in the Center cafeteria."

"Uh, no, Aaron. That will be all for now. Savannah? Are you two … uh, getting to know each other?"

"I'd like to get to know her better. Not sure if she feels the same about me though," said Aaron, glancing away momentarily. "She's quite a girl, Aaron. It'd be awfully hard to find one better."

Chapter 59

Aaron entered the Barnett Center cafeteria and found Savannah Richards seated at a table near the back of the room. He waved to her, thinking how beautiful she was, dressed in a light blue blouse and dark blue skirt, her lab coat opened. He said as he approached her table, "Hi Savannah, sorry I'm late. I was in a meeting with Kristian."

"No worries, I just got here," said Savannah. "I'm starved, let's get some food."

In the cafeteria line, Savannah picked up a pre-made cob salad and bottled water. Aaron stood by the grill while his cheeseburger was cooked, which he got with fries and a chocolate milkshake. While standing in line for the cashier, Savannah said, "I wish I could eat like you … guys. I'm always trying to behave and eat my bunny food when there's nothing I'd like better than a burger and fries."

"You should reward yourself once in a while," said Aaron, as the chip in their company identification badges transmitted the executive code to the cashier's check-out register indicating they were Barnett executives. A perquisite of being an executive at Barnett was one got all the free food one wanted from the cafeteria. This perk was designed to encourage the executives to mingle with the staff in an informal setting.

"So, what exciting projects does Kristian have you working on, Aaron?" asked Savannah, as they sat down to eat.

"Well, I need to be careful as I am under non-disclosure agreements with Barnett, but I can say that my primary project is…groundbreaking. It is dealing with the transmission of wireless signals to devices including smartphones, tablets and IOT, Internet of Things, devices," said Erik, hoping he had spun his response to deliberately bore Savannah and avoid any more question regarding his work.

"Don't IOT devices include automobiles, appliances, and even surgical robots being used remotely?" questioned Savannah. "Uh-oh," thought Aaron, thinking he had just opened a can of worms for himself given Savannah's apparent technical savvy. "Yes, any device that can communicate via the Internet is a possible IOT device," he said. "So, what are you currently working on?" he asked Savannah, hoping to change the subject.

Well, we are making good progress on our ability to stop the advancement of ALS. We have begun trials using humans diagnosed and in the early stages of the disease. Recall that our initial goal is to be able to stop the disease before it becomes debilitating. The second goal, developing an actual cure that will reverse the damage the disease causes is our ultimate goal, but that is likely years away."

"I'm sure you and your team will achieve that goal, Savannah. Everything I have seen so far is utterly amazing, groundbreaking. You're the future," said Aaron, smiling.

"We do work hard, and it helps when we achieve the solutions and treatments that truly help people continue to lead long and healthy lives."

As their lunch concluded, Aaron said, "Hey, would you like to play some tennis after work one evening? How about tomorrow?"

"I'd like that, if you promise not to go too hard on me," said Savannah. "Meet you on the court at 6 PM?"

"Perfect. See you then."

Aaron returned to his office and must have been grinning walking down the hall, excited that Savannah had accepted his invitation for a tennis date. His assistant greeted him with, "What are you so happy about? You look like the cat that ate the canary." "Oh, it's just been a really great day, so far," he said, still smiling.

Chapter 60

Erik and Captain Barnes rode in a ramp services vehicle to the F/A-18 they would be flying to Groom Lake. "I'm looking forward to flying again, sir," said Erik. "It's been several years since I flew a fighter."

"You did get a chance to do a check ride in the simulator, Commander?" said Barnes.

"Yes, sir."

Erik performed his pre-flight walk around, examining the external components of the F/A-18 including wing surfaces, landing gear, and service ports. Erik and Captain Barnes then climbed up the ladders to take their seats in the cockpit. After strapping in, Erik prepared the cockpit systems for flight. The cockpit display systems were the latest generation and virtually allowed the pilot to provide commands using multiple inputs, including touch, verbal, and eye control provided through an advanced helmet. These enhancements to the F/A-18 were completed in the mid-2020s along with addition of conformal fuel tanks that enabled a strike range of one thousand nautical miles.

Once the aircraft was ready for takeoff, Erik contacted the tower at Joint Base Andrews. "Tower, Viking requesting taxi and runway instructions," said Erik into the microphone in his helmet, using his aviator call sign which he used at military-controlled airports.

"Viking, taxi to Runway 19L and Hold," responded JBA Tower control.

"Runway 19L, Viking," said Erik, repeating the instruction per proper flight control protocol.

"Tower, Viking requesting takeoff clearance Runway 19L."
"Viking, take Runway 19L and hold."

"Tower, taking Runway 19L and holding, Viking"

An aircraft landed and rolled down the runway in front of Erik's F/A-18.

"Viking, you're cleared for takeoff. At three zero (3,000) feet set your heading to two-seven-zero."

"Rolling, Viking. Have a good day," said Erik as the F/A-18 began its takeoff roll, climbed to three thousand feet and banked right to a heading of two-seven-zero, westbound for Nevada and Groom Lake. To conserve fuel Erik avoided entering a Military Climb using the jet's afterburners but did manage to roll the jet a few times once their cruising altitude of 37,000 feet was attained. "Great to be flying again!" exclaimed Erik. "Wish I could light up this baby and go supersonic."

"Copy that, Commander," said Captain Barnes. "Let's just make sure we have enough fuel to get to Groom Lake."

"Yes, sir. So, what are we going to see at Area 51?" said Erik. "Oh, an alien spacecraft or two and some little green men," said Barnes.

The time passed slowly. Erik said, "Can you imagine flying like this for a living? I have a friend who left the Navy to fly for Delta. Says he misses flying upside down."

"I know, my ass is beginning to ache," said Barnes. "But those big airline cockpits have much more comfortable seats than an F/A-18. And you can easily get up and walk around and stretch." Three hours and forty-five minutes after departure from Joint Base Andrews: "Viking, Homey Approach Control. Clear to land, Runway 13R, wind two-one-zero at twelve". The Area 51 airport at Groom Lake was officially named Homey Airport (KXTA) in 2008. After the airport received its ICAO airport code, the joke immediately became that the airport code stood for extra-terrestrial.

"Homey Tower, clear to land Runway 13R, Viking," said Erik.

After landing the F/A-18, Erik was instructed to taxi to an

unidentified hangar at the end of the ramp where a black SUV was parked. As they came to a stop, the driver and an additional armed man stepped out of the vehicle and stood at the door.

"Good afternoon, Captain Barnes, Commander Richards. I am Captain Sean Miller, USAF. With me is Staff Sergeant James." All four saluted each other. Please place your personal items in the back of the vehicle. "Captain Barnes, please join me in the front seat. Commander, please join Sergeant James in the back seat. We will take you to meet our base commander, Colonel Jacobsen."

"Captain Barnes, Commander Richards, welcome to Area 51," said Colonel Joseph Jacobsen, base commander of Area 51 who extended his hand to shake the hands of his guests. "I understand you will be with us for a couple of days. We have much to show you. I have received orders directly from the President that we will share with you the most secret intelligence known about this base."

"Thank you, Colonel," said Barnes. "Then you know that our top-secret assignment is the building of the Earth's first starship. We need to learn as much as possible regarding the integral workings of the … alien craft that landed near here almost one hundred years ago."

"Colonel, are you aware of my … background?" questioned Erik.

"Yes, you were nearly killed in the accident aboard the Elon Musk but survived to face a life of paralysis and pain under conventional medical care. Instead, you were given a new, artificial body. Your mind has been downloaded to the electronic brain in that body."

"Correct. So, you understand my curiosity in seeing the origins of this body."

"Yes, Commander, we will be including those … origins on your tour here," said Jacobsen. Captain Miller will escort you to the areas that will benefit your assignment. But in the meantime, please follow me for a virtual tour of Area 51."

In the base briefing room, a one-hundred-twenty-inch, clear screen was lowered from the ceiling. Sitting at a table facing the screen were Colonel Jacobsen, Captain Barnes, and Erik. Standing in front of the screen, Captain Miller clicked through a series of photographs of Area 51 and described the purpose of the facilities shown in each. Near the end of the briefing, the audience was shown the side of a mountain not far from the base. This picture was actually a video that showed a large section of the mountainside fade away and reveal what appeared to be large hangar doors. The doors opened and the camera zoomed inside the facility to reveal an oblong, windowless craft that resembled a small dirigible in shape. It appeared to be floating a few feet above the floor.

"What you are seeing, gentlemen, is the craft that crash- landed near Roswell, New Mexico in 1947," said Colonel Jacobsen. The United States has denied the existence of this craft for nearly one-hundred years and continues to deny it exists today. Approximately seventy years during this period have been spent trying to figure out how it works – what it's made of, its method of propulsion, and who built it. In the early 2020s we were finally able to determine these things and began to reverse-engineer some of its components and systems. But much earlier, beginning in the 1950s, we were able to begin to incorporate some of its basic designs into aircraft like the A-12, the SR-71 Blackbird, and later into the B-2 Bomber. During those years, we were decades ahead of any other country regarding stealth aircraft design. The large hangar facilities behind the illusionary mountainside were created with the assistance of high-powered laser cannons. The mountainside illusion covering the hangar doors is an ultra-high-resolution video beamed from hidden transmitters on the mountain. The airspace above the mountain is part of the protected airspace surrounding the base. Aircraft that violate that airspace are warned that they are subject to being shot down should they enter the protected airspace. If they persist, laser cannons hidden on the mountain will fire and destroy the aircraft instantly by literally reducing it to atoms. There are no remnants of the aircraft nor human remains. The video transmitters on the mountain also block all visibility from space."

"Colonel, did I understand you correctly, that we now know who built and flew that craft?" asked Erik.

"We have the ... bodies of the crew that flew and crashed it.

And we believe we have been able to figure out the navigational systems on the craft and determine the star system it came from." "It's getting late in the day. Captain Miller, please escort these gentlemen to our BOQ (Bachelor Officers Quarters) where they can stow their gear and freshen up. Gentlemen, I hope you will join me for dinner in my quarters at 1900 hours where we can continue to answer any questions you may have thus far."

The next day Captain Miller and Staff Sergeant James met Captain Barnes and Erik at the officer's mess hall where they were having breakfast. "If you both are ready, we'll take you out to the stealth hangar facility where we can show you the true inventory of alien artifacts and the current status of our efforts to contact the aliens who've been observing the planet for at least one-hundred years."

They followed the paved road from the mess hall in the general direction of the mountain housing the stealth hangar until the pavement ended and turned into a dirt road. There were no signs, not even signs warning not to approach the mountain. The area was desolate as far as one could see. As they approached the mountain, Captain Miller reached up to the SUV's sun visor and touched a remote device that looked like a garage door opener. Miller's fingerprint was authenticated to the portal management system in the mountain. If a fingerprint other than Miller's was scanned, the device would disintegrate. The face of the mountain began to slowly dissolve revealing the one-hundred-foot-tall hangar doors. The doors opened just enough for the SUV to enter the hangar. Just inside the hangar, an SR-71 Blackbird spy plane could be seen. The hangar doors closed immediately. Once closed, the image of the SR-71 dissolved revealing the alien spacecraft they had seen the day before in the video. There were also armed guards wearing camouflage fatigues and carrying combat weapons posted on either side of the spacecraft. It was evident that there was maximum security around the spacecraft as well as within the hangar.

The alien spacecraft was oval, wider towards the center than at the front and rear, tapering on the edges to a flat, narrow wing that appeared to be about one-meter wide that surrounded the craft. The craft measured twenty-two meters long, sixteen meters high and sixteen meters wide at the center. There were no windows or hatches visible from outside the ship. The material used for the external skin appeared to be aluminum but seemed to be moving slightly as if alive. The craft floated about four feet above the hangar floor.

"We believe the ship to be from a much larger spacecraft, similar in concept to our aircraft carriers," said Miller. "Similar craft have been seen and filmed by military jets on several occasions beginning early in this century. Before that, we believe their stealth capabilities coupled with their incredible acceleration effectively hid them from our most advanced camera technologies."

Miller continued, "We believe the craft is capable of trans-atmospheric flight, enabling the craft to leave Earth's atmosphere. It is equipped with cabin-pressurization, inertial dampening, and life-support systems that are sophisticated enough to allow up to four crew members to sit comfortably inside the craft without requiring the need of sealed and pressurized space or G-suits, despite the craft's perceived ability to pull incredible-G turns that stress normal airframes and pilots often to the breaking point.

It is apparent, by the near-perfect condition of this ship, that the craft has the capability to successfully complete re-entry into a planet's atmosphere at least as dense as Earth's. When this craft was found, it was embedded in a crater some forty-feet deep. Much of the forward hull was crushed including the flight deck. After it was excavated from the crater under the cover of strict military security it was taken to Wright-Patterson Airforce Base in Ohio. Later it was taken to Area 51 when the first hangar was retrofitted with advanced, state-of-the-art security systems."

"The forward hull was crushed?" asked Captain Barnes. "It looks perfect."

"After a few days it became apparent that the craft was ... healing itself. After about a month there was no evidence that the craft had been nearly destroyed in the crash. We still don't know how that happened but do know that the material in the exterior hull is nothing like we have here on Earth."

"What about its crew?" asked Erik.

"Despite numerous rumors regarding the condition of the crew, two actually survived for a time. What we found appeared to be biological remains, but they were anything but. All four, we later determined, were completely synthetic. The materials used for their bodies were mostly not of this world but were finally discovered by the DARPA project to create a human cyborg."

"Will we be able to go aboard the craft?" asked Erik.

"Yes, one thing we were able to find when the forward hull was still damaged was a lever that opened a hatch just forward of midships. That is how we were able to board the ship and how we found the remains of the crew. Fortunately, once inside the ship we were able to locate the position of the lever once the ship repaired itself. If you gentlemen will follow me, let's get on board."

The three men climbed the ladder and entered what appeared to be the flight deck of the alien craft. Captain Miller stepped forward, between two rows of two seats each, and waved his hand over a dial on the cockpit display panel. The forward section of the hull appeared to dissolve revealing a completely clear, floor- to-ceiling view of the hangar doors in front of the craft. On the armrests of the two forward seats were joysticks, like those in a fly-by-wire jet aircraft that appeared to be for navigation and weapons control. Multiple screens could be seen on the cockpit display panel but were all dark until Miller placed his hand on one of the forward seat armrests. Then the screens came alive, displaying what appeared to be the status of different systems on the ship, but with characters heretofore never seen by Captain Barnes or Erik.

"The size and shape of the seats indicate they were for beings similar to humans," said Erik.

"I believe you will be astounded at how much the alien cyborgs look like humans. The little green men and other movie portrayals of alien beings were mostly figments of active imaginations," said Miller. "Not much else to show you at this time, but if you follow me, we'll go and have a look at the aliens." The three men exited the craft by descending the ladder from the hatch and walked towards another set of doors, bordered by another set of heavily armed guards. Upon reaching the doors, Miller looked into a glass orb on the wall next to the door.

"Welcome back, Captain Miller," a voice said.

"I have two guests," said Miller to the voice.

"Please have your guests look into the glass orb and say their name and service branch or government agency as they enter," said the voice.

Erik and Barnes stepped up to face the orb, "Richards, Erik, Commander, United States Navy," said Erik.

"Barnes, Jeffrey, Captain, United States Navy," said Barnes.

The three entered a stark, white hallway that had no visible doors as far as they could see. Miller, followed by Erik and Barnes, walked about thirty feet when Miller turned to face the right wall. A portal opened into a large room housing a long, oval conference table and chairs. Once they were inside, the far wall dissolved, revealing a clear glass wall where four metal operating tables could be seen. On each table there was a body.

Erik and Barnes were dumfounded by what they saw. Both men walked slowly from one end of the glass wall to the other, speechless for what seemed like minutes. The bodies they saw appeared to be remarkably similar to human bodies. The bodies appeared to be hairless from head to foot. The legs were long and thin, and feet narrow by human standards. The arms and hands were also thin. The torso was very human-like and what appeared to be male reproductive organs were visible in the groin area. The hands had four long fingers and the feet had four large toes each.

The hands and feet appeared proportionally larger than human hands and feet. The head appeared to be elongated with a high, wide forehead and very narrow chin. The eyes were larger than human eyes, rounded and tapered in an Asian-like appearance. The nose was long and narrow and appeared to have only one nostril. The mouth was small but very human-like, and there were no apparent lips.

"Gentlemen, what you are seeing are not bodies of biological beings," continued Miller. "These bodies are artificial. Near as we can determine, they are specifically designed for long space travel. The materials used are a combination of known synthetics that have compatible Earth material, and of initially unknown synthetics that took years for us to determine their atomic structure."

"There were initially two survivors of the crash in 1947 that lived for several weeks. Unfortunately, our mid-20th Century medical technology coupled with our lack of knowledge of the physiology of the beings prevented us from saving their lives. It was determined later that their bodies were kept functioning by way of nanoscopic batteries incorporated into their skin. We theorize that this could enable solar charging when available, negating the need to be tethered to a power source. Had we realized this at the time, we may have been able to keep them alive longer. In any case, without the ship to provide recharging of their batteries, the bodies died. However, what we did discover is that the functioning of the electronic brain depended upon modelling one of their biological beings. By examining the recharging port at the back of their neck, we determined that their minds, if you will, were downloaded from a permanent database, likely located on a mother ship."

"All … of this sounds very familiar, Captain Miller," said Erik. "I see where Dr. Barnett and her team were able to create a human cyborg using this advanced technology. Once they were able to determine the atomic structure of the alien material used in the cyborgs, they adapted it to human physiology. My batteries are not nano particles in my skin, which sounds incredible. Perhaps later versions of our cyborg bodies will include this feature."

As Erik and Captain Barnes prepared to leave Area 51, Captain Miller and Staff Sergeant James met them at the BOQ.

"Good morning, gentlemen," said Miller. We have set you both up with log-in credentials to the data containing information regarding everything you have seen here over the past two days. Regarding the alien spacecraft, you now have access to all of the findings, both proven and speculative, regarding its origin, materials, construction, flight capabilities, and planned continued investigation of its functional design."

"Thank you, Captain," said Barnes. "May we contact you should we have questions as we review this information?"

"Of course, Captain. We will remain at your disposal."

Eric and Barnes climbed the ladder to their F/A-18, Erik taking the command seat with Barnes in the WSO (Weapons System Officer) seat in the rear.

"Homey Departure Control, Viking awaiting taxi and take off instructions," said Erik.

Chapter 61

It was Monday, June 9th, 2042 at 2:12 PM PDT when Kristian heard his digital assistant's chime. "Go ahead, KB."

"I have Senator Richards' office on the secure line. Shall I connect you?"

"Yes, yes, by all means," said Kristian.

"Hello, Kristian, Bradley Richards. I have news that I expect you will be pleased to hear. Barnett Industries has been added to the DARPA project team working with telecommunications mind control for the military."

"Excellent, Senator, thank you!" said Kristian. "When and where do we get on board?"

"My office is setting up the first virtual meeting. Attendees will include the DARPA Director, Jim Hanson, Project Director, Inger Beck, Jonathon Brahe, CEO of Find Corporation, you and Phil Preston (Aaron Adams), and me. Look for an appointment request to your digital assistant in the next day or so. It was decided to meet by holoprojection to eliminate your need to travel, at least for now. In the meantime, you and Mr. Preston will need to complete non-disclosure forms and have your security clearances upgraded to Top Secret. The appropriate federal office will be in touch with you regarding these requirements."

"Thank you, Senator. We will comply with all requirements as expeditiously as possible," said Kristian.

Approximately one month was required for Kristian and Aaron

to obtain the required Top-Secret security clearances. Kristian was especially pleased that Aaron's true identity was not revealed during the clearance investigation. The meeting with Senator Bradley Richards, Kristian, Aaron and the DARPA project team was scheduled on Tuesday, July 8th, 2042, at 1 PM EDT. Senator Richards began the meeting with introductions and then said, "Ladies and gentlemen, I don't need to take up time stressing the importance of this project. The Russians and Chinese are well on their way to establishing mass mind control through telecommunications. What we must do is develop our own technologies to accomplish this while at the same time determining how we block any attack they may launch. I know this will be an extremely challenging task but one I believe we can accomplish. That said, I will turn this meeting over to Director Hanson and Inger Beck."

"Inger, can you give us an update on the status of the project?" said Hanson.

"I will start with an overview of the project for the benefit of Messrs. Barnett and Preston," said Inger Beck. "Intelligence gathered regarding activities of other nations regarding the use of telecommunications technologies for mind control was first brought to DARPA a number of years ago. We knew that the Russians and Chinese, specifically, were experimenting with mind control in the 20th Century but that little progress was made. In the early 21st Century, with the proliferation of smartphones throughout the world, using telecommunications technologies to send subliminal suggestions to masses of people offered a possible means of influencing people without them being aware of the intrusion. The DARPA project's mission is to investigate, test, and prepare for the eventual implementation of a system that would use telecommunications technology to deliver a message to targeted subjects that would alter their reality and bend it to a desired outcome. For the military, this would mean delivering controlling messages to the enemy that distorts their reality and bends it to what we want them to see. On the battlefield, hypothetically we could blind the enemy to approaching troops and equipment. In the air, we could blind enemy aviators against ground targets and opposing combat aircraft."

"Wow," said Kristian. "All of that sounds pretty far- fetched. How would an enemy on the battlefield receive telecommunications messages while engaged in battle? And a combat pilot moving at speeds exceeding Mach One?"

"At this point, we are simply considering the possible outcomes associated with the concepts of subliminal suggestion and mind control. What I described is arguably at the boundaries of possibility," replied Beck.

"It seems it would be less challenging to deliver thought controlling messages to government and political leaders than to soldiers in battle," said Jonathan Brahe, CEO of Find Corporation. "If you can crack their secure phones, just leave a voicemail that would infect their thought processes and influence their decision making."

"Very true," said Beck. "I'm glad you used the term 'infect'. What we are currently looking at is emulating the way a virus infects the body with a telecommunications signal that opens the mind to subliminal suggestion. With the mind 'opened', the afflicted individuals would accept the message as reality."

"But in the years following the CoVid-19 Pandemic, a universal vaccine against viruses was developed. Since about 2028, there has not been a major virus outbreak anywhere in the world," said Kristian. "Could a vaccine, in the form of a security application, against a telecommunications virus be developed?"

"That certainly would be technically possible. But only after the technology behind the virus was discovered, which may take years," said Beck. "A means of blocking or disabling the telecommunications signal would have to be developed. Once the signal is delivered by means of hearing or seeing it in a text message, it would be too late. It is unlikely there would be a cure as there is with biological viruses."

"In order to move the project forward, we need to make some assignments for the team to undertake," said Beck. "Kristian, if your team from Barnett Industries could begin leveraging your technologies that are employed today in many cities and by the military to distribute signals to control automated vehicles. We believe that has promise relative to this project."

"Absolutely, Inger. We'll get right on it," said Kristian. "Jonathon, we will need your software engineers to engage in the development of the actual virus and the delivery technologies for subliminal messages and commands."

"Yes, Inger, we have already begun research regarding solutions in these areas. But I believe we need to enlist cellular technologists on this project. I have recommended this before but have not seen any reaction from DARPA. I personally know the CEOs of two of the major cellular providers that I could approach, but I am currently restricted by our project security requirements."

Kristian and Aaron glanced at each other following Brahe's statement, recalling the participants they saw at the failed demonstration of the mind control technology in 2052.

"Kristian, how do you feel about enlisting cellular companies for the project?" asked Inger Beck.

Kristian thought for a moment and decided it would probably be better to get the future culprits involved early, and said, "It probably would be a good move. However, Barnett's technology is a special derivative of cellular designed for the delivery of critical messages. Our systems are depended upon for real-time life and death situations. But the cellular companies may have something to offer that would complement our systems."

"With that, I have no more issues for this meeting," said Inger. "Unless someone has any additional items, let's adjourn. We will schedule update meetings quarterly for the entire team. To minimize the issues regarding travel for Kristian, I recommend we hold our quarterly meetings at the Barnett Center for Neurological Restoration. In the meantime, I would appreciate a monthly update in the form of a holographic meeting from each sub-team that will state progress and raise any questions or issues. Thank you."

Chapter 62

It was a typically beautiful California evening at the Barnett mansion with temperatures in the mid-seventies and a slight breeze that carried the breath of the Pacific Ocean inland. Senior Barnett Industries executives were provided access to the mansion's tennis courts and locker rooms. "Thirty-Love," yelled Savannah as she prepared to serve the ball to Aaron with the second set game score at 5-2. Aaron lost the first set 6-4 and had been surprised by how well Savannah played.

Savannah's serve nicked the back-right corner of the service area as it spun away from Aaron's swing. Although his racket tipped the ball, his return spun out of bounds. "Forty-Love," yelled Savannah.

"Hey, I thought you were going to go easy on me. I've only taken up tennis recently!" whined Aaron. Savannah hadn't told Aaron that she was a tennis All-American at Stanford during her undergraduate years.

"I am taking it easy on you," Savannah shot back. "You're flat-footed during the serve. You should be standing on the balls of your feet with your knees bent, ready to pounce as soon as I hit the ball."

Aaron followed Savannah's advice, and returned Savannah's serve to her backhand, near the baseline. Savannah couldn't resist and unwound her two-handed backhand, sending the ball deep to Aaron's backhand. The ball was so fast Aaron couldn't get a solid return and hit the ball into the net.

"Game, set, match," yelled Savannah. "6-4, 6-2. Guess that means that you are buying me dinner!"

"You've got me there," said Aaron as he approached the net and reached to shake Savannah's hand. "I'll call an Uber to pick us up in front of the mansion after we shower and change."

"That's OK, we can take my car," said Savannah. Meet you in fifteen minutes at the lot?"

"Perfect."

"Nice car," said Aaron, complimenting Savannah on her 2042 silver-blue Mercedes E-93 AMG Cabriolet.

"Thanks," she replied, as she stepped into the light-blue leather driver's seat. "This is the perfect climate for a convertible." She started the engine and touched a button to lower the soft top. "I sometimes go for a drive along the shore and park at my favorite beach to soothe my nerves after a particularly challenging day. So where are you taking me to pay up on our bet?"

"The Bel-Air Restaurant. I've eaten there before, and it was excellent," Aaron said, recalling his dinner with Ansley.

"I've eaten there a few times and found it quite good," said Savannah.

Savannah instructed the Mercedes' GPS to take them to the Bel-Air Restaurant. Verbal instructions as well as a live view of the road with turn-by-turn instructions superimposed appeared on the car's thirteen-inch screen in the center of the dash. As virtually all automobiles manufactured since the late 2020s were electric, the Mercedes silently backed out of Savannah's named parking space and proceeded to follow the route to the restaurant. They were seated right after entering the restaurant and the server asked if she could take their drink orders. "Water for me, with lime," said Aaron.

"Could I see your wine list?" asked Savannah.

"Of course," said the waitress as she handed the wine list to Savannah. "I'll come back in a few minutes to get your wine order."

After a few moments of silence, Aaron broke the ice. "I'm still in awe over the fact that I have been resurrected from the nearly dead and now exist in a near-perfect, possibly immortal body. That I won't face the decline that comes with age."

Savannah looked up from the wine list and her eyes caught Aaron's blue eyes. "Yes, that is quite astounding when you think about it. The implications for medical science and human longevity are amazing. One of the possibilities and challenges we envisioned are the effects on the human mind regarding the concept of virtual immortality. The true unknown is not the synthetic body but the human mind it is hosting. At some point does the mind age to the point where it becomes trapped in the synthetic body? And then what does it do when it wants to cease to exist? As one of the first humans to live with these concerns, what are your thoughts?"

"I … I guess I haven't given those questions much consideration. As long I am enjoying life, why would I want to cease to exist, as you put it?" said Aaron, his hand rubbing his chin.

"OK, let's look at a hypothetical. Say, someday you fall in love with someone. You see her as your soulmate. You have a wonderful life, even have a couple of kids who grow up to be successful and bring you several grandchildren. First, your soulmate ages and passes away, which devastates you. Eventually, your children die, as well, as your grandchildren. How will you deal with a litany of death every succeeding generation?"

The server returned to take the wine order. "I'll have the Burgess Chardonnay 1980," said Savannah. "Aaron, does that wine meet with your expectations?"

"Yes, sounds good."

"Well," said Aaron thoughtfully. "I suppose grief that is repeated continuously could result in one wanting to end one's existence. But, alternatively, at some point could one invest themselves in starting over, so to speak? While always remembering the life one enjoyed for a while, start life anew with new experiences and with new people."

"And here's another thought. If we look at human aging as a disease and not an inevitable outcome of our life cycle, could we give people the choice of a synthetic body? How would this choice be any different than the choice I was given? Could my soulmate choose to stay with me in a synthetic body?"

"Interestingly, viewing aging as a disease has been done for some time," said Savannah. "Once the possibility of obtaining an advanced synthetic body becomes common knowledge, the concept could grow legs very quickly."

The server returned with the wine, poured a bit for Savannah to taste. Then poured a glass for Savannah and Aaron.

"May I take your dinner orders?" the server asked.

"I'll have the chicken breast, and sautéed spinach for the side," said Savannah.

"Sir?"

"I'll try the braised short ribs," said Aaron. "Appetizer or a side?"

"Scalloped potatoes."

"There will be many issues that will need to be addressed before synthetic bodies can be offered on a wider scale. The costs associated with developing synthetic bodies for you, Kristian, and Erik were well into the billions of dollars. If we were able to develop rapid production of synthetic bodies, the issue of cost must be addressed. That, along with ethics, strain on human population, and religious concerns will take years to be settled. By then, we will hopefully have eliminated all disease and enable humans to live their full theoretical life span, well past one- hundred years of age," said Savannah.

"Yeah, I guess we won't be able to solve the wide scale use of artificial bodies today," said Aaron. "What about you, Savannah? You are one of the preeminent clinicians in the world. With all your amazing accomplishments, who is the person behind the genius?" Savannah laughed, "Genius? I don't think so. But I've been completely consumed by my work for nearly twenty years. I've not allowed myself much in the way of fun. I have not had a meaningful relationship with anyone. But I am waking up to the fact that there is more to life than my science, the lab, and saving humanity. I bought the Mercedes on a whim one weekend and immediately went for a drive along the ocean. Until recently, I wouldn't have allowed myself a tennis date and a dinner out with a man. I think I'm ready to expand my horizons."

"Oh, maybe I can help you with expanding your horizons," laughed Aaron.

Savannah smiled but had no reply.

Savannah and Aaron finished their meal and returned to the Barnett mansion where Aaron was still staying in a guest house. Savannah stopped the car in front of the walk to the door and said, "I had a really great time this evening, Aaron."

"Thanks, Savannah, so did I. Let's do it again," said Aaron. "I'd like that. Give me a call," she said as she leaned over and kissed Aaron on the cheek.

Chapter 63

Ansley Barnett's digital assistant pinged her smartphone with the familiar sonar tone. Ansley picked up the smartphone. The assistant immediately detected her touch and said, "Dr. Barnett, you have a call from Director Hanson waiting. Do you wish to connect, or shall I send the call to your voicemail?"

"Please connect the call," said Ansley.

"Ansley, I have some news from SecDef (Secretary of Defense). A few months back, a Naval Aviator, Lieutenant Scarlett Bross, crashed her F-35 onboard the USS Donald Trump. The ship was conducting night-time Pitching Deck exercises in twenty- foot seas in the South China Sea while reassuring the Chinese of our strength in the region. Lt. Bross had attempted to land twice and missed the ship's arresting cables both times, and was waved off into the Bolt, or Wave-off pattern. On her third try to land, the ship's deck rose quickly as she slammed down on the deck and bounced over the arresting cables. Her aircraft went off the side of the ship into the ocean. Bross was recovered but sustained serious, mostly unrecoverable injuries. SecDef wants her evaluated for a synthetic body."

"Jim, you know we have not created a female cyborg. I do have a prototype in the final stages of development, but we have not completed testing."

"Ansley, I strongly suggest that you use Lt. Bross to complete your testing. SecDef is growing increasingly impatient with our lack of progress on creating more cyborgs for the military. He has the ear of the President and could easily scuttle our project.

I strongly suggest you and your team evaluate Lt. Bross for a synthetic body. Lt. Bross is at the VA Medical Hospital in San Diego. Your contact is Commander Brett Lewis, chief of the spinal cord injury unit."

Savannah reached for her smartphone. Before she could say hello, she heard, "Savannah, this is Ansley. Are you available for a trip down to San Diego? There's been another accident that has disabled a naval aviator. The Secretary of Defense wants her evaluated for a synthetic body."

"Yes … I suppose so. Did you say her? Is the candidate female?" "Yes," replied Ansley.

"But … but I thought you weren't ready to accept a female candidate."

"I'm not. But it may be possible to use Lt. Bross, the Navy pilot who was injured, in the same way we did with Aaron as a test case. This time it would be for a female. When could you go with me?" asked Ansley.

"I have nothing critical scheduled the rest of the week. Is tomorrow too soon?"

"Perfect, I'll meet you at the Center's helicopter pad at 8 AM. We'll fly directly to the VA hospital."

Ansley and Savannah boarded the Barnett Center chopper promptly at 8 AM and departed for the San Diego Veterans Administration Hospital. "Savannah, please don't forget our visit will be under top-secret conditions. Our liaison at the hospital is Commander Brett Lewis, chief of the spinal unit. Commander Lewis has not been cleared for knowledge of the cyborg project.

We will be interviewing Lt. Bross under the guise of bringing her to Barnett Center for advanced spinal recovery with artificial limbs." "Got it. But how do we address DARPA's involvement in this?" said Savannah.

"DARPA has been involved for quite some time developing

high tech artificial limbs, so that shouldn't be a problem. I'm sure Commander Lewis is aware of this."

"On another note, I hear that you had a date with Aaron. How did that go?" said Ansley, still wondering if her secret tryst with Aaron was safe.

"We had a genuinely nice time. He is fun to be around and can be … persistent," said Savannah.

"Oh, in what ways?" asked Ansley, recalling Aaron's unrelenting pressure on her to … fully test his synthetic body.

"I … really can't say specifically. I just got the impression he was … trying hard not to push things too fast." "So, will you be dating him again?"

"Yes, yes, I told him I would like that, and I would," said Savannah, with a slight laugh.

The Barnett helicopter landed on the rooftop landing pad of Building One of the San Diego Veterans Administration hospital complex. Ansley and Savannah exited the chopper, ducking to avoid the swirling blades. They were greeted by a doctor on Commander Brett Lewis' staff.

"Good morning, Drs. Barnett and Richards. Welcome to San Diego. I am Lieutenant Seth Jackson, physician on staff with Dr. Lewis." Jackson was a young African American man, Naval R.O.T.C. graduate of Auburn University, and the University of Florida Medical School. He appeared to be more than six-feet tall with an athletic build and an attractive demeanor that didn't go unnoticed by both Ansley and Savannah. Jackson, who was a walk-on, had been an Auburn Tigers starting wide receiver during his junior and senior year.

"Good morning, Dr. Jackson. Nice to meet you," said Ansley, smiling until catching herself momentarily captivated by his deep brown eyes.

"Please follow me to Dr. Lewis' office. We are housed in Building Eleven, the spinal center."

Ansley and Savannah followed Dr. Jackson into Dr. Lewis' office. Dr. Lewis stood and walked around his desk to greet them.

"Good morning, Doctors, welcome to San Diego. I understand that you will be evaluating Lt. Bross for admission to Barnett Center's advanced spinal and limb restoration program. What you were able to accomplish with Commander Erik Richards was amazing."

"Yes, that is correct, Doctor," said Ansley. "We would like to begin by interviewing Lt. Bross to gain insight into her current psychological state. The regimen for the ... restoration program is quite challenging. We need to make sure the patient, who has been through a life-threatening trauma, has a strong will to succeed."

"My opinion of Lt. Bross' mental state is that she is strong and prepared to undertake whatever course of treatment is needed to restore at least some of her mobility," said Lewis. "I believe she has accepted the fact that she will never fly again, but she is looking forward to a new, productive career. Would you agree, Dr. Jackson?"

"Yes sir, given her extensive injuries, and current paraplegic condition coupled with the loss of her left limbs, Lt. Bross is exhibiting a strong 'can-do' attitude," said Jackson.

"What is your prognosis for Lt. Bross' recovery?" asked Savannah.

"Frankly, not good," said Lewis. "We know she could be outfitted with artificial limbs. Unfortunately, the condition of her spine, or more accurately, what little remains of her lower spine, would not support a prosthesis for her left leg. Fortunately, her spinal injuries were concentrated in the area of her S1-L4 vertebrae, which allowed her to recover much of her upper body mobility including respiration. Had the injuries been higher on her spine she likely would not have survived, and at best be completely paralyzed."

"Are you ready to meet Lt. Bross?" asked Dr. Lewis. "Yes, definitely," said Ansley.

Drs. Lewis, Jackson, Barnett, and Richards entered Lt. Scarlett Bross' hospital room. Because of her injuries and required care, she had a private room.

"Good morning, Scarlett," said Dr. Lewis. "You have a couple of visitors. Meet Drs. Ansley Barnett and Savannah Richards from the Barnett Center for Neurological Restoration. Barnett Center is known worldwide for its advanced treatment of spinal and limb restoration. They would like to speak with you about possibly taking advantage of their programs."

"Good morning, doctors," said Scarlett. "I guess Dr. Lewis has described the extent of my injuries as well as my prognosis for recovery to you. I've been here for about three months. What is the Barnett Center's protocol for spinal recovery? Do I have a shot at regaining the feeling in my right leg? If I do, perhaps I would have an opportunity to get an artificial leg."

"Yes, many things are possible," said Ansley. "But we need to get some information from you in order to assess your opportunities for success at the Center. Do you feel up to spending a few hours with Dr. Richards and me today?"

"Yes, absolutely," said Bross. "I'm ready to do anything to get well."

Ansley and Savannah spent the next three hours interviewing Scarlett Bross. They had her describe her accident aboard the USS Donald Trump.

"Night Pitching Deck exercises are, I feel, the most challenging situation a Naval Aviator can undertake," said Scarlett. "Landing on a carrier in the dark with smooth seas is challenging. When the deck is moving up and down vertically as much as thirty feet, the conditions are as frightening as I've ever encountered. I'd rather be a in a dogfight with a Mig than land on a pitching deck in the dark. A pitching deck is a Naval Aviator's worst nightmare."

"I had already missed the traps, the arresting cables on the deck, twice. But I had enough fuel to attempt a third landing. I was on approach to the carrier and could see the deck moving up and down vertically. The deck was sinking, and I thought I'd lined up with the motion pretty well. I thought this time I would snag the trap and land. But just as I was about to touch down, the deck rose violently. My F-35 hit hard, really hard, and bounced up, causing me to lose control of the aircraft. The plane began to roll left. Before I could get control, it hit the side of the deck and fell into the ocean. I didn't have time to eject. That is the last thing I remember until I woke up about a week later in the hospital."

"Wow, that is a horrific story. The fact that you're alive is a miracle!" said Savannah. "What was your reaction when you regained consciousness and realized the extent of your injuries?" "When I opened my eyes, a nurse happened to be changing my bandages. As soon as she saw I was conscious she paged the attending resident physician. He came into the room shortly and asked me if I knew where I was. He asked if I knew my name, and other questions to see if I was aware. He then pulled up a chair and sat down next to my bed. He described my injuries to me and said my prognosis didn't look good, that I may never walk again, even with a prosthesis. He then offered to give me a sedative after seeing my reaction to the news that I would be in a wheelchair for the rest of my life. I declined and asked to be left alone. I then tried to absorb the state I was in, but all I could do was cry. I wept for what seemed like hours."

"Now, you seem to have accepted your fate and want to move on to the next stage of your life," said Ansley.

"Losing my limbs and my paralysis were like part of me dying. My career as an aviator that I worked so hard for was over. But after a week or so of grieving and feeling lost, I began to realize that I was indeed still alive, my mind was intact and undamaged, and there were other things I could do with my life."

"That's a great attitude," said Savannah. "Many people would've have just given up."

"Quitting has never been in my vocabulary."

"Scarlett, we are going to recommend you for the Barnett Center's physical restoration program. This will mean you will be transferred to Barnett Center where we will further evaluate your condition and prescribe the best course of treatment to restore full functionality of your body. It will likely mean months, if not longer, of staying at the Center, as well as arduous physical challenges. Do you believe you can accept the challenges associated with the program?" said Ansley.

"If there is a chance that I could achieve most, if not all, of my pre-accident abilities, I am most certainly willing and able to try," said Scarlett.

Later in Dr. Lewis' office, Ansley advised that they believed Lt.

Bross to be an excellent candidate for the Barnett Center's restoration and rehabilitation program and needed to have her transferred to Barnett Center as soon as possible. The transfer would be arranged using air-ambulance services.

"Also, Dr. Lewis, we will need all of Scarlett's medical records to facilitate her participation in the program.

"No problem, Dr. Barnett. I've arranged for you have access to Scarlett's records by the time you return to Barnett Center."

"Thank you, Dr. Lewis," said Ansley.

Ansley and Savannah returned to Barnett Center later that same afternoon and immediately contacted Director Hanson from DARPA.

"Hi Jim, Ansley. We have completed our preliminary evaluation of Lt. Scarlett Bross and find her to be a likely candidate for a synthetic body. We will need to conduct further testing, but at this point, we see nothing preventing us from proceeding. However, we will need to explain the risks associated with the procedure to ensure her full understanding about that which she is to undertake. We will also require her to accept the non- disclosure agreement. In the meantime, please have her security clearance elevated to the level necessary for us to continue with the procedure. We'll need this as soon as possible."

"I'll notify SecDef as soon as we hang up," said Hanson. "I'm sure he'll be satisfied with your recommendation."

Chapter 64

Aaron lay down on his charging bed after connecting the cables to the back of his neck. "I really enjoyed time with Savannah this evening. She is nearly perfect. Her golden hair descending to her shoulders, her captivating green eyes, her amazing intelligence, and her athletic body. She moves like a cat on the tennis court. I hope I didn't make too big a fool of myself out there!" The cyborgs did not sleep in the conventional human sense, but they were taught techniques that enabled them to clear their mind and enter a restful state. The emulation of sleep was needed to keep the human mind functioning. It also contributed to the speed for the backup of the mind to the central data center. An active mind could slow down the backup process considerably. It took Aaron longer than usual to enter a restful state because he kept returning to his thoughts of Savannah. But he finally drifted off and was able to shut his mind down.

In his mind, Aaron could see a mist forming in his bedroom. At first it was light and transparent. But it quickly filled the room. He then saw a human shape form in the mist.

"Aaron," said The Guardian. "We have work. There is a rift in a timeline that is in danger of going awry. We need to correct the errant path this timeline is trending towards. Otherwise, life as you know it is at risk. Take my hand and travel with me to the location in time where we will intervene and correct the timeline."

The next moment, Aaron found himself standing with The Guardian in the White House Oval Office. Sitting at the large, decorative desk was President Franklin Delano Roosevelt. Seated in desk chairs in front of the President were Democratic Party chairman Robert Hannegan, Postmaster General Frank Walker, New York Democratic party chief Ed Flynn, and Democratic party treasurer Edwin Pauley. These men were meeting with the President to discuss the 1944 election and FDR's choice for vice president.

The Guardian then described the rift in the timeline and what needed to happen to correct it. "Where the timeline was beginning to go astray was with FDR's choice for vice president for FDR's next term. Henry Agard Wallace, the thirty-third vice president of the United States, and FDR's former secretary of agriculture had been chosen by FDR in 1940. FDR chose Wallace because of his strong presence in the agricultural community, and for his support of the New Deal programs. FDR believed, at the time, that should anything happen to him, Wallace would continue promoting the New Deal with fervor. Democratic Party leaders, however, were highly skeptical of Wallace. They felt that Wallace, a former Republican, would not fit well with the Democrats in Congress should he become president. FDR persisted with his support for Wallace, and even threatened the party leadership with withdrawing from the 1940 election if Wallace was not the vice-presidential candidate."

"When the 1944 Democratic presidential convention neared, the party leadership was even more adamant to remove Wallace. Now," continued The Guardian, "I will show you why we must ensure that Wallace is replaced on the 1944 Democratic ticket by Harry Truman."

Visions from World War II began to play before Aaron's eyes. The Japanese attack on Pearl Harbor on December 7, 1941 showed the devastation to the United States Naval fleet and the sinking of the USS Arizona. Japanese fighter-bombers unleashed torpedoes on the shallow harbor, wreaking havoc. The visions then showed several battles, including the Philippines, Iwo Jima, and Guadalcanal, where thousands of soldiers lost their lives. Then, the visions showed the death of President Roosevelt and the subsequent swearing in of Henry Wallace as president.

The next scene was in the Oval Office, shortly after Wallace was sworn in. Henry Stimson, Secretary of War, and (and soon to be Secretary of State) James F. Byrnes, briefed Wallace on the Manhattan Project. The Manhattan Project was kept so secure that not even Wallace knew any details of the program until Roosevelt's death on April 12, 1945. After Wallace took the oath of office, both Stimson and Byrnes finally informed him of the project. While Byrnes heralded the bomb enthusiastically as the object that would allow the US to dictate its own terms to end the war, Stimson provided the president with a more sobering outlook on the technology. He stressed its powerful ability to change international order and that it required a revision of international methods for obtaining peace.

Wallace appreciated Stimson's nuanced position on the bomb and made it clear that, on the surface, he was against using lethal force on Japanese civilians. The increasing success of the nuclear facilities, meanwhile, sent the program hurtling towards a final completion of the bomb, necessitating a formal decision on whether to use the technology.

The Guardian continued, "While the Interim Committee created by Stimson existed to debate the issue of using an atomic bomb against Japan, the ultimate decision came down to Wallace. Upon hearing the Interim Committee's recommendation on June 1, 1945 to use the bomb as soon as possible against Japan without prior warning, Wallace disagreed with the recommendation, saying there must be other alternatives for forcing Japan's surrender. Wallace did agree that using knowledge of the Atomic Bomb and its destructive capability with Japan to achieve a surrender was prudent. Scientific estimates informed Wallace that the first bomb would be ready by August 6, the second around August 24-information that he used in planning when to give Japan a final chance to surrender. Ultimately, Wallace refused to authorize use of the bomb after the Japanese refused to surrender despite the nuclear threat. Japan believed, rightly, that Wallace was not strong enough to use the bomb."

The next series of visions showed the invasion of Japan in January of 1946 by the allied forces in the Pacific. Included with the allied Pacific forces were the Russians. Visions depicted eighteen months of battle, over a million military and civilians killed, and the capture of Japanese Emperor Hirohito. Aaron witnessed the execution of Hirohito by firing squad for crimes against humanity.

"But what happened following the conquest of Japan is where history takes a bad course. When talks of withdrawal of allied forces from Japan began in the late 1940s, Russia, under Stalin's rule, refused to withdraw. The refusal contributed to the growing rift between Russia and the United States. President Wallace, known and despised by many for his friendly relationship towards Stalin and Russia, appeared weak, even condescending to Russian aggression in Japan. China was livid over Wallace's refusal to insist the Russians withdraw."

Aaron then saw more visions that were, by far, the most horrifying. The USSR, which had acquired nuclear bomb technology during the period of the Japanese invasion, threatened China with the atomic bomb should they attempt to repel Russia from Japan. China did not relent in pressing against Russian aggression. Aaron saw the vision of mushroom clouds ascending over China. Aaron then saw mushroom clouds rising over New York City, Chicago, and Washington, D.C. in the East, and Los Angeles, San Francisco, and Seattle in the West. In response, Henry Wallace had no choice but unleash the United States nuclear arsenal on Russia. World War III had commenced and resulted in the destruction of much of both the Western and Asian worlds.

Chapter 65

"Guardian, what you are saying is that if the United States does not drop the Atomic Bomb on Japan, killing thousands, civilization will be set back hundreds of years. Much of the human race will be extinguished in a nuclear holocaust and the nuclear winter that follows. How do we alter this timeline and ensure Truman is nominated for vice president over Wallace?" said Aaron.

"We will observe President Roosevelt in separate settings over the next few months. You will see that FDR was beginning to waiver on his support for Wallace, but that he definitely liked the way Wallace promoted the progressive ideology and the New Deal programs," said The Guardian.

Aaron then found himself standing in The Oval Office. The President was seated behind his desk. Henry Wallace was seated across from him. The time was May 1944. "Henry, I would like you to plan a trip to Russia and China," said FDR. "I would like for you to inspect lend-lease materials [industrial equipment provided to the USSR during WWII] that are in operation in Soviet labor camps. After touring Russia, I want you to go to Chungking, China to begin trying to solve China's major wartime problems. I believe we both want to see resolution come to the differences between Chiang Kai-shek's Nationalists and the Communists. You need to prod the Nationalists into stepping up their campaign against the Japanese. Are you up to these tasks, Henry?"

"Yes, Mr. President," said Wallace. "I have developed an excellent relationship with Premier Stalin. I see this trip as a way to solidify the relationship between Russia and the United States as the beginning of lasting world peace once the war is ended."

"What actually transpired during Wallace's tour was that he was completely duped by Stalin and The Soviet Union. By 1944, relations had become so comfortable that the unsuspecting Wallace was invited to Kolyma to personally inspect the USSR's biggest and most deadly labor camp. Wallace was presented with a temporarily polished-up commune full of well-fed and happy citizens, most of whom were shipped in for the occasion. Buying into everything he was told, the unwitting American inadvertently let colossal human rights abuses slip from right from under his nose, and even labelled the GULAG, "clear evidence of the most outstanding and gifted political leadership," said The Guardian. "This was followed by his failure to establish any cooperation between Chinese Communists and Nationalists, and solidified the Democratic Party's position that Wallace should not run for vice president."

"The Asian journey allowed Wallace no time to campaign and made him vulnerable to political attack. When Wallace returned to Washington's National Airport, he faced reporters who asked if he planned to withdraw from the race. The vice president replied, "I am seeing the president at 4:30. I have a report to make on a mission to China. I do not want to talk politics."

Back in The Oval Office on July 11, 1944, Wallace was again seated across the desk from FDR. "I am sorry, Mr. President, but I do not believe we will achieve much cooperation between the Chinese Communists and Chiang Kai-shek's Nationalists."

"I am disappointed that we could not motivate them to settle their differences and get the Nationalists to step up their efforts against Japan," said FDR.

"Mr. President," began Wallace. I am hearing that there are those among the Democratic Party leadership that are against my running for another term as your Vice President."

"Yes, Henry, it is pretty much the same group that opposed you in 1940. You know I threatened not to run then if you were not the vice-presidential candidate," said FDR.

"By 1944, Vice President Wallace was a hero to both organized labor and the increasingly powerful African American communities in America's biggest cities. But among the Democratic elite, opposition to him was even more fervent than it had been in 1940," interjected The Guardian. "You may recall the 2016 election and the battle between Hillary Clinton and Bernie Sanders for the Democratic presidential nomination. The way the 1944 election went down was eerily similar, with the Democratic Party elite supporting Clinton but millions of the rank-and-file Democrats supporting Sanders."

"Yes, sir, and I greatly appreciate your support," said Wallace. You are aware that I have the support of labor leaders and rank and file Democrats. Would you be willing to write a letter stating your support of my candidacy to the Democratic Party leadership? Your support, I believe would convince the Party of the need for my nomination."

"Yes, Henry, I will do that," said FDR thinking that he was not nearly as strong a supporter of Wallace's nomination as he had been in 1940."

After Wallace departed The Oval Office, FDR began to pen the letter he had promised Wallace that he would write.

"Aaron, this is the critical moment that restores the timeline to the one we know," said The Guardian. "You will enter the President's mind, but you will not take complete control. Rather you will observe what he writes. Roosevelt's letter needs to emphasize that he has no desire to dictate to the Democratic Party convention. This approach will leave the door open sufficiently for the Party to draft Harry Truman as vice president. To accomplish this, you will infuse your thoughts with Roosevelt regarding the content and tone of the letter and continue to raise doubts about Wallace. Note that I am not suggesting you take control of the President's mind. He is not in good health and will eventually pass from a stroke. We do not want to rush that outcome."

"Guardian, this is different from what I've done before. Before, we just took control of the subject's mind and forced the desired outcome. How do I influence Roosevelt to do what we need?"

"I agree that this method will be more challenging for you. But you have the power to influence and gain the desired outcome. Try it now. The President is drafting his letter."

Aaron entered FDR's mind. When he did, Roosevelt blinked and looked up with a startled expression on his face. He then took a breath and continued writing.

In that conversation on July 11, Roosevelt appeared sympathetic to keeping Wallace on the team. Aaron began to bring thoughts to FDR's mind of Wallace's failures over the past four years. Roosevelt paused, looked up and thought, "I must write this so the party leaders will feel they have discretion regarding the vice-presidential candidate."

Continuing the letter, Roosevelt stated that he could support Wallace as the candidate but was not going to dictate to the party whom they could select. This should provide the party with sufficient cover should they reject Wallace. The completed letter was signed and delivered to Democratic Party Chairman Robert Hannegan the next day.

The 1944 Democratic Party convention nomination of the vice-presidential candidate was far from a shoo-in for Harry Truman. Wallace came close to defeating the Party bosses' choice, Harry Truman. On the second day of the Convention, there was a huge pro-Wallace demonstration. Claude Pepper, the Florida senator, later said that if he had managed to place Wallace's name into nomination that evening the Vice-President would have kept his position—and become President upon Roosevelt's death. When Pepper was only a few steps from the lectern, Democratic Party leaders succeeded in having the session adjourned. The next day, the nomination went to Truman. In fact, on the first ballot, Henry Wallace scored a significant majority of votes, although not enough to achieve the nomination. By the third ballot, Truman had gained enough votes for the nomination.

The Guardian continued, "On April 12, 1945, President Franklin Delano Roosevelt passed away due to a massive stroke. Harry Truman was sworn in the same day. When Truman was briefed for the first time on the Manhattan Project, he immediately reflected a favorable response. Truman did stipulate that he wanted Japanese manufacturing cities targeted and as few civilians taken out as possible. He did not want Tokyo to be a target for this reason. The bombs were dropped on the manufacturing cities of Hiroshima and Nagasaki. The Japanese surrendered a few days later, ending World War II."

"Aaron, you can see that, despite the horror of the Atomic Bomb, it was necessary to use it against Japan. Had Henry Wallace been President instead of Harry Truman, the world would be a much different place today."

The next moment Aaron found himself lying on his charging bed as if nothing had happened. The mist in the room was gone, as was The Guardian. Recalling his college course in Greek Mythology, "My God, how will The Guardian challenge The Fates next," he wondered, as he tried—unsuccessfully—to relax his mind.

Preview of Sequel

Kristian and Aaron continue to pursue a means of blocking Find Corporation's cellular wave technology that will enable subliminal commands to be transmitted to control the masses via a secret network. Members of the DARPA team continue developing both the technology and a corresponding antidote or digital antivirus while Kristian observes what Find and its telecommunications partners are doing. Ultimately, will a digital antivirus be developed that will prevent the mass distribution of subliminal commands? Will the CEOs of Find and its telecommunications partners be charged with criminal intent by the U.S. Department of Justice? Will the elected government of the United States in 2056 fall into communist hands?

Lt. Scarlett Bross will debut as the latest and first female synthetic cyborg. Ansley and Savannah guide her transformation and recovery as a cyborg, which will include some unforeseen challenges involving the emotional side that is felt more strongly than with the male cyborgs. Being a female F-35 Naval Aviator, her injuries were widely publicized in the media. That she returns to duty, apparently fully recovered including her amputated limbs, arouses the interest of the media which raises the questions of how her complete recovery was accomplished. The media attention puts Ansley, DARPA, and the Defense Department in a bind to explain Bross's recovery. Photos of her taken secretly when she was hospitalized clearly show her left appendages missing. More recent photos show Bross, after returning to active duty, climbing into an F-35 on an aircraft carrier. The more the media attacks the story, the greater the clamor from the public to reveal the secrets behind her recovery. In addition, as Kristian is seen appearing to be recovered from ALS, the media again begins to clamor that something is going on to revive hopelessly ill and injured patients to full recovery. Ultimately, Ansley's affiliation with DARPA becomes the center of focus as to how these miraculous recoveries are happening.

Commander Erik Richards and Ksenia Anderson continue their long-distance romance, she as a bridge officer for Viking Cruise Lines, and he on a secret Navy Space Command project to develop a starship using technology acquired from the alien craft that crashed near Roswell, NM in 1947. About a year after meeting Ksenia in 2042, Erik proposes to Ksenia during another visit to the Anderson family estate in Norway. Erik and Thor's friendship continues to grow as memories of Arya's death aboard the USS Elon Musk under Erik's command fade over time. But before Erik proposes he reveals his secret to Ksenia. What will that do to the relationship? Will Ksenia become a cyborg and become immortal?

Will the U.S. government continue to fund Erik's starship project? If so, who will command the first expedition into deep space? Who will be members of the crew? The first mission will most likely span several years. If Erik goes on the first mission, what will that do to Ksenia?

Aaron and Savannah will continue to develop their relationship. Will Aaron propose to Savannah? Will she accept his proposal?

Will The Guardian return to correct a historical timeline gone awry? Which of the cyborgs will be tasked with correcting the timeline?

About the Author

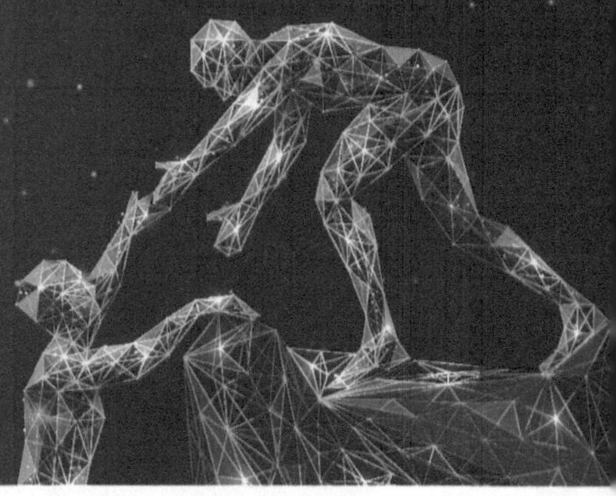

Kiel Barnekov is an information technology executive who has led innovative airline and airport technology projects for over thirty years. He was Director of Information Technology for Tampa International Airport and Manager of Information Technology at Orlando International Airport. He was also the Business Technology leader for Delta Air Lines Airport Customer Service Division during the 1990s. Well known in the airport industry, Mr. Barnekov has chaired the Airports Council International - North America Information Technology Committee. Mr. Barnekov as appeared on CNN and several local news stations to demonstrate airport technologies and airport processes. Shepherds of Destiny is Mr. Barnekov's first novel. He was born in 1951 in Washington D.C. His father was a federal government intelligence executive & captain in the U.S. Naval Reserve. His mother was a federal government employee at several agencies. His grandmother, Fleur Conkling, was a published author of children's books. Mr. Barnekov lives with his family in Ormond Beach, Florida.